[Nathan Walpow] is a hell of a

—LEE CHILD, AUTHOR OF **KILLING FLOOR, DIE TRYING** AND **TRIPWIRE**

PRAISE FOR
Death of an Orchid Lover

"The second Joe Portugal mystery is as much of a delight as the first. The mystery unfolds as beautifully as the orchids of the title. Walpow transports readers into his fabulous botanical world, populated with quirky characters who the reader will want to spend time with again and again. *Death of an Orchid Lover* is a winner."

—PAUL BISHOP, AUTHOR OF THE FEY CROAKER LAPD CRIME NOVELS

"With great wit, Nathan Walpow offers up a hothouse of quirky plant-crazy suspects."

—JERRILYN FARMER, AUTHOR OF THE MADELINE BEAN MYSTERY SERIES

"*Death of an Orchid Lover* is as complex and enthralling as orchids themselves. . . . Nathan Walpow's Los Angeles has streets every bit as mean as Raymond Chandler's, and his way with dry wit and great characters is every bit as original and entertaining as the master's."

—HELEN CHAPPELL, AUTHOR OF THE HOLLIS AND SAM SERIES

PRAISE FOR
The Cactus Club Killings

"Walpow brings the [gardening mystery] genre to the West Coast with short, snappy Chandleresque dialogue."

—*LOS ANGELES TIMES*

"Crisp and witty dialogue makes a fast-paced read of Nathan Walpow's spirited first mystery."

—ANN RIPLEY, AUTHOR OF *MULCH* AND *DEATH OF A POLITICAL PLANT*

"The book is a delight. Mr. Walpow writes well—clearly, concisely, and with a wonderful subtle sense of humor."

—*THE MYSTERY READER*

"Walpow has penned a mystery that anyone will find funny and riveting."

—*THE ORANGE COUNTY REGISTER*

Dell Books by Nathan Walpow

The Cactus Club Killings

Death of an Orchid Lover

DEATH
of an
Orchid Lover

A Joe Portugal Mystery

NATHAN WALPOW

A DELL BOOK

Published by
Dell Publishing
a division of
Random House, Inc.
1540 Broadway
New York, New York 10036

This novel is a work of fiction. Names, characters, places, and incidents either are the product of the author's imagination or are used fictitiously. Any resemblance to actual persons, living or dead, events, or locales is entirely coincidental.

ISBN: 0-440-23492-1

Printed in the United States of America

Published simultaneously in Canada

April 2000

10 9 8 7 6 5 4 3 2 1

OPM

For Andrea . . .
again and always

Acknowledgments

My thanks go out to the membership of the Malibu Orchid Society—especially Brian Derby, Richard Klug, and George Vasquez—and to Rod and Janet Carpenter, for their invaluable help with orchid lore.

Thank you to the members of the Los Angeles and Internet Chapters of Sisters in Crime for constant support and clear thinking. To Linda Thrasher, without whom *Death of an Orchid Lover* might still be looking for a title. To Emy de la Fuente Jr., Kevin Burton Smith, and Jerry Wright for Web site stuff. To Alice Fundukian-Anmahouni and Vicken Anmahouni, for *aboush*.

And thanks to my agent, Janet Manus, and my editor, Mike Shohl, for doing what they do.

Thanks to my editor, Mike Shohl, for figuring out what was wrong with this book and showing me how to fix it.

And special thanks to my agent, Janet Manus, for support and enthusiasm that continually go far beyond the call of duty.

1

THE SCENT EVOKED MEMORIES OF MY FATHER AT THE kitchen counter with a hammer and a brown hairy thing.

"Coconut," Gina said. "What smells like coconut?"

The guy who looked like Humpty Dumpty overheard her. He snatched a potful of plant off a table and rushed over. It was a mass of long skinny leaves erupting from bulblike bases. Its flowers, maroon and yellow and about an inch across, resembled old-fashioned airplane propellers with spotted tongues.

He stuck the thing in Gina's face. *"Maxillaria tenuifolia,"* he said.

"Very nice," she said. "Would you please get it out of my nose?"

Humpty's forehead creased as he considered his faux pas. He pulled the plant back, cradling it against his substantial gut. "I only wanted you to enjoy the fullness of its fragrance."

"Which she couldn't do with leaves in her nostrils," said Sam Oliver.

We were at the Palisades Orchid Society's spring social.

Throughout the spacious house overlooking Mulholland Drive, people darted from plant to plant, uttering "oohs" and "ahs" as they alit on one orchid or another. There were plenty for them to alight on. A pot or two on each table, a bunch on shelves near the windows and sliding glass doors. In a corner at least a hundred miniature plants grew under lights on an antique rack.

Why we were there was Sam, the goateed elder statesman of the Culver City Cactus Club. A friend of his was hosting the event and had insisted he come. Sam—who wasn't particularly into orchids—had dragged me along. I, in turn, had dragged Gina.

I took the plant from Humpty. "Is this thing an orchid?"

His eyes flitted from me to Gina to Sam and back to me again. Then, as plant people are apt to do, he spewed. "It is indeed. Not being orchidists, you probably think orchids all resemble the corsages teenagers wear to proms. But there's an infinite variety. There are large orchids, small orchids, white orchids, red orchids, orchids of every hue. Except black. There are no black orchids. Not true black, anyway. Oh, some of your growers say they've created a black orchid, but it isn't a true black, just as there isn't a truly black rose." He took back the plant, brought it to his nose, took a big whiff. "If you like scented plants you might consider *Oncidium* Sharry Baby, with a chocolate fragrance. And of course vanilla comes from an orchid, and—but I'm forgetting my manners." He reached a pudgy hand over to me. "Albert Oberg."

"Our host," Sam said.

I took the hand. Albert surprised me with a solid grip. I'd expected a mackerel. "I'm Joe Portugal," I said.

"Gina Vela," said Gina.

Albert looked to be around sixty, though I suspected his

chubby face was hiding a few years. His features were slightly too close together, accentuating his resemblance to one of those stuffed pantyhose dolls. His head sprouted an incongruous mushroom of luxurious blond hair. He was tall as well as round, several inches more than my five-ten, and he had one of the most impressive stomachs I'd ever seen. It wasn't like a beer belly, suddenly erupting somewhere south of his nipples and hanging off him like he was about due for a cesarean. Instead, it slowly rose just below his shoulders, climbing smoothly to its full rotundity and tapering off equally gracefully, eventually beveling into his stick legs. He didn't seem to have any room for genitals, but with looks like his, he probably didn't need them very often.

To his credit, he wasn't one of those fat guys who wear size 34 pants by slinging them below their guts. His belt threaded directly across his huge expanse of stomach like a pipeline traversing the Alaskan wilderness. The pants were wide-wale corduroys. A herringbone sport jacket over a pale yellow dress shirt completed the picture.

"Well, Albert," I said. "I'm sure these are all fine orchids, and I'm sure there's a lot of interesting things I could learn about them, but I'm more of a succulent kind of guy."

"Succulents?" He said the word like it was an expletive, like I'd told him I collected Nazi war helmets or Charles Manson memorabilia. "Succulents?" He turned to Sam, received a dirty look, came back to me. "What is it about those spiny things that makes them so attractive to some people?"

"We've had this conversation a million times," Sam said.

"So we have. Well. Come along, Sam, I want to show you my new eulophia."

Sam turned to me. "Coming?"

I shook my head. "I've seen enough eulophias for a while."

The two of them wandered off. "What's a eulophia?" Gina asked.

"I have no idea. Come on, let's explore."

We walked into the living room, where a group had gathered around a big flameless stone fireplace. They had the look of plant people. Dressed subtly behind the times, with conventional hairstyles and earnest expressions. One pair stood out, a middle-aged woman standing behind an older one in a wheelchair. Each had a moon-shaped face, watery gray eyes, and a British accent.

Two guys were discussing fertilizers. One said he liked 10-10-10, and the other told him that was fine for growth but not for blooming, and the first said, "Oh, you and your manure." Mr. Manure retorted by saying a lot of the winners at the Santa Barbara show had been over-potashed.

I listened awhile, nodding at appropriate places. When a woman wearing a muumuu decorated with Day-Glo hibiscus began haranguing a man in a priest's collar about tissue culture, I caught Gina's eye and we moved into the kitchen. There, three or four people were dissecting the cancellation of *Ellen*. Gina rolled her eyes and went outside to get a snack. I stood near the sink, looking busy fixing myself a Coke. Someone invaded my space. "Hi," she said. "I think I know you."

She was blond, average height, a few years older than my forty-five, with a look of ethereal intensity. She wore a well-tailored lavender blouse and cream-colored pants. She seemed vaguely familiar, but anyone will if you look at them long enough.

"I'm Laura," she said.

"Joe. Wait. I've got it. The Altair. *Boondale,* right?"

"That's it." We managed a half-assed hug. "How *are* you?"

Fifteen or so years before, when I managed the Altair Theater, Laura Astaire—no relation to Fred—had done two shows there. The first, about the decline and fall of a West Virginia coal mining town, was called *Last Train to Boondale.* It was one of the occasional plays I acted in, portraying Laura's brother, a ne'er-do-well who ended up getting run over by the eponymous train.

Laura followed that with a fine turn in the title role in *Lysistrata,* one of our rare dips into the classics. She'd been an excellent actress. It was a pity that she was mired in the Equity-Waiver scene.

"I'm good," I said. "And you? Still acting?"

"I am. Things have never been better. I did the lead in an *Unsolved Mysteries* last year."

I hadn't seen her in fifteen years and the best she could come up with was an *Unsolved Mysteries*? Things couldn't be *that* much better.

"And how is your career going?" she asked.

"I'm not into acting anymore."

"Then what do you do?"

"I grow cacti and succulents."

"For a living? How unusual."

"For pleasure."

"Then what work do you do?"

"I kind of make a living doing commercials."

"I thought you said you weren't into acting."

"You call commercials acting?"

"Good point. What does 'kind of make' mean?"

"It means if I didn't live in my parents' house I would have to find real work, but since I do, I don't."

"You live with your parents?"

"No. My mom's dead. My father lives in another house."

I remembered one of the things I'd most associated with Laura. "You still into est?"

Back at the Altair I'd suffered a plague of actors who were into pop-psych crazes, of which est was the worst. I couldn't go an hour without one of them buttonholing me with talk of commitment and intention and keeping your word and the great works of Werner Erhard, the movement's founder. One show we did, five out of six actors were into the thing.

I didn't know if est had survived into the late nineties. It seemed to have been replaced by Scientology as the acting fraternity's pop-psych drug of choice. Maybe poor Laura here was the last remnant, still spouting commitment and intention, a sad reminder of something deservedly left in the past.

"No," she said, to my considerable relief. "I stuck with it for several more years. Then I somehow stopped being involved."

"I see. So are you an orchid person now?"

"I'm becoming one. Isn't it odd? For half a century I wasn't at all interested in plants, and now suddenly I'm starting to know about cymbidiums and dendrobiums and all those other -iums." She looked around. "Too noisy here. Let's go outside."

We passed through a den of sorts, filled with more orchids and featuring a big array of framed diplomas on the wall, like you'd see in a doctor's office. An open door led us out into the fabulous mid-April day. Up above, a cloudless sky promised a fine growing season. A windstorm the night before had blown away most of the smog, and I got a good view of the mountains, with a smidgen of snow still on their peaks.

The place was landscaped to the hilt. Mostly tropicals, not the kind of stuff a succulent guy like me generally goes for, but I had to admit it was gorgeous. There were mature palms and huge split-leaf philodendrons. An enormous clump of giant bird of paradise lorded over one corner of the lot. At the far end of the property, an impressive greenhouse sat reflecting the midday sun.

We stopped in the shade of a big king palm. Unseen speakers played classical music. Several blooming orchids sat on a small wrought-iron table. One had a three-foot stalk with scores of inch-wide yellow and red flowers. The inflorescences on the others were much shorter, with roughly half a dozen blooms apiece.

Laura reached into her purse, pulled out a pack of Virginia Slims, gracefully lit one. "You really should think about acting again," she said. "Real acting. Not just commercials."

"Oh?"

"No one ever really stops being an actor."

"Is this going to turn into some airy-fairy thing?"

"No. You were good. I hate to see talent going to waste."

"I didn't have that much talent. Not like you."

"Thanks. But I just think you ought to consider—"

I smiled and shook my head. "Just drop it, okay? I'm not going back to the stage."

She didn't say any more, but I got the feeling I hadn't heard the end of the conversation. She reached out and plucked an orchid off the table. The flowers were three inches across, shaped sort of like moths, mostly white with some dull red around their throats. There were only two leaves, straplike, hugging the surface of the potting mix. Laura reached a finger out toward one of the blossoms, stopped a fraction of an inch short. "One mustn't touch the flowers," she said, in the tone of a child who's just learned some important rule. "Our fingers have oils."

She carefully replaced the pot. "He gave me a few seedlings and keikis. That's how I got started."

"Who did?"

"Albert. He's always giving people plants. Hello."

Gina had magically appeared at my side. I made the introductions. Then: "Maybe you two met at the Altair. Gina worked there too."

"Actress?" Laura said.

"Set design," Gina said.

"Do you still do that?"

"Not exactly. I'm an interior designer."

"I see. So are you two . . ."

"We're just friends," I said.

Laura looked amused. "Well," she said. "I suppose I ought to mingle some more. But I'd love to get together, talk about old times. Let me give you my card." She looked at her cigarette, which she hadn't puffed on since she lit it, rubbed it out on the underside of the table, laid it down. She produced a business card from her purse. Above a phone number with a Hollywood prefix, it said, *Laura Astaire,* then, *Actor*. There weren't any actresses anymore, it seemed. The Screen Actors Guild had awards for best performance by a male actor, and best by a female actor. Not that I'd ever be up for any of them, but by virtue of my commercial work I got to vote on them.

Laura handed over the card. She waited for me to produce one of my own.

"I don't have one," I said.

"My, my. You really *are* out of the game." Out of her purse came a pen and tiny leatherbound pad. "Tell me your number."

I did. She wrote it down, snapped the pad closed, made it disappear. Suddenly her arms were around me. The est people were into hugging. This was a typical est hug, where you stick your butt out in the air so there's no possibility of any midbody contact. "Good to see you again, Joe. I'll give you a call. We'll talk about acting." She looked at Gina, who seemed horrified at the prospect of being hugged, picked up the dead cigarette, and walked back toward the house.

"You want her," Gina said.

"I don't think so. A little too brittle for me." I looked her in the eye. "Do you?"

"Probably not. Anyway, I'm being faithful to Jill."

Something put my radar up. "Trouble in paradise?"

She shook her head a mite too quickly. "No. Everything's great. Come on, let's go get some ribs."

We moved on to the food area and filled our plates. Albert had brought in mass quantities of barbecued ribs and chicken. The rest was potluck. We found a couple of relatively isolated lawn chairs, but in a few minutes we were surrounded by the orchid people. They did their best to draw us into conversation. We did our best to stick to our own. We didn't do badly, except for a woman who told us more than we'd ever care to know about pleurothallids, whatever they were.

2

SAM CAME OVER HALF AN HOUR BEFORE I WAS DUE TO LEAVE for a bug-salesman gig at Beverly Center. "Albert wants to make sure you don't go without seeing the greenhouse."

I got up from the soft patch of grass I'd found myself and looked around for Gina. She was deep in conversation with one of the guys from the kitchen. They were discussing bull-nose edges. Interior design talk.

I walked to the greenhouse, a structure maybe fifty feet long and twenty-five wide, with the summit of its peaked roof eight feet or so above my head. The clear parts were glass, and the metal frame looked like it could have withstood an 8 on the Richter scale. Quite a difference from my flimsy construction of fiberglass and two-by-fours.

A sign asked that I close the door behind me. I complied. Then I turned and wandered through, taking in the spectacle.

There must have been several thousand orchid plants. There were white flowers and purple ones and more white ones and more purple ones. Big red ones and little yellow ones and some in a peculiar pale green. Some had two colors and some had three, and the count went up from there.

Some of the orchids would have looked at home on a high school senior's wrist on prom night. Others I wouldn't have suspected were orchids, were they not in an orchid house. Their blooms had weird wings, long spurs, whiskers, other appendages. Sizes ranged from dessert plate down to a quarter inch or less. Some of the flower stalks poked up to eye level; some dangled over the lips of pots. Every once in a while I would catch a whiff of scent. Sometimes I could track it down, sometimes I couldn't.

The walls were hung with plaques of wood and bark and other natural materials, each with one or more plants magically attached and doing just fine in the absence of any noticeable trace of soil. Metal pipes crisscrossed overhead, and scores of plants descended from them in hanging pots, or in wooden baskets with no discernible potting mix in them, with roots gnarling around the slats and dangling below.

Every few minutes mist burst from nozzles on the pipes. It made it nicely cool and slightly humid, a far cry from the hothouse conditions I thought orchids liked.

In keeping with my taste in plants, I found myself attracted not so much to the ones that were traditionally beautiful, but more to the odd ones. I found one that resembled a bumblebee and one that looked like a tiny mountain man with a hat and beard. Nature found infinite ways to put a few basic flower parts together in order to attract pollinators and perpetuate the species.

Through the glass I noticed an outdoor bench full of plants with lots of colorful flowers, and I went back out to investigate. They were in one- and two-gallon pots and had long leaves like lilies' Like most of the orchids, they were potted in a fine version of the bark chips people dump in their yards for mulch. The average size was a half to three quarters of an inch. There was a little perlite in there too, puffy white particles that would inevitably float to the top of the pot, wash out, and litter the ground. I also saw a Styrofoam noodle or two.

The flower stalks bore a dozen or more blooms apiece, in colors from deep purple to white and everything in between, with all sorts of mottlings and stripings and other markings. The flowers were splendid. But I couldn't help thinking how ugly the plants would be when they weren't in bloom.

"You like those cymbidiums?" It was the older of the British ladies from the group by the fireplace. She was trundling her wheelchair along the concrete path.

"They're very nice," I said.

"They're wretched most of the year. But my daughter Mo is fond of them, so we have some around the place. She doesn't know orchids, of course. She grows roses. Did you know that?"

"I didn't."

"I'm the orchid person, not her. If it has to do with orchids around here, I know about it. I'm Dorothy Lennox. Everyone calls me Dottie."

I introduced myself and held out a hand. She reached out and took it. Hers was thin and bony, the skin translucent, but her grip was firm. She leaned forward, spoke quietly so only I could hear. "My dear mother, God rest her soul, called me Dot, and I always hated that, but I never told her."

"Then I won't either."

Dottie thought that the height of hilarity. Her laugh was a good-witch cackle. "You're a funny young man. You should come to the orchid society meetings. It's a bunch of fussbudgets. All those people worrying about the judging."

"Then why do you go?"

"It gets me out of the house. I don't get out of the house very often, you know, what with my affliction and all." She slapped the bony tops of her thighs. "These don't work too well. Oh, dear. Here comes Albert. I was going to steal a division of his *Dendrobium smillieae*, but now I won't be able to."

She'd obviously said it for his benefit. "If you want some of my *smillieae*, Dottie," he said, "you shall have it."

He entered the greenhouse. We watched through the glass as he produced a plant shears from who knew where, dipped it into a bucket of God knew what, and snipped off a chunk of a plant that looked to me like dozens of others surrounding it. He shook off debris, came back outside, presented the cutting to Dottie. "Here you are, dear."

"Thanks ever so much, Albert." She turned to me, gave me a big wink. "That Albert. Such a dear. If I were just ten years younger . . ." She shook her head. "I had better find Mo. She gets into trouble."

She opened the big crocheted bag in her lap, pulled out a pencil and a scrap of paper. "You'll come see me. I'll show you my plants. Come anytime." She wrote on the paper, held it out until I took it, then wheeled away.

"She's quite a character," Albert said.

"Seems to be." I glanced at the paper. Dottie lived in Hawthorne, a small city south of the Westside. I didn't think I'd ever been there.

Albert led me back inside, made an expansive gesture, and said, "What do you think?"

I stuck Dottie's address in my wallet. "It's very impressive. But not what I expected. I thought orchids liked heat and a closed-up atmosphere."

He shook his head. His blond mane jiggled. "Folklore. In the early days, because the plants came from the tropics, they were grown in structures called 'stoves,' with coal fires and no ventilation. It made the plantsmen ill to work in there. Finally they deduced that orchids are mostly epiphytes. That means they live in trees."

I smiled. "I know the term. Epiphytic cacti, you know?"

"Of course." He momentarily bowed his head to acknowledge my wisdom. "Once those old plant people realized that, they began to tailor conditions better. These days, we know how to simulate the plants' natural situation pretty darned well. Although people are always coming up with new wrinkles."

"Such as?"

"The latest is—wait, I have a few here, let me show you." He rooted around among the pots and brought me a four-incher that appeared to be filled with little pieces of rubber. "Shredded auto tires," he said. "It shows a lot of promise as a medium. It doesn't compact like bark does."

"Seems weird. What about nutrients?"

"That's what fertilizers are for." He put the plant back. "One has to try strange things if one is to be successful with plants. I've seen so many odd experiments over the years."

"How many years?"

"I've collected for over a quarter of a century. But I've really been seriously at it since I retired and moved to Los Angeles eight years ago. The climate back east made it difficult to maintain much of a collection." He got all dreamy-eyed. "I love nurturing them. Bringing a plant along from a tiny seedling to what the catalogues call a 'mature, blooming-size plant.' Of course, even getting to the seedling stage can be tricky. Orchid seed is incredibly fine. There are thousands in each pod. And they are very difficult to germinate. Many people send their pods out for germination. I do my own." He was beginning to sound like PBS.

"Years ago," he went on, "growers tried all sorts of media, and met with little success. They finally determined they had the best luck sowing the plants at the base of the mother plant. Eventually it was found that micorrhizae, symbiotic fungi in the medium, were instrumental in germinating the seed. Oh, just listen to me go on."

He picked up one of the plants with strap-shaped leaves, like the one Laura'd nearly defiled. Its stalk poked up ten inches or so, held in place by an elegant wire mechanism. The flowers were orange-red, with little yellow dots. "Look at this phalaenopsis," he said. "Or moth orchid, to the layman. I made this cross myself. One reason hybridization is so difficult is that the results of a particular cross can vary widely, even if your stud plants are wonderful. You have to go through many inferior specimens to find the good ones."

He handed me the plant. "This is one of the good ones. I got an Award of Merit on it. One step short of the best. And I have high hopes for the next generation."

"Don't we all."

He smiled, nodded. "Well. I suppose I ought to go back to my guests. Feel free to look around, and if you see something you want a piece of, come after me."

"Thanks."

"I know you're thinking that won't happen. But you probably didn't expect to get involved in succulents either, did you?"

"Now that you mention it."

"You'll see a plant you want and suddenly you, too, will have orchid fever." He made his way outside.

I replaced the plant on the bench and checked my watch. Nearly time to collect Gina and head back to the flatlands. I cruised a little more. No. It wasn't going to happen. I had way too many plants as it was. No need to get launched on a whole new botanical family.

I stopped by some big frilly orchids like the ones in corsages. Lots of pinkish-purples, with an assortment of other colors. Each erect stem had just a few leaves, but new growth sprang from the base of the old and the plants filled the pots. One bloom had a lustrous white surface that begged to be touched. I reached out to do so.

"Shouldn't touch the flowers," someone said.

I whipped my hand back, turned to see who it was. A woman wearing an enchanting half-smile was watching me.

"Right," I said. "Our fingers have oils."

My first impression was that she was well over fifty, but I quickly realized that was simply because her hair, pulled back in a French braid, had all gone silver-gray, a nice mix of darker and lighter tones. Once I got past the hair, I realized she was probably a few years younger than me. She had deep brown eyes. Her weight was appropriate to her height, which was nearly equal to my own. She wore loose black jeans and a white sleeveless top that revealed well-toned arms.

She walked over, dug around the base of one of the orchids with her fingers, removed a dead leaf. Then she looked at me. "Go ahead and touch it. No orchid ever pooped out because someone touched it."

As I fondled the petals, another plant caught her eye. More digging turned up a second brown leaf. She saw me watching her, gave me a slightly embarrassed smile, and tossed the debris into a bucket marked COMPOST. "I heard someone say you're into cacti," she said. "I don't quite understand that."

Were the plant police on duty? "Cactus-collecting invader on premises. Beware."

"It's hard to explain," I said. "It's like, when you see a

plant and you like it, you buy it. It just happens that most of the plants that I like happen to be succulents. They're kind of . . . primeval, I guess is the best word, although actually they're among the latest-developing plant families." Now *I* sounded like PBS.

"I wasn't faulting you."

"I didn't think you were," I said. "And you? What's the attraction with orchids? I mean, when they're not in bloom they all look pretty plain, don't they?"

"The attraction comes out when they *are* in bloom."

"Maybe that's the difference between your people and mine. You guys are willing to wait for the good stuff. We're into instant gratification." I pointed outside at the cymbidiums. "Take those, for instance. The flowers are nice, sure. But is it really worth looking at an ugly plant fifty-one weeks a year just for a week's worth of bloom?"

"They bloom much longer than that. At least two months."

"They do?"

"Sure. Most orchids are long-lasting. Some aren't, some last a week or less, but most go on for several at least. Not like cactus flowers. One, two days and that's it, most of the time. Am I right?"

"I don't really grow cacti for the flowers."

"And I don't really grow orchids for the plants themselves."

"Why do I have the feeling we're having an argument here?"

"It's a discussion, not an argument." She saw my discomfort, smiled, shook her head. "I'm sorry. I'm afraid I'm a bit of an evangelist sometimes."

"It's okay." I fingered a leaf, stuck my nose into a greenish-yellow flower, picking up a pleasant if faint scent. "They're interesting, I guess."

"*Interesting* means a person hates something."

"Well . . ."

"Cymbidiums can take direct sun, which most orchids can't. You can grow them outside all year here in southern California. You can even put them in the ground. They're terrestrials."

"As opposed to extraterrestrials?"

Her smile told me she got the joke and knew I could do better. "As opposed to epiphytes. Plants which—"

"Grow on trees. I know about epiphytes. I have a patio filled with epiphytic cacti. Rhipsalis and epiphyllums and stuff like that. I have an orchid too."

"What kind?"

"An epidendrum. Someone gave me a cutting, and I stuck it in a pot and it took off. Flowers all the time. Kind of neat."

She nodded. "Well. I think I'll go freshen my drink." She didn't have a drink.

She stuck out a hand. "Nice meeting you . . ."

I told her my name. "And you're?"

"Sharon. Sharon Turner." She looked into my eyes for a couple of seconds, turned, walked away.

I watched her go out, then followed. When I got outside, she'd already disappeared. I wanted to talk to her some more. How could I arrange that?

It would have to wait. All my greenhouse conversations had put me behind schedule. I tracked Gina down and we bid adieu to Albert and to Sam. As we reached the front door, I scanned the place for Sharon. I spotted her in the kitchen and caught her eye. She smiled slightly, gave me a half-wave, turned away. I watched her a second or two more before going.

3

My Datsun pickup was stopped at a red light at Laurel Canyon and Mt. Olympus. I had Procol Harum in the cassette deck. "Conquistador" was on, not the live-with-orchestra version they play on the classic rock stations, but the one on the first album, the one only people with their musical heads still stuck in the sixties know.

Cassette deck. It still sounded weird. My millions-of-years-old eight-track had finally given up the ghost the previous fall. After nearly mail-ordering a new one from the J.C. Whitney catalogue, I'd moved on to the nineties. Or at least the late seventies.

"That woman," Gina said.

"Laura?"

"No. The one you sort of said goodbye to when we left."

"Her name's Sharon."

"You're going to go out with her."

"Not that I know of. I'll probably never see her again."

The light changed. We pulled away, continued down the hill, past Sunset, where Laurel Canyon turns into Crescent Heights. I thought about what Gina had said. I felt like a teenager whose mom had asked, "You like Susie, don't you?"

But Sharon was certainly intelligent and attractive. And we shared an interest in plants. Maybe asking her out would be an interesting idea.

As we turned onto Santa Monica, a couple of blocks from Gina's condo, she said, "You will, you know."

"Will what?"

"Screw her."

"I love it when you talk dirty."

"Stop joking. This is serious."

"Why is it so serious?"

"Because I don't need you getting mixed up with some orchid woman."

"I'm not mixed up. Look, you're acting weird. Will you tell me what's wrong?"

She shook her head. I dropped her at her condo and headed for Beverly Center.

Most days I hung around the greenhouse, then maybe did some volunteer work at the Kawamura Conservatory at UCLA. Commercials paid well and made few claims on my time. And I didn't really need much money. My father refused to accept any rent for the house, not that I pushed him very hard on it.

My agent, Elaine Chen—who's also my cousin; Chen is her married name—sent me on a couple of auditions a week. I got lucky on a fair percentage, and stole jobs from people who put all their waking hours into making themselves appealing to casting directors. I did maybe a half-dozen commercials a year, say twenty thousand dollars' worth, and that was plenty. My daily rate had inched up to over a thousand, and with residuals I made out okay.

The previous year I'd done a series of spots for Olsen's Natural Garden Solutions, and somehow the chemistry between my "wife" and "kids" and me had touched a chord. People came up to me on the street and said, "It takes a bug to catch a bug," and smiled knowingly. And I'd get embarrassed and hide in a doorway.

Now, with warm weather breaking out and aphids having a field day with people's roses and such, they'd brought the commercials back. And someone at Olsen's ad agency had gotten the bright idea to take Diane Shostakovich—the actress who played my wife—and me, and dump us in kiosks at shopping malls, surrounded by stacks of biological controls, and have us tell the public all about them. Rather, Diane would tell them and I would act ignorant, the same role I played in the commercials.

They'd scheduled a whole bunch of these appearances, which struck me as an easy, if inane, way to supplement my income. Plus, I got to go to exotic locales like Pasadena, home of the Tournament of Roses, and Northridge, home of the Northridge Earthquake.

My dog and pony show at Beverly Center began at one. I put on my fake wedding ring in the parking structure, then spent several hours listening to Diane spout interesting facts like "The descendants of a single female ladybird beetle can eat two hundred thousand aphids in one season" while we sold dozens of packs of them. And of lacewing larvae. And of parasitic wasps.

Actually, I let Diane handle the parasitic wasps. Even though I knew they were minuscule and couldn't possibly hurt me, I couldn't get over the fact that they were wasps, a type of insect I have a completely irrational fear of. Diane, fortunately, had caught on to this back when we were shooting the commercials.

We were off at five. Diane wanted a snack, so we went to the food court for frozen yogurts. She was thin, short, blond, in her late thirties. She'd been moderately successful in commercials and as a day player on TV, and did a lot of theater too. Regional, New York for a while. I'd met her long ago when she did a show at the Altair.

A play she'd been rehearsing was opening the following weekend. I'd asked her several times to tell me about it, but she kept blowing me off. She seemed sheepish about it, making me think it was one of those shows you do for exposure but would just as soon your friends didn't know about. I told her I wasn't going to let her leave the table until she filled me in.

She shook her head. "It's experimental yet commercial."

"That usually means at the end everyone takes their clothes off."

She laughed. "It's really not bad. And only one person takes her clothes off."

"You?"

"No, not me. The playwright's the producer of *Huff and Petty,* you know, the cop show? And he's getting some important people down to see it, and I have a pretty meaty part. Exposure, you know?"

"What's it called?"

"*Go Down Moses.* It's about a fictional conspiracy between Grandma Moses and Robert Moses."

"Who's Robert Moses?"

"Some New Yorker who was involved in transportation improvement and things like that. He was a boyhood hero of the playwright."

"When should I come see it?"

"You don't have to, you know."

"I want to."

"You're sweet. Can you come next Saturday? Friday's opening, we've papered the house to make it look good for the critics, but we're trying to get some people in Saturday so we have an audience to work with. I can probably get you comps." Theater talk for freebies. From the word *complimentary*.

"Comps are good."

"I can get you at least two. Do you want to bring someone? I don't really know a whole lot about you, Joe. I know you're not married, but do you have a girlfriend or anything? Wait, I shouldn't assume. Not in this business. A boyfriend?"

Gina would go with me. We'd spent years being each other's dates when the occasion demanded.

Then I thought of Jill. Even after four months, I was having trouble remembering that Gina wasn't available for me every Saturday night. And with Jill in San Francisco this weekend, there was a good chance Gina'd be tied up with her all the next. Maybe I could wait until later in the run to—

"Joe? Hello?"

"Sorry. Two for this Saturday would be great. And I'm straight, by the way."

"Good," Diane said. "I mean, good that you're coming. It really doesn't matter to me if you're straight or not."

"I don't know why I said that."

"You'll meet Tom Saturday. My other husband."

"I'm looking forward to it."

Gina came over at seven. We drove to Trader Joe's and picked up some frozen shrimp and stir-fry vegetables and cheap portobello mushrooms. Then we went to the Baskin-Robbins on Venice and got a couple of hand-packed pints. I asked the teenage girl behind the counter why two scoops cost $3.55, while a hand-packed pint, which was twice as big, was only a quarter or so more. Gina berated me for giving the poor kid a hard time. "Why doesn't the American public figure this out?" I asked, and Gina gave me a glare and I shut up.

We cooked everything except the ice cream in my electric wok, then sat watching a *National Geographic* special on the giant squid. I complained that they never actually showed the beast, except in animation. Gina pointed out that they couldn't do that, since nobody had ever seen a live one, and I said, "Still," in that way you say "still" when you know the other person's logic is faultless and you wish it weren't.

A commercial came on. Gina got up to spoon out dessert. I cycled the remote, stopping on the lipstick commercial with Ziggy Marley prancing on the beach with Tyra Banks and some other models. Gina came back in, with huge dishes of ice cream in hand, and saw me watching it. She seemed as if she wanted to say something, but she refrained.

Three hours later. We were still on the couch, still munching, still soaking up mindless television. Ziggy Marley and his harem came on again. I perked up.

"You know," Gina said. "It's really okay with me if you go out with the orchid woman."

"Thank you, O One-who-gives-permission."

"I mean, you do need a girlfriend."

"Tell me about it."

She twisted around on the couch, put her hands on my shoulders, looked me in the eye. "We've been over this a thousand times. It's not you."

"I seem to be the common denominator, don't I? Jeez, I haven't had a Real Date since, what, last July with Iris." In recognition of the ongoing spottiness of our social lives, Gina and I had long ago given Real Dates the capitalized status usually reserved for events like the Age of Reason and the Summer of Love.

I focused on Gina, realized she didn't know what to say.

"I'm sorry, Gi. I shouldn't lay this on you. You have a nice relationship. I shouldn't bore you with my lack of one."

"Yeah," she said. "I have a nice relationship."

There it was again. "What's wrong?"

"Nothing. Everything with Jill is fine."

"Gi, we've been friends long enough that I can tell when you're bullshitting. What's wrong?"

"It's nothing."

"It's something. What?"

She let go of my shoulders and slumped back in a corner of the couch. She doesn't slump very often. She looked very small. "I think she's seeing someone else."

"Why do you think that?"

"I don't know, it's just a feeling I get, like she has something to tell me that she can't get up the courage to tell me. I know she's up in San Francisco visiting friends, but I can't help wondering if she's really with somebody else. Because otherwise why wouldn't she invite me?"

A small admission: some part of me was happy at the prospect of Gina and Jill breaking up. Because, no matter that our relationship hadn't been romantic for seventeen years, sometimes I wanted Gina all to myself.

I shook my head. "She's not good enough for you anyway. And if you break up, you'll find someone else. You always do."

"Oh, eventually I do, but they never stick."

"Carlos would have stuck, if you'd let him."

"Carlos's chief attraction was his ass."

"And a fine ass it was."

"Not fine enough to make up for his . . ." She reached out a hand, as if expecting to pluck the word from midair.

"*Vapidity* is the word you're looking for. Okay, you're right about Carlos."

She looked at me sadly. "Sometimes I think . . ." She stopped, seeming to wonder if she should go on, and phrasing in her head what she would say if she did. The telephone rang.

We looked at each other stupidly. "Are you going to answer it?" Gina asked.

"I guess so." I checked my watch. Ten after midnight. I pulled myself up and went to the phone. "Hello."

"Joe?" The voice was familiar but not instantly identifiable.

"Yes?"

"It's Laura."

"Oh. Hi." A sequence of thoughts cascaded through my head. She wanted to convince me to get back into acting. She'd had a sudden urge to reinvestigate est and wanted me to come along. She wanted to ask me out on a date. "How are you?"

"Not good."

"What's going on?"

"It's Albert."

"Albert? Albert-from-this-afternoon Albert?"

"Yes. He's dead."

"Dead? What happened?"

"He was murdered. And they think I did it."

4

GINA WAS PRACTICALLY JUMPING UP AND DOWN ON THE couch, trying to get me to tell her what was going on. I held up a hand to get her to wait.

"What do you want me to do?" I asked Laura.

"Get me out of here."

"Where's 'here'?"

"The police station on Wilcox. They said they're about done with me. They offered to drive me home, but I don't want to be home by myself. Wait." I could hear her talking to someone else. When she came back on, she said, "Please come get me."

"What just happened?"

"Some new detective is here. He wants to ask me more questions. Just come get me, all right?"

"I'm on my way." We hung up.

"Give," Gina said. "Who's dead?"

"Our friend fat Albert. Come on."

Gina and I sat in the lobby of the LAPD Hollywood Division, wondering why Laura had chosen me to call. Maybe, we thought, it was because I was fresh in her mind. Or maybe she didn't know anybody else well enough to call. All this time in L.A. and she had no friends. How tragic. How nice of us to make up a whole life for poor Laura.

Time stretched. I kept catching whiffs of cigar smoke from somewhere in the back. Cops escorted an assortment of lowlifes through. Big burly guys who'd had a bit too much to drink. Little men with anxious faces, speaking a variety of incomprehensible languages. Hookers from many lands, wearing hot pants and tube tops and shoes time-warped from the days of disco. The cold fluorescent lighting made them all look sick.

We sat twiddling our thumbs until someone said, "Jeez. Look what the cat dragged in."

I looked up. The man standing in front of me was short, with a fringe of dark hair surrounding a bald pate. He had accusing brown eyes with well-defined bags under them, and a pair of half-glasses perched on his nose. He wore a well-cut gray suit, a pale blue shirt, and a tie with pheasants on it.

His name was Hector Casillas. He was an LAPD homicide detective. The previous spring my friend Brenda Belinski had been murdered. I'd been Casillas's number one suspect. He was all over my tail, trying to prove I did it, showing up on my doorstep at inopportune times to ask me inflammatory questions. He was good at what he did, but he was a giant pain in the ass while he did it.

"What the hell are you doing here?" I said.

"The real question," he said, "is what the hell are *you* doing here?"

"I'm picking up a friend."

"Let me guess. Laura Astaire."

I nodded.

"Figures."

"How come you're up here in Hollywood?" I said. "You been transferred?"

He shook his head. "I'm in Robbery–Homicide now, not that it's any of your business. Which means I get to deal with killers all over the city. Isn't that nice for me?"

"What about Burns?" Detective Alberta Burns had been Casillas's partner.

"She's still at Pacific Division. Got a new partner now. What do you care?"

Good question. Damn. Who needed to see Casillas again? "So you're involved in the Albert Oberg case?"

"Sure am, not that that's any of your business either. Look. Don't get in my hair again. *Capiche?*"

I managed not to say, "What hair?" Instead I told him that I capiched fine and asked where Laura was.

"I'm right here." She came around a corner, looking haggard and drained. "They're done with me now, so can you please take me home?"

"Sure thing." I brushed past Casillas, took Laura's arm, and shepherded her toward the door.

Laura lived in Beachwood Canyon, up above Franklin. An area with a certain cachet, like the people who live there are on the good side of the hipness bell curve. In reality, the lower part, where Laura lived, is a bunch of apartment buildings just like the ones all over the rest of Hollywood and West Hollywood and North Hollywood and everywhere else unsuccessful actors live.

Her building—the same one she'd lived in way back

when—was like a million others in L.A. Two stories, eight apartments, with the front ones on the second floor jutting out over the parking area. Dingbat style, they called it. Decorations mounted on the taupe outside walls looked like alien hieroglyphics from a science fiction movie. Beneath them, a house number spelled out in words clung grimly, although the *Seven* was short a screw and dangled at an angle its designer never intended. There was a big jacaranda out front, with only a smattering of flowers.

Gina parked her Volvo on the street, and she and I got out. After a few seconds Laura realized we were waiting and emerged too. Just as she'd done the second we left the police station, she lit a cigarette, took a puff, stubbed it out on the sidewalk. She led us up the sloping driveway, around to the north side of the building, to her ground-floor apartment. A couple of orchid plants sat by the door. They didn't look good. Probably weren't getting enough light.

Laura unlocked the latch and the deadbolt and led us into her living room. Judging from the layout, and having been in dozens of similar apartments, I was almost sure it was the only room, other than the kitchen and, I assumed, a bathroom.

I couldn't help sniffing when we walked in. But there wasn't any cigarette odor. Either Laura only smoked outside, or, at one puff per cigarette, the stink just never accumulated.

She kept the place neat. A few more orchids were scattered around on tables and the counter that separated the living room and kitchen. The walls were jammed with pictures, awards, and posters. A photo of Werner Erhard. Three Drama-Logue awards, one for a play I'd actually heard of. Everyone in town had Drama-Logue awards. Most of them put them on their resumés, even though six hundred or so a year were given out. Even I had gotten one, for a mediocre performance in a dreadful play. The critic was a little old lady who swore I looked just like her nephew. "I'll remember you," she'd said, and she did, with one of her myriad awards.

Laura asked if we wanted anything. We told her we didn't. She insisted we did. We compromised on tea. She went into the tiny kitchen to make it. I sat on a worn sofa that felt like it had a bed inside, which it more or less had to. Gina considered an old easy chair resembling the father's on *Frasier,* though minus the duct tape. The orange tabby upon it looked up at her and yawned. Gina wrinkled her nose and sat beside me.

Laura came out with tea in big green mugs and a plate loaded with Chips Ahoy! or their close relatives. She set them on a glass and fake wood coffee table and sat in the easy chair. The cat jumped onto the arm of the chair and crouched, looking peeved.

Laura took a sip of tea, a bit of cookie. "I suppose you're wondering why I called you," she said.

"Kind of," I said.

"I went through all the people I knew, and I didn't want to be with any of them. Is that sad, or what? And you were fresh in my mind."

It was as good an explanation as any. Which was why I didn't like it. "There's something else, isn't there?"

She nodded. "After you left this afternoon, I remembered reading about you in the paper last year. When your friend was killed."

The Brenda business. After I stumbled upon the murderer's identity, I'd been a media sensation for about a day and a half.

"I felt sheepish, not having remembered about that when I talked to you. Then, when all this police activity happened,

I thought you might be able to give me some help. Since you'd been exposed to them before."

That explanation worked a little better. But not much. I decided not to push her on it. "Tell me what happened," I said.

It took her a beat or two to get started. "I was the last one to leave the party. I stayed on to help Albert clean up. He insisted his cleaning lady would come in and take care of things, and I said—but you don't care about that, do you?"

"Not particularly," Gina said.

"In any event, I left about seven."

"Where'd you go?" Gina asked.

"I was with a friend."

"Which friend?"

Laura stared at her before turning to me. "She's as inquisitive as that Detective Casillas."

"And," Gina said, "she loves being talked about in the third person."

"Sorry. I'm under a strain."

Gina avoided saying something inappropriate and mounted a conciliatory smile. "You were about to tell us where you went."

"Like I said, I was at a friend's house. Helen Gartner. We had dinner."

"Where's she live?" I asked.

"Tarzana." A residential area in the San Fernando Valley, so named because it grew up around Edgar Rice Burroughs's ranch.

"How long were you there?"

"A few hours."

"Anyone else see you there?"

She shook her head. "Her husband was at a hockey game in Anaheim. I left before he came home."

"Why didn't you call this Helen when the police came for you?" Gina said.

It took Laura a second. "I just didn't think of it. I thought of Joe."

"And after you left her place?" I said.

"I came back here to feed Monty."

"Then?"

Laura looked blankly at me, going inside herself, as if doing some prep work before delivering a particularly difficult line of dialogue.

"Laura? After you fed the cat, you . . ."

"I went up to Albert's."

"How come?" Gina said.

"Well."

"Well, what?"

She got up, opened the door, lit a cigarette, stood half in and half out of the house. "Albert and I were involved."

"Romantically?" I said.

She indulged in a second puff before stubbing out the cigarette. She came back in, sat back down. "Is it so hard to believe? I know Albert isn't—wasn't the most handsome man, but he was intelligent and caring and—"

"Whoa." I held my hands up. "No one's putting down your choice of boyfriend." I saw my hands up there, decided they didn't need to be, dropped them to my lap. "And what happened at Albert's?"

"I found him on the floor in the living room. He looked like a sleeping little boy. Except for the blood." She focused on me. "I suppose I screamed. That's what people seem to do in that situation, and I suppose that's what I did. I called 911, but I was certain he was already dead."

"How?" Gina said.

Laura shifted to face her. "I just was, all right?" She

gulped some tea and absently petted Monty, whose crouch had transmuted into a meat loaf position. "And I was right. The police said he would have died within minutes after those wounds, that there was nothing anyone could have done."

"What kind of wounds?"

"Gunshot. The first thing they asked me was whether I owned a gun. Of course I don't own a gun. What kind of person owns a gun?"

Gina and I exchanged looks. Gina owned a gun.

"In any event," Laura said, "the paramedics came, and the police, and the hours after that are a bit of a blur. Eventually they took me down to the station, and asked me the same questions over and over. When they were done I called you, but while we were on the phone that Casillas character came along, and he asked me the same questions yet again, along with some new ones."

"What kind of questions?" I asked.

"Mostly about where I was tonight, and my relationship with Albert. And if anyone would have had any reason to kill him."

"What did you say to that?"

"I couldn't come up with anyone. Albert was a lovely man. He didn't have any enemies that I knew of. He really had few contacts outside the orchid world. Orchids were his life."

"He ever have arguments with any of the people in the, uh, orchid world?"

"He's had disagreements with various members of the orchid society, but nothing serious. No one in the group gets along with everyone." She shook her head. "No. I haven't a clue who might have shot him."

Gina and I kept pushing Laura for someone who might have wanted Albert dead. She kept insisting she knew of no one. I also worked the conversation back to why she'd chosen me to call, but she insisted it was because of my previous association with the police. She seemed to be telling the truth, but she was, after all, an actress.

Eventually she became less receptive to our questions. I drained my cold tea and stood. "We should get going. Come on, Gi."

Laura nodded. "I need to get to bed." She got to her feet as well, and Gina followed suit. Laura led us to the door, but instead of opening it, she turned and leaned against it. "Could I ask a favor?" she said.

"Sure thing," I said.

"It's rather a big one."

"What is it?"

"Would you find out who killed Albert?"

"What makes you think I can do that?"

"You did it once before."

"That was a fluke."

"Then why were you—and you, Gina—asking me all those questions?"

"It seemed like the thing to do."

She managed a weak smile. "Admit it, Joe, you're intrigued by this. You want to ask more people more questions. I could see it in your face the whole time we were talking. Doesn't he, Gina?"

"That would be my guess," Gina said.

"What?" I turned to her. "You're ganging up on me."

"Maybe."

I drew a deep breath, faced Laura again. "I'll see what I can scout up."

"That's all I can ask," she said. "There's an orchid show at the Church of God in Torrance tomorrow. Maybe you could go there and find something out." She pushed herself away from the door, opened it, let us out into the cool darkness. No hug, est or otherwise.

When we got out to the curb, I realized Laura's car was probably still up at Albert's. I thought about going back and offering to help her get it. But she was a big girl. She'd figure something out.

When we got back to the car, Gina said, "You don't believe her, do you?"

"Not totally. You think she killed the guy?"

She shook her head. "My gut says no. But there's something she's not telling us."

"I got the same feeling."

By the time Gina dropped me off at home, it was nearly four. I set the clock for eight and went to bed.

5

THE REASON I SET MY CLOCK FOR EIGHT ON A SUNDAY morning, thus ensuring myself no more than four hours sleep, was that I was due at a yard dig in Westwood at ten, and I had to whip up a batch of my succulent eggplant salad before I left. I needed to prepare my signature dish because the Culver City Cactus Club—which I was president of—was having a board meeting at my place at seven that evening, and I'd promised to make the eggplant, and the other board members would whine if they didn't get it. I could have waited until afternoon, but I didn't know how long I'd be at the orchid show. Besides, the stuff tastes better when it sits in the refrigerator for a few hours. The flavors meld, and all that.

I put on a robe and karate slippers and started some water for tea. I grabbed the two eggplants I'd bought the morning before, poked them with a fork, stuck them in the oven. When the water boiled, I made a cup of Darjeeling and carried it out the back door to the greenhouse.

It was cool out, with a cloud cover that threatened rain. The last remnants of El Niño, I supposed. I pulled my robe tighter around me, stepped into the greenhouse, began my rounds. I did this every morning, checking for buds and bugs, inspecting for new growth and unexpected flowers, drawing strength from the plants.

It was that glorious time of year when most of them were breaking dormancy. A couple of pachypodiums had already popped their yellow flowers, and the rest were leafing out, ending the close resemblance to cacti they bore when they were asleep. The Madagascar euphorbias were adding leaves too, and many of the cacti had the lighter green at their crowns that marked the resumption of growth.

It was time for my semiannual application of Cygon. It was the only thing that would keep scale and mealybugs from feasting on all the new growth. But I knew I was going to skip the dousing, as I'd missed the one the previous fall. I'd have to find some other, less noxious way to control the pests. The horrid odor of Cygon would forever be associated with Brenda's death in my mind.

I found a surprise among the discocacti. They're small globular species from Brazil, equipped with cephalia—furry flower-bearing heads that sit atop their bodies—and remarkable for how quickly their buds develop. One morning you'll see a white cone, the tip of a bud, poking out of the cephalium. A couple of hours later it's noticeably longer. By that evening it's a couple of inches long, and it blooms and fills the greenhouse with its almost sickly sweet scent. The next morning it's a limp cylinder of tissue. As Sharon, the woman I'd met at Albert's, had pointed out, one of the problems with growing cacti. Ephemeral flowers.

The surprise was on my *Discocactus nigrisaetosus*. A bud peeked from its cephalium. I made a mental note to check back that evening. But I knew I would forget. As the Big Five-O had begun looming in my consciousness, I'd become more and more aware that I was forgetting things. They had a name for my condition. CRS. Can't Remember Shit.

I went in the house, checked the eggplants. Not soft enough yet. I visited the canary room, dealt with food and water, changed the paper at the bottom of the floor-to-ceiling cage. I had a little conversation with the birds. As usual, I did most of the talking. I asked them if they missed their mommy. Brenda'd been their mommy. I'd taken the birds in when she died. I was thinking of Brenda a lot that morning.

I took a shower, washed away some of the lack-of-sleep feeling, returned to the kitchen. The eggplants still weren't cooperating. I chopped the tomatoes and scallions and mixed the spices. While I was squeezing the lemon, I noticed a couple of ants wandering along the wall above the counter. Argentine ants, merely an eighth of an inch long. They're ubiquitous in the Los Angeles area, digging their tunnels all over your yard, carrying their little larvae and pupae to safety every time you run the sprinkler. They habitually wandered into my kitchen, occasionally causing a problem big enough for me to do something about, but I hadn't seen any in weeks. There weren't enough yet to worry about, and often they'd go away by themselves.

The eggplants, I decided, were done enough. I took them out and left them to cool. I filled a bowl with Grape-Nuts, tore off a banana, poured a glass of Trader Joe's pear juice. I went out to the Jungle, which is my banal name for the patio on the south side of my house, the place I'd mentioned to Sharon. It's shaded by an immense elm tree next door, and on it I grow a lot of epiphytic cacti and viny ceropegias and other plants that don't need a lot of sun.

I lasted only a couple of minutes out there. The extended family of weirdos next door was playing *The Best of Iron*

Butterfly at a volume of eleven. Too much for a guy with four hours sleep. I went inside and ate at the coffee table, then threw together the salad, got dressed, and went off to the yard dig.

Once a year or so some club member or previously unknown succulent enthusiast got tired of collecting, or got old and couldn't care for their plants, or died. Someone would contact us, and we'd dig up the stuff for our collections or to sell at the annual show. Without the proper direction, most of the members would wander around aimlessly and get themselves spined. As president of the CCCC, it was my responsibility to see that they didn't.

As usual, most of the folks who showed up were old and frail. Austin Richman and I were the only ones capable of any significant work. Austin was the club's vice president and librarian, and a living relic of the sixties, a guy who could say things like "out of sight" and get away with it. His blond hair, parted in the middle, hung down the back of his overalls to the top of his butt.

I'd been there about an hour, supervising the removal of everything from giant columnar euphorbias to tiny rosettes of echeveria, dumping stuff in boxes and loading up station wagons, when Sam showed up. He grunted a hello to a few people and started in on a big patch of a climbing aloe that had gotten itself entwined in an oleander. I let him have a few minutes, moseyed over, waited until everyone else was out of earshot. "I have some bad news," I said.

He snipped off an aloe stem with a pair of pruners. Another cutting for the freebie table at the next meeting. "About Albert? I know already."

"How?"

"Heard about it on the radio."

"How much do you know?"

"Just that they found him shot and they have a suspect."

"They don't have a suspect. They have an aggrieved girlfriend." I filled him in.

When I was done, he shook his head. "I'm probably next."

"What, you think there's a serial plant-lover killer on the loose?"

"Not from the maniac who killed Albert. Just from whatever."

"Sam, you'll live to be a hundred and fifty."

"Right." He attacked another recalcitrant stem, had it undone, accidentally broke off the tip. "Damn."

"This has you a little more upset than I expected."

"Albert was a good friend."

"When Brenda died you acted as if nothing had happened. Said something about spending the morning feeling bad being all you could afford."

"It's still morning. Stroke of noon, I lighten up. You want to ask me a bunch of questions, don't you?"

"As a matter of fact, I do."

"Let me save you the trouble. Here's what I know about Albert. He's been collecting orchids for a long time. He moved here eight or nine years ago."

"I already know that."

He fixed me with a look. "Fine, then. I'll just work on this goddamned aloe and keep my mouth shut."

"Sorry. Go ahead."

"I first met him five years ago at one of the cactus clubs, I forget which. He gave a talk on CITES." The Convention on International Trade in Endangered Species. "Big shot that I am, I thought I was up on all that stuff, so I wasn't paying much attention, but suddenly I realized I was hearing information and views I hadn't heard before. I—young man, will you please stand still?"

"Sorry." I was doing my dance-around-like-a-nitwit routine, keeping my distance from the yellow jacket that had flown in to see what Sam was up to. Finally it lost interest and flew off. "You were saying?"

Sam glared at me. "He had a lot to say, is what I was saying, so I collared him after the meeting and we went for coffee. We've been friends ever since. He always tries to get me interested in orchids, and of course I am, you know me, I have some of everything around the place, but he wants to get me *interested* in them. And I never let him forget about succulents. About the only thing we have in common, plantwise, is eulophias."

"Right. He was showing you one at his place."

"It's a genus of terrestrial orchids. They grow with succulents in South Africa, and have big pseudobulbs." He saw my look. "The thickened part at the bottom of the stem." He climbed to his feet. "My boy, I'm going to leave that aloe for someone younger."

"I've never heard you say that before."

"There's a first time for everything." He stripped off his garden gloves. "We write letters and we go to meetings and probably none of it ever saved one species. Sometimes I think CITES is a big joke."

"You think the people you're working against have anything to do with his death?"

"I suppose it's possible. Didn't we go down this route with Brenda?"

"We did. Can you think of anyone else who might have held a grudge against Albert?"

He mulled it over. "It sounds ridiculous, but . . ."

"What?"

"Albert's an orchid judge. A couple of times he's said things to me about someone who didn't like the way their plant was judged. Somebody will act like a jerk because they don't get the right score."

I wondered if Sam knew he was still talking about Albert as if he were still alive.

"Orchid judging's far more rigorous than what we do. And they do it more often. Some clubs have judging at every meeting." He took a look at the aloe, put his gloves back on, knelt down to renew the attack. "They have a fancy point scale, and if you get a certain number of points you get to put some letters after the name of the plant, and if you get more points you get better letters. Pain in the ass, if you ask me. But the letters make the plants more attractive to buyers, so I guess if someone were pissed off enough at their score they could hold it against the judge."

He jerked the stem from the ground, said, "Aha," stood back up. "You're going to play detective again, aren't you?"

"I don't want to, but Laura asked me to."

"Of course you want to."

"I do?"

"Yes. You enjoyed it last time, my boy. I've never seen you so excited."

"Well . . . I was sort of thinking of going to the orchid show in Torrance."

"See? You're at it already." He licked his lips. "They have anything to drink around here?"

"There's some water over on the patio."

"I think I'll go get some. And you'd better see what those two ladies over there are doing. It doesn't look good."

I turned. Rowena Small and Vera Berg, two of the more problematic members of the club, had somehow managed to unearth a six-foot *Lemaireocereus marginatus,* a.k.a. fence post cactus. They were carrying it God knew where and had managed to get Vera pinned up against a yucca.

I went to the rescue. They both emerged unscathed. I came out of it with a spine in my thumb.

6

I STOPPED AT HOME, TOOK A QUICK SHOWER, MADE IT TO the Church of God in Torrance by a quarter after one. The name seemed redundant. Who else would it have been a church of?

A big orange sign with black lettering was propped up outside the boxy beige building:

ORCHID SHOW TODAY
.50 CENTS ADMISSION
GET READY FOR MOTHER'S DAY

The colors said get ready for Halloween. And someone had gotten hold of some black crepe paper and made a border around the edges, twisting the paper over and over to give it a kind of unintended—I hoped—festive look. Up in the corner someone had hand-lettered TODAY'S SHOW IS IN MEMORIUM OF ALBERT OBERG. Plant club people are not known for their spelling.

I stopped at a table in the lobby to give up my .50 cents admission. I was tempted to give the woman seated there a penny and ask for my .50 cents change, but didn't think it was a good time to be irritating the orchid people. So I handed in a dollar bill and got back two quarters and a little red ticket. "It's for the door prizes," the woman said. "We have some nice cymbidiums."

"My favorites," I said.

I walked into the display area, a small auditorium, and began checking out the show plants. I stopped at a table labeled CATTLEYA ALLIANCE. I asked an Asian woman with a name badge—I was beginning to realize a lot of Asians went for orchids—what the alliance thing was about. She said an alliance was a group of genera centered around one popular one. So the cattleya alliance included not only *Cattleya,* the big, frilly orchids they put in corsages, but also *Brassavola* and *Laelia* and several more, botanically similar and all judged together in the show. She pronounced the genus "cat-lee-uh," with the emphasis on the "cat." Whenever I'd seen it in plant books, I'd thought it was "cattle-yuh" and thought of cows.

I moved on to phalaenopsis, the moth orchids Albert had shown me in his greenhouse. The crewcut guy guarding the table told me, "They sell more of these than everything else put together."

"Who's 'they'?"

A voice from behind me answered. "Flower shops. Supermarkets. People at swap meets."

It was Sharon Turner, the woman from Albert's I'd vaguely considered asking out. She had on a T-shirt commemorating an orchid show and, again, black jeans. Her gray hair was in a ponytail. "Phals are easy to grow," she said. "They bloom well in indoor light. Visitors say, 'Ooh, what pretty flowers.' " She shrugged.

The crewcut guy nodded solemnly and turned back to his table. "Not your favorites, I take it?" I said to Sharon.

She smiled, a nice, even smile that showed nice, even teeth. "They're just so . . . common."

"Yet Albert, the big orchid expert, went for them."

"He went for everything. Now I have it."

"Have what?"

"Where I know you from. You're the it-takes-a-bug man on TV, aren't you?"

"Uh-huh."

"An actor."

"That's pushing it. I do commercials." I sought something clever to say. "So. How's the mood?"

"The mood?"

"Yes. Albert dying, all that."

"Oh. The mood." She made a what-can-you-do gesture with her hand. "Life goes on."

"Any idea who might have wanted him dead?"

"Now, there's a question. Why do you care?"

"You know Laura Astaire?"

"Yes."

"Well, there's this police detective who's got a bug up his ass—sorry."

"For what?"

"For saying *ass*."

"That's charming."

"It's charming to say *ass*?"

"It's charming to think I might be offended. You were saying . . ."

"He's got it in his head that just because Laura found the body, she's the logical suspect. She's asked for my help in proving she didn't do it."

"And you know she didn't because . . ."

"She has an alibi. She was out to dinner with a friend."

Sharon had a smile on, a tolerant one like a mother wears when her kid is talking gibberish. "What do you think of the show?" she said.

"I just got started, but it's a little overwhelming. Too many genera."

"Want a guided tour?"

"Sure."

"Come."

By the time we were done an hour later, I knew enough about the family Orchidaceae to hold my own in any second-rate orchid conversation. They were characterized by having three sepals and three petals, which were modified in a bunch of weird ways to give the flowers their unique forms. The lowermost petal was called the lip, and its shape and color were often the most prominent features.

Sharon showed me dendrobiums, with conelike stems from an eighth of an inch on up, some resembling miniature bamboo forests. And oncidiums, plants with tall flower stalks—or, as the orchid people referred to them, spikes—like the one on the table outside Albert's house. There was an *Oncidium* Sharry Baby, which Albert had told me smelled like chocolate. It did, but only vaguely.

I met the vanda alliance, some of which had purple-and-white-spotted flowers that I found appealing. They grew in hanging wooden baskets, with their roots dangling below. Rather than putting out a few leaves on each stem and popping new growth from the base, as so many of the orchids did, the vandas instead grew a succession of leaves on the same stalk. This growth form, Sharon said, was called monopodial; the other, the base-branching one, sympodial. When she told me this she seemed to study me, as if my reaction to this semitechnical bit of information was important. Whatever I said must have shown me to be on the proper wavelength, because she smiled, nodded, and went on. I'd passed my first test.

The last group Sharon showed me was the paphiopedilums. Their common name was slipper orchids, because the lip formed a semienclosed structure that resembled the front of a slipper. They tended toward thick, glossy petals, and their colors and textures made them look like they came out of one of the *Alien* movies. They gave me the creeps.

Sharon picked up on my reaction right away. "They do have that effect on some people."

"I can't help it. It's some inborn thing. Take me away from them."

As I learned about the plants, I tried to pick up what I could about orchidists. I'd already noticed how many Asians there were. Another thing: The orchid people seemed more affluent than the cactus crowd. I couldn't put my finger on why I felt that; a little better cut of clothes, perhaps.

We went outside to the sales area. They had three portable fabric pavilions set up, each housing half a dozen or so dealers. As soon as I hit the first table, the seeming affluence of the orchidists began to make sense. The plants were, in a word, expensive.

At a cactus show you'll find table upon table of plants, neatly labeled, mostly in plastic pots. Leafy ones, spiny ones, weird ones. You see rare plants at fifteen, twenty, thirty dollars on up, but the majority are five or less. Seedlings or rooted cuttings might go for two or three dollars. On the donation table you can pick up club members' excess plants for a dollar, even a quarter for the little bitty ones. Thirty bucks at a cactus show will fill your windowsill.

But not so here. The cheapest plants I saw were five dollars, and those were unrooted divisions, three-inch fragments lying forlornly in a tray. The least expensive potted plant was eight dollars, for one of the phalaenopses Sharon held in low regard. Everything else was ten bucks and up, with the emphasis on the up. Four-inch pots routinely went for twenty dollars. Numbers in the thirties and forties were common. Higher ones showed up with alarming regularity.

Yet the prices didn't seem to be stopping anybody. There were as many customers as I'd ever seen at a cactus show, snapping up plants left and right.

Finally I asked Sharon about the prices. She'd been showing me a stanhopea, and telling me how old-time growers had tried in vain to bloom them until one day a "crock boy" accidentally dropped a pot and discovered that the flower spikes grew downward, into the medium, and hadn't reemerged to bloom because the pot was in the way.

I checked the tag. Thirty-five dollars. "Are the prices related to how hard it is to raise orchids from seed?"

"Now how did you know about that?"

"Albert told me. Saturday, right before I met you."

"That *is* a factor."

"The reason I ask is that succulents are a lot cheaper, and they're easy to grow from seed. You don't have to send the seed off to some expensive lab. You sow them, you keep the fungus off, in a couple of years you have decent plants. Sometimes you don't even have to sow them. My greenhouse is full of volunteers. Baby cacti at their mothers' feet. Dorstenias, fat little ficus relatives, that spit their seeds all over the place and root in teeny little patches of dirt. I have anacampseros everywhere. Little African leaf succulents, related to portulaca. Rose moss, you know, or moss rose, the plant books can't seem to decide. I'm babbling, aren't I?"

"Yes."

"Make me stop."

She smiled. "You already have."

Sharon went off to the rest room, and I went over what I'd seen. Aside from the higher prices and a slight modification in the ethnicity of the average attendee, there wasn't a whole lot that was different from a cactus show. You had your pompous dealers pontificating on botanical trivia, and your perceptive ones who realized some customers just wanted something beautiful and easy to care for. You had folks who wore business suits on a Sunday afternoon rubbing shoulders with people schlepping shopping bags and holding conversations with themselves.

There were many familiar sights. Collectors running into each other and exchanging information about their latest discoveries. The looks of excitement on people's faces when they stumbled across something they'd been looking for. The expressions of "Oh, what the hell" when that something cost more than they wanted to spend.

A plant caught my eye, a tiny specimen, with slightly succulent leaves, attached to a piece of tree bark. It was a common method of display, in both the show and sales areas, and I remembered seeing dozens of them in Albert's greenhouse. The combination of plant and mounting had a certain gestalt that I thought would work well in my Jungle. The price sticker said nineteen dollars.

A guy with a persistent smile, maybe a few years older than I was, staffed the table. I plucked the plant from the chicken wire it was hooked to, waited while he finished selling an orange-haired old lady two hundred dollars' worth of plants that would have fit in a shoebox, and asked him if my choice was a rare species.

"No, not particularly rare."

"Then why is it so much money?"

"There's a lot of labor involved."

"I see." I checked out the orchid, a *Nanodes discolor,* more closely. A couple of the heads had the beginnings of flower spikes. "I'm just starting. I don't know that I want to spend this much on such a tiny plant."

"No problem." He smiled, as if he were just as happy to have me look at the plant as to buy it.

I hung it back on the rack and said, "Maybe I'll come back later."

"You will be back. That plant's meant for you." He broadened his grin and turned to the young couple and their shirt-tugging kids who were clamoring for his attention.

Sharon came back. She'd taken the elastic thing off her ponytail and her hair hung handsomely on her shoulders. I found myself wondering what it would look like if she masked the gray.

I told her I was orchided out. She said she could use a rest too, and we found seats in the back of the auditorium. Over to the right, tiny snores escaped a sleeping man. He had the look of a plant spouse, dragged to the show by his significant other. He'd probably gamely walked the tables for ten minutes before sneaking off to napland.

I turned to Sharon. "So how did you get involved in orchids?"

"A friend. She was in the club, she brought me to a meeting."

"I see." I looked out at the crowd. "Funny to think one of those people might be a murderer."

"*Funny* isn't the word I would have chosen."

"You know what I mean. You're sure you don't know anyone who had it in for Albert?"

She looked at me. She seemed to be gauging whether to trust me. Then: "Well . . . no, it's probably nothing."

"Let me be the judge of that." Right. Detective Portugal. Arbiter of who's a valid murder suspect and who's not.

"All right, if you insist. There's a couple. Helen and David Gartner."

"And?"

"It's probably nothing."

"You said that."

"All right. They had some sort of business dealings with Albert."

"Oh?"

"I overheard something at an orchid society meeting. Something about contracts."

"And, what, you think these dealings went sour and these people got mad enough to whack Albert?"

She looked sheepish. "It does sound pretty silly."

But, I thought, worth following up on. "Where would I find these people?"

"I could get their number from the membership list. They run a tire store in Reseda. Gartner's Tires."

Hearing the name again helped me make the connection. "Gartner, you said. Helen Gartner."

"Yes. What about it?"

"That's the woman Laura had dinner with last night."

"How coincidental."

A heavy guy wearing a hideous checked jacket walked by

with a box full of plants. "See the one with the tall pseudobulb and the two little leaves at the top?" Sharon said.

"Uh-huh."

"That's a schomburgkia. Sometimes the pseudobulbs are hollow and ant colonies live in them."

"We have those too. *Hydnophytum*. They call them ant plants. Would you be interested in going out with me sometime?"

She looked at me and smiled. "Nice segue."

"I'm nervous."

Her eyes looked sad. "I'm very flattered. But I don't think so."

I'd been so sure she'd say yes that when she didn't, it took me several seconds to formulate a reply. When I did, it was no gem. "Well, you can't blame a guy for trying."

"It's just that—well, it doesn't matter what it is."

"I see." I got to my feet. "I ought to get going."

"I hope I haven't hurt your feelings."

"No," I said. "Not at all. I just have to get home to check on my eggplant."

7

LOTS OF PEOPLE BUY THINGS WHEN THEY'VE SUFFERED DISAPpointments. Clothing. Banana splits. BMWs. I buy plants. I found the vendor with the little plaques and bought the one I'd been looking at. His name was Yoichi Nakatani, and he invited me to visit his nursery. "The address is on the receipt," he said. "I'm usually there." I glanced down. His place was in Stanton in Orange County. The receipt was written with that peculiar slant some left-handed people have.

When I got home, I hung the orchid in the Jungle, then took the Sunday *Times* into the canary room. I sat with the paper unopened, wondering why Sharon had turned me down, finally deciding it was her loss, not mine. Yeah, right, I told myself. And if you believe that, I've got some swampland in Fresno to sell you.

I pulled out the Calendar section and read Robert Hilburn's facile ramblings about the rock music flavor of the month. In Opinion I discovered that crime was down and learned why the experts thought that was. I looked in the magazine section and read about a restaurant I would never go to.

I put the paper down and stared out the window. Shadows crept up the wall as I listened to the canaries' chirping, wondering what it would be like not to have to worry about anything except where your next dish of seed was coming from.

I got up and called Gina. "I was just getting in the shower," she said. "Jill's back and she'll be over in twenty minutes."

"You want to hear about my detecting adventure today?"

"I'd love to, but I'm standing here naked—"

"Oh, baby."

"—and I'm freezing my ass off. So call me in the morning." The phone clicked.

I put out the eggplant salad and some pita bread and chips and pretzels, arranged soft drinks and beer in the fridge. I dug out Laura's card, gave her a ring, got her machine. Very concise, very professional. None of the show tunes or whooping birds actors like to put on their recordings. No piteous supplications on the order of "If this is a producer or casting director, please, please, *please* find me."

I began to leave a message. Laura picked up. "I've been screening my calls. So many people have been calling. Reporters. Can you believe it?"

"I can," I said. "Look, I think we should talk some more."

"Now?"

"No, I'm tied up. How about tomorrow sometime? I've got an audition in the morning at Stoneburg Studios, not far from you. I could come over after that."

"I'm working on a scene with my scene partner at nine. How about eleven?"

"Sounds good."

The doorbell rang. I looked at the clock. Seven on the nose. I said goodbye to Laura and hung up.

Vera Berg was at the door. Vera wasn't on the board, but we always made a point of inviting all the club members to board meetings. No one who wasn't on the board ever came, except Vera, who would commandeer the chair most convenient to the snacks and spend the evening hogging them.

Some more people showed, including Austin and his wife, Vicki Neidhardt, she of the beautiful red hair. She wasn't on the board. She wasn't even a member. But she was an investment banker—which somehow meshed with Austin's hippie routine—and she was going to advise us on what to do with five thousand dollars recently willed to the club by a member who'd gone to that big cactus garden in the sky.

Rowena Small came in next. She has radar. It homes in on whoever's least interested in hearing her chatter. Much of the time this is me.

"Did you hear?" she asked.

"Hear what?"

"About that orchid man who was killed."

"Yes, Rowena, I heard about that orchid man who was killed."

"But did you hear the latest?"

"The latest?" Okay, I was interested. "What's the latest?"

"It was on the six o'clock news. The police think a ring of plant thieves might be responsible for his death."

"You mean smugglers?"

"No, Mr. Smarty-Pants, I mean thieves. They think someone came to his house to steal his plants and he found them and . . ." She mimed shooting a gun. She appeared to be enjoying it.

I tuned Rowena out—not difficult with all the practice I'd

had—and thought about what she'd said. I'd heard the tales through the years. How the cycads disappeared from Manny Singer's place in the Valley. How a huge bursera walked out the door at Grigsby's in San Diego. How several hundred valuable seedlings were stolen from Arid Lands in Tucson. These seemed isolated incidents, but what Rowena had said might have merit. What if there were organized plant thieves? Orchids would be a better target than succulents. The plants were more valuable. And they probably traveled better; dump a bunch of succulents in a loot bag and they'll all spine each other. Suppose someone had invaded Albert's greenhouse to glom on to some of his plants. He stumbled upon them. They panicked, shot him, and ran away without any booty. The theory had a sort of simplistic attraction.

Nearly two hours later. Austin, Vicki, and I were lounging around the living room. Everyone else had left except Vera Berg, who wouldn't be gone until the last crumb of food was.

The doorbell rang. I went to answer it. Eugene Rand stood at the door.

Eugene was thirty-five, short, and bald, with a discolored spot shaped like Argentina marking a failed hair transplantation attempt. He was an odd little guy who was never very comfortable around other people. He'd been Brenda's assistant at the Kawamura, and when she died he'd more or less taken over the place. This increased responsibility, coupled with some serious therapy, had gone a long way in the last several months toward taming Eugene's antisocial tendencies. He was still a weirdo, but one a lot nicer to be around than he'd been the previous spring, when his chief positive attribute was that he'd probably saved Gina's and my lives.

"Hi, Joe."

"Hi, Eugene. The meeting's pretty much over."

"I didn't come for the meeting. But I knew you'd be here because of it, and I wanted you to be meet someone."

He turned and gestured out to the lime-green Renault Le Car parked in front of the house. A woman emerged and came up the walk.

Eugene's "someone" was at least four inches taller than he was. She was thin, just this side of Ally McBeal. Fine brown hair hung to her shoulders. In fact, everything about her was brown. Her clothes. Her shoes. Her eyes, bright, curious, with a hint of mischief.

"This is Sybil," Eugene said.

I shook her hand, invited them in, and offered them something to drink. They declined. Everyone stood around awkwardly. Then we all sat, maintaining the awkwardness level. Eugene clutched Sybil's hand.

"Eugene's told me so much about you," Sybil told me.

I gave him a look. "Well, he's been keeping you a secret."

Eugene fluttered his eyes. "I, uh, I didn't want to jinx things by telling anyone I had a, uh, a . . ."

"A girlfriend," Sybil said.

"Yes," he said. "A girlfriend. Isn't it odd? Isn't it strange?"

I stopped him before he broke out into a chorus of "Send In the Clowns." "It's not so strange, Eugene. You're a good-looking guy." I was stretching things there, but the cause was just. "Why shouldn't you have a girlfriend? And a beautiful one at that."

The two of them turned various shades of red. "Oh, Joe, you're too sweet," Sybil said.

We made chitchat. Eugene and Sybil, mostly Sybil, told us

about their ice-skating date at the rink over on Sepulveda. But it was clear a crowd of five—Vera didn't count; she was by this time in the kitchen clearing out my refrigerator—was more than Eugene was comfortable with. "Come on, Syb," he said. "It's time to go back to—to go."

I escorted them to the door. Eugene hadn't let go of Sybil's hand for an instant. "You'll be at the conservatory Tuesday afternoon to help move the euphorbias, right, Joe?" he said.

"Sure will."

"Good. See you then."

I shut the door behind them. When I got back to the couch, Vicki stood and gave me a hug.

"What was that for?" I said.

"For being so sweet. For telling her she was beautiful."

"She thinks I'm sweet. You think I'm sweet. Yesterday my bug-commercial wife Diane thought I was sweet. Every woman in the world thinks I'm sweet. So why can't I get a date?"

Austin rolled his eyes. "Not this again."

"No," I said. "I mean it this time. I mean, even Eugene Rand's got a girlfriend, for Christ's sake."

"I've heard you say he was making great strides," Vicki said.

"Yeah, but he's only been seminormal, and thereby eligible for a girlfriend, for a month or two. Whereas I, whatever strangeness I may exhibit, have been in the running for years. Decades, even. So what gives?"

"Man," said Austin. He was shaking his head. His ponytail swung from side to side.

"What?"

"How many times have I told you?"

"Jeez, Austin, don't start in about Gina again."

"I don't know, man. You're like oil and vinegar together."

"Austin, honey?" Vicki said.

"Yeah, hon?"

"Oil and vinegar don't exactly mix."

"Yeah, but they go well over salad." He pulled out his pocket watch. "Time to go."

Austin shook my hand, and Vicki hugged me again, and they went home. Eventually Vera went away too, and I was left alone, picturing Gina and me lying limply on a bed of romaine.

The phone rang while I was washing up. I would have let the machine get it, but it had a something's-wrong ring.

"She dumped me," Gina said.

"She what?"

"She tried to make it sound like it was all about a job, but I know she's just moving to San Francisco to get away from me." Her voice was a little off.

"Have you been drinking?"

"A little. I downed the wine after she left."

"A glass of wine's not so much."

"Not the glass. The bottle. She came over and gave me five minutes and then she sprang it on me. 'A great opportunity,' she called it. 'Everything I've always wanted in a job.' Bullshit."

"She'll change her mind."

"She won't change her mind. We talked for hours, for Christ's sake. After a while we were talking about other stuff, and I realized I was already thinking of her as a former lover." She wasn't crying, but she was close, and that had me worried. The only time I ever saw Gina cry was at her father's grave.

"I'll be there in twenty minutes," I said.

I actually made it in eighteen, though I nearly ran over a late-night skateboarder in doing so. I buzzed and ran up the stairs. She was waiting in her doorway. I wrapped her in my arms and held her. I could smell the wine on her breath, but she was entitled, I guessed, to get a little tipsy in a time of romantic trauma.

After I got her inside and onto the sofa, I kept an arm around her and stroked her hair, just letting her go on about how she couldn't keep a relationship going with anyone, and how she was so lucky to have me around to try to make things better.

And still, she didn't cry.

Finally, when she was quiet, I spoke. "How long have I been here?"

She looked at me like I was insane. "I don't know. Fifteen minutes? Twenty?"

"And in all that time did you even once mention Jill?"

"What? Of course I did."

"No. The last time you mentioned her was on the phone. And even then you didn't say her name. All you've been moaning about was how you can't have a relationship with anyone. You're more upset about that than about any particular person."

She considered it for a while. "You're wrong."

"It took too long for you to say I was wrong for me to be wrong. Admit it. You weren't that much into her."

"Sure I was. We really had something going."

"You could move to San Francisco with her."

"That's ridiculous. I'd never move up to America's Most Impressed With Itself City just to—" She looked up at me, pursing her lips. Her eyes might have been wet. "Damn you, Portugal, you know me too well."

Silence for several minutes. Then she said, "I need to get drunk."

"You *are* drunk."

"No, I mean *really* drunk."

"Is this a good idea?"

"Who gives a shit? I'm always in such control, and now I have a perfect reason not to be." She shifted her position so she was looking squarely at me. "Come on, Joe, get drunk with me."

"Why drag me into it?"

"Because it's no fun drinking alone."

"You don't drink enough to know that."

"I heard it on *Oprah*. Come on. Let's tie one on."

I wouldn't have done it for anyone else. "Okay."

She wanted vodka, which she was out of, so we went out and walked to the all-night Mayfair Market on Santa Monica Boulevard. We passed a pizzeria on the way, and Gina decided we needed a pizza. So we ordered one and continued to Mayfair while it was baking. Gina grabbed a couple of pints of Häagen-Dazs, then said we needed some beer to go with the pizza. I pointed out that she hated beer, but she said something about penance, and since she's Catholic and I'm only half I figured she knew what she was talking about.

When we got back, we dealt with the pizza in short order, each consuming a beer or two in the process. Then Gina filled a water glass half full of vodka and topped it with V-8 juice. She asked if I wanted one. I said, what the hell, why not. Soon we were seated on the sofa with our drinks and our ice cream.

I brought her up to date on my visit to the orchid show. I

left out the part about Sharon turning me down. One miserable social life an evening was enough.

We turned on the TV and watched a terrible TV movie with Tori Spelling, which is probably redundant. We kept packing away ice cream and cut-rate Bloody Marys, and an hour later we were both in rather sad shape, sprawled at opposite ends of the sofa, with our legs in a jumble somewhere in the middle.

"I'm going to pass out," Gina announced.

"Thanks for the update."

"I need to go to bed."

"A fine idea. You'll sleep it off, and everything will look better in the morning."

"Everything will look like shit in the morning. And I won't have the booze to make it look better."

"I'm glad to hear this trauma isn't turning you into an alcoholic. Come on, I'll tuck you in."

"No."

I tried to figure out what "no" meant. My vodka-saturated brain finally decided she was concerned about my well-being. "Don't worry. I won't drive home drunk. I'll sleep on your sofa."

"You hate sleeping on my sofa."

"I'm not going to throw you out of your bed."

"So we'll sleep in the same bed."

"Didn't we have this exact same conversation about a year ago?"

"Yes. And then we didn't share the bed. Now I think we should."

"Bad idea," I said. "Because when we *did* sleep in the same bed a couple of nights later—"

"Nothing happened."

"But it almost did."

"And, if it had, would that have been so bad?"

"That's the alcohol talking."

"I don't think so."

I sighed. "It would have changed things."

"There's a fresh toothbrush under the sink. Go use it."

I went and used it. When I came out of the bathroom Gina was sitting on the side of her bed in T-shirt and panties. She popped up, nearly lost her balance, righted herself, headed for the bathroom. When the door closed behind her I listened for retching sounds. When there weren't any, I undressed. I kept my underwear on. It wasn't as if she hadn't ever seen me naked. But the last time had been seventeen years before, and it didn't seem the right moment to break the string.

I slid under the covers. Soon she came back in. "You're on my side of the bed," she said.

"Right. Sorry." It was my side too. But that time a year before when we'd shared a bed, we decided that, if we ever did it again, the one whose place we were at would have dibs on it. I shoved over.

She turned out the light, got under the blanket, snuggled up next to me. She was cold, her feet like ice cubes. But she warmed up nicely.

Eventually she said, "This is nice and cozy. Why don't we do this more often?"

"Because Jill would have minded."

"Maybe I wouldn't have told her."

I felt her pressed up against me. It was, indeed, nice. It was, indeed, cozy. My loins stirred. I willed them not to. Gina and I were, after all, just friends. My loins ignored me.

"Do you think it would?" she said.

"Do I think what would what?"

"Making love. Screw up our friendship."

The moon was behind a cloud. I couldn't make out her expression. I could, though, smell the alcohol on her breath. "I don't know. This isn't the right time to find out."

Half a minute later she said, "You're probably right."

"You don't sound too sure."

"I'm not. But how do we know?"

"We don't. Go to sleep, Gi. We can talk about this some other time. When you're not quite so vulnerable."

"You promise? You promise we'll look into being lovers?"

"I promise." I gently kissed her dry lips. "Now go to sleep." Within a minute or so she did, and as soon as I saw she was safe in dreamland I joined her there.

8

I LURCHED OUT OF BED A LITTLE BEFORE NINE. GINA'D MUMbled something during our alcoholic interlude the night before about having to be at the Pacific Design Center at noon, so I let her be.

Outside, it was a bright Monday morning. Fluffy clouds floated over the Hollywood sign. I took La Cienega south, driving slowly, letting the cool spring air chip away at my hangover. Jefferson Airplane's *Surrealistic Pillow* was in the cassette player. Traffic was light. Young women walked their dogs; joggers reinforced their hearts.

As I pulled across Melrose I had to stomp on the brakes to avoid being squashed by a bus. I sat in the intersection screaming obscenities, staring as a bus-side placard, which told me I should watch *Nash Bridges* Friday nights on CBS, swept by six inches from my bumper. A man in a toga saw me yelling and gave me the peace sign. At his feet a lava lamp stood idle, with its white goop congealed at the bottom of the purple liquid. Then he held up a sign. THOU SHALT NOT LEND UPON USURY UNTO THY BROTHER. As I drove away I gave him back the peace sign.

At home, I dealt with the canaries and went out to the greenhouse. I didn't have time to do my rounds properly, but I thought I'd breeze through and see if anything startling had happened. I stumbled across the discocactus. The bud had done its thing. The spent flower lay across the cephalium. I cursed, told myself there'd be more buds, wondered about the conversation I was having with myself.

Stoneburg Studios was on Hollywood Boulevard, east of the run-down tourist disappointment around Vine. All the street parking was metered, and I didn't have any change. I parked in the lot at the Pep Boys across the street, went into the store through the lot entrance and out the front, jaywalked over to the studio.

It was an audition for Mighty Blue toilet bowl cleaner. The copy reinforced my recent pigeonholing as the dumb husband with the smart wife. I was to be scrubbing my fixture when she came in with her squeeze bottle of Mighty Blue and showed me what a cleaning ignoramus I was. The tag was, "Don't spend so much time in the bathroom."

I knew the actress I read with—you see the same faces over and over at these things—and afterward we stood on the sidewalk and talked. She told me she'd been in a pilot that had a good chance of making the next year's midseason replacement schedule. She described it as "*Melrose Place* in Santa Fe." She seemed very happy about it, and I congratulated her. She asked what I'd been up to. I told her about the Olsen's mall things. "Wow," she said. "Sounds great. Easy money. Ever do any near Studio City? I'll come visit you." I had one scheduled for Sherman Oaks that very weekend, but told her no, they did them only on my side of the hill. I didn't want people I knew seeing me stand around a mall selling ladybugs.

She went off to an acting class. I went off to the Pep Boys and thence to the truck.

There were a couple of beat-up bikes lying in Laura's driveway, with a couple of eight- to ten-year-old boys standing over them. At first I thought they were playing hooky. Then I remembered that a lot of the schools in L.A. are on a year-round plan. At any particular time, a third of the students are on the streets. The kids are in school for four months, take two off. Then four more on, two more off. No wonder they're mixed up.

I nodded a hello. The kids grunted back. I headed to Laura's apartment. One of the cars under the overhang was a Honda Accord, close to twenty years old. Its light blue paint was wearing off in that peculiar way you always see on old Hondas. The car hadn't been there the other night. Laura'd had a similar model back in the Altair days, and I was willing to bet this one was hers.

She came to the door with Monty the cat flung over her shoulder, wearing jeans and an ancient red sweatshirt that said YOU'LL NEVER KNOW IF YOU DON'T TRY. I looked at her and asked myself, Could this woman have committed murder? It didn't seem likely. But I still wasn't sure.

She ushered me in, gave me some iced tea, pointed me toward her sofa, took the *Frasier* chair. Monty sniffed my pants leg and lay down at her feet on the one-step-up-from-shag carpeting.

"You know," I said, "I still can't get over how we hadn't

seen each other in fifteen years and now I'm playing Paul Drake for you."

"Paul who?"

"The detective on the old *Perry Mason* series. The guy that went around digging up clues for Raymond Burr."

"You're upset that I called you. Your resent that I brought you into this."

"*Upset* is too strong a word. *Puzzled* is more like it. I still don't know why you didn't call your friend Helen when the cops took you to the station. Or a lawyer."

"I don't know any lawyers. And I can't afford one. As for Helen, she has problems of her own."

"What kind of problems?"

She shook her head slightly. "That didn't come out how I meant it. All I meant was that I didn't think to drag her into this." She smiled. "I thought to drag you into it."

"Because of my vast knowledge of the criminal justice system."

"Yes."

There was a pay stub from Apple One, the temp agency, on the coffee table. "You're still temping," I said. She'd been temping when I'd known her fifteen years before. She'd be doing it forever.

"I can't hold myself down to one job," she said. "When you get a role, it can tie you up for weeks at a time, or take you far away, and I would violate my responsibility to my employer if I were to leave suddenly."

It all came back to me, all the psychobabble her crowd had favored in the Altair days. *Responsibility* was another big word, like *commitment* and *intention,* and they flapped it around in the breeze like they were the only ones who'd ever heard of such a thing.

"Did you ever consider just giving it up?" I said. "Saying,

fine, I've given acting my best shot, but it just wasn't in the cards, and now it's time to move on with my life. Maybe doing community theater, just to keep the old chops honed."

She wasn't angry, wasn't sad, only amazed that I'd come up with such an idea. "Of course not. An actress is who I am. To be anything else would be to reject who I am. I couldn't live that way."

I took a sip of my tea, stood, went to the photo of Werner Erhard. Werner—the est-holes all called him by his first name, like they were close personal friends—stared out at me with benevolent antagonism. His name was a pseudonym, I remembered. He was really Jack Rosenberg. Hiding his Jewishness. "So why's Werner's picture still up?" I asked.

She shrugged and got up. "I guess I keep him around to remind me of the old days." She went to the door, lit a Virginia Slim. "Why does anybody put things on their walls, other than those that are there for the pure aesthetics of it? Pictures of your family, things from when you were a child."

I thought of the Jefferson Airplane poster in my hallway. "Because they mean something to you. A remembrance of things past."

"Well put, Mr. Proust. And that's exactly why Werner's still up there. That was an important time in my life. I'm not going to repudiate it because I'm not into those things anymore."

She came back in, got rid of her cigarette, stood close to me. "Can I ask a favor?"

"Sure."

"Would you throw me some lines?"

"Didn't get enough work with your scene partner?"

"He got an under-five on *The Young and the Restless* and couldn't make it. We're putting the scene up in class tomorrow, and I feel if I don't work on it at all today I'll lose my momentum."

"I haven't read anything but commercial copy in years."

"I just need to hear the lines. If we can run it a few times, I think I'll be all right until tomorrow morning."

"I'll give it a shot."

"Wonderful." She picked a Samuel French script book off her tiny dining table. Actors are always carrying them around. Any play that ever gets a semi-significant production eventually ends up in one, or one by French's competitor, Dramatists Play Service. Many were the hours I spent at the French store on Sunset Boulevard, scanning the shelves for interesting material.

I looked at the cover. *Chapter Two*. "GORNS?" I said.

"I'm perfect for Faye."

GORNS. Good Old Reliable Neil Simon. Let the artsy types scoff. "So I must be Leo."

"Right. This is the scene where he and Faye almost sleep together. Here, let me show you where it starts." She found the place and handed me the book. I smiled when I saw the penciled-in cuts, the pink-highlighted Faye lines, the places in the margin where Laura'd made notes to herself. *Take a beat. Let him come to me. Just like snarvx.* At least it looked like *snarvx.*

"You're supposed to have your shirt off," she said, smiling. "But I think we can skip that."

"If it would help . . ."

"No, that's okay. Let me just get ready."

I was afraid getting ready would entail much fluttering of eyes and elephantine breathing sounds, but all she did was take a couple of deep breaths. "Let's go."

I read off the first line. She responded. We traded back and forth. As Laura invested the lines with the sadness behind the laughs, I remembered how good an actress she'd been. Now, with more years of tedious life experience behind her, she was wonderful. When we finished the scene, I told her so.

"You helped a lot," she said.

"No, I—"

"Stop it, Joe. I don't know why you quit. Can we go through it again?"

"Okay. You want me to do anything differently?"

"No. You're fine. You're perfect."

We did the lines again. I was able to raise my head from the script a bit more, give her more eye contact. When we were done she said, "Can I tell you something?"

"I guess so."

"You're already better in this scene than the actor I'm working with in class."

"I can't believe that."

"Believe it. I mean, he has the lines down, and he knows the blocking, but I'm really getting more out of you than I ever do from him."

We went through it twice more, then took a break. We discussed her motivations in the scene, and then we were off onto pacing and nuance and back story.

We started up again, and ran the scene until a warning light went on in my head. Danger, Will Robinson, point of diminishing returns approaching. It always happened; you'd do a great run-through, but the next would be slightly less satisfying, and after that nothing useful would come out of the rehearsal. Eventually you'd both give up, and sit around munching pretzels and badmouthing people.

So we tried a time or two more, but it was pointless. Out came the pretzels. Laura began telling me about some of the plays she'd been in since I'd known her before. It was time to deal with what I'd come there for. "Have the police been by lately?"

She seemed startled that I wanted to discuss Albert's murder. "A couple of calls to clarify things, but that's it."

I nodded. For a guy who wanted to ask a bunch of questions, I was having trouble deciding which ones to ask. "So how did you and Albert get together?"

Monty the cat materialized in her lap. She stroked him absentmindedly. "When I met him at an orchid club meeting, I thought he was a big bore. Talking about his hybrids all the time. But one day he talked me into coming up and visiting his greenhouse. Then I stayed for dinner. It all happened rather quickly. I think we were both surprised."

"You do make, keeping up the Neil Simon theme here, an odd couple."

"You're speaking of his appearance."

"He was a fair amount older than you."

She shook her head. "I know what you mean. He was a big man. Fat."

"But that didn't bother you."

"No. He cared about me." She pointed at a miniature orchid sitting on a windowsill. It had a dozen tiny orange flowers. "And he showed me beautiful things."

"Did you ever hear about any business dealings between him and Helen and David Gartner."

"Helen? And David? Gartner?"

"Yes. You're friendly with Helen, having dinner with her and all. I thought she might have told you something."

"No." She was looking down at Monty, and he up at her with a big contented cat smile. "There's nothing." She glanced, too casually, at her watch. "Look what time it's getting to be. I've got a movement class at two."

"It's not even one."

"It's in Santa Monica. You know what traffic is like."

She stood, I stood, Monty jumped to the floor. Laura got some clothes from her closet and went into the bathroom, shutting the door partway behind her. "Look on the coffee table," she called out a moment later.

"What am I looking for?"

"The orchid society's newletter. It's cerise. You can't miss it."

It was far more elaborate than what my cactus club managed to get out, twelve pages, nice fonts, pretty pictures. "Okay, I've got it, now what?"

"There's a meeting tonight. The address is on the front page. Maybe you can go."

I found the meeting notice. 857 Iliff Street in Pacific Palisades. One of the cactus people lived on Iliff. Nice area. "Maybe I can."

She emerged a minute later wearing her leotard. She saw me looking and smiled. "Not bad, eh?"

"You look great, Laura."

She threw a sweatshirt around her neck, grabbed her Day-Timer, herded me to the door. As I reached to open it, she put a hand on my arm and spun me half around. "I want you to do something."

"And what would that be?"

"Come to my scene study class tomorrow."

"Why would I want to do that?"

"I thought you might want to get serious about acting again."

Joe Portugal, hero of several dozen commercials, returning to the stage. What a ridiculous idea.

"That sounds good," I said.

"Wonderful."

"Where and what time?"

"It's on Santa Monica Boulevard, at the Richmond Shepard Theatre. That is, it used to be the Richmond Shepard, and that's how I still think of it. Ten o'clock. You live where again?"

"Culver City."

"Why don't you come by at nine-thirty, and we'll go together."

"Okay."

"Good. Go to the meeting tonight, would you?"

"Are you going?"

She shook her head. "There are auditions for a new show at the Tiffany. One of the parts is perfect for me, if you can believe what they say in Drama-Logue."

"Break a leg."

"Thanks."

She gave me an est hug and we went out. She got in her car. I was right about it being the Honda.

9

I GOT HOLD OF GINA AND CAJOLED HER INTO GOING TO THE orchid society meeting with me later on. Then I drove over to my father's house in the Fairfax district. Dad's housemate Leonard answered the door. He's legally blind, though slightly sighted. As usual, the blue yarmulke in the middle of his bald spot hung there by some special dispensation from God.

He ushered me in. "Your father's in the back with Catherine," he said. "He's planting posies again. Me, I'm watching MTV. You know that Carmen Electra? She's a hot one." He returned to his position six inches in front of the screen, tossed some popcorn in his mouth, fashioned a rusty lascivious smile.

Out back, Catherine, the third member of the household, sat at the teak table reading the paper. She was dark-haired and feisty and looked more than a little like my mother, something my father continually denied. She said hi and went back to the sports page.

Dad patted the soil around his latest patch of impatiens, pushed to his feet, came and gave me a hug. "So," he said.

"What's the big special occasion that brings my son to see me?"

"No special occasion, Dad. It usually isn't."

"What have you been up to?"

"Not much. I went to a plant show yesterday."

"A cactus show?"

"Not exactly."

"What kind, then?"

"An orchid show."

"I'm not surprised."

"Oh?"

"No, it doesn't surprise me one bit that my son should be getting interested in orchids at this time. Does it surprise you, Catherine?"

She looked up from the paper. "Stop picking on the boy, Harold."

"Picking? Who's picking?"

"What are you getting at, Dad?" I said.

"This." He plucked the *Times* Metro section from the table, leafed through, pointed at a headline. DEATH OF ORCHID AUTHORITY STILL A MYSTERY. Dad cleared his throat and read to us. " 'Police refused to say if actress Laura Astaire, 53, who discovered the body, was a suspect in the murder.' " Fifty-three? Laura was older than I'd thought. "This Laura Astaire, she wouldn't happen to be someone you know."

"As a matter of fact, I was just over at her place."

"Wasn't nearly getting killed once enough for you?"

"I'm not doing anything dangerous. Just asking a few people a few questions."

"I'm sure he's being careful," Catherine said.

"Please, young lady, this is between my son and me."

Catherine gave him a look and went into the house.

"She's right, Dad. I'm being very careful."

"You were being very careful last time. Then the guns came out."

What could I say? He was right. The guns came out and suddenly my little investigatorial game became a matter of life and death.

"You think you know about murderers," he said.

Uh-oh. Here it was. I'd broached the subject back when the Brenda business happened, and by unsaid agreement we'd sealed it back up after the crime was solved. "Do you really want to talk about this?"

"I can tell you're not going to give up this cockamamy thing you have about playing policeman. So I need to remind you about murder again. It is not a game."

"Don't go there," I said. But he did.

I first figured out my father was a criminal when I was ten, after a week of two-a-day *Highway Patrol* episodes. He was involved in truck hijackings, among other things. He was a smalltimer, never making that one big score, not even pulling in enough to keep the family going. But my mother had a part-time job at the May Company, and we got by.

One day in 1966 things went awry. Another gang of bumblers picked the same truck on the same night. There was a scene that, from what I've pried out of Dad and Elaine, would have been comical if it weren't so tragic. When it was over, one of the other band of hijackers lay dead, and my father had the murder weapon in his hand.

He spent thirteen years in prison. When he got out, I was twice as old as when he went in. He came back to our house for a while, before moving up to Fairfax, "where the Jews are." As far as I could tell, he'd stayed on the straight and narrow.

"Murderers are dangerous people, Joseph."

"I know that."

"Even the ones who are honest all their lives, and then they kill someone, they're dangerous. Like that—"

"I remember."

"So you think you'll just ask your questions, and if one of the people you ask them of is the murderer, they'll just say, oh, he's just poking around, he's harmless, I'll just let him go on his way."

"What else am I going to do?"

"Let the police handle it. Trouble is their business."

It was tempting. Laura would understand if I backed away. She was overwhelmed when she asked me to take a look into things. Not reasoning properly. She didn't really expect me to uncover anything, at the orchid society meeting that night or anywhere else.

And I'd make my father happy, wouldn't I? So there was no reason not to drop the whole thing, was there?

"I can't give it up," I said. "It makes me feel like I'm accomplishing something, that I'm doing something useful instead of sitting on my ass collecting residuals and playing with my cacti."

He watched my face silently for a good thirty seconds. "I knew you would say that," he said at last.

I said nothing.

"Do you want a gun?"

"No. What would I do with a gun?"

"You might need a gun. In case by some chance you trip over the actual killer."

"I don't want a gun. And if I need a gun, Gina still has hers, and she knows how to use it, which I don't."

He stuck out his lower lip. He put it back in place. "You want to help me plant some posies? And after, you can stay for dinner."

"Posies, yes. Dinner, only if it's early."

"Dinner can be early. But tell me why it has to be early."

"I've got to go to Pacific Palisades to an orchid—"

"Stop. I don't want to hear about it."

"You just told me to tell you—"

"Joseph, you're old enough now, you should know when to lie to your father." He walked toward the house. Just before we got inside, he stopped and turned. "You'll—"

"Yes, Dad," I said. "I'll be careful."

10

THE PALISADES ORCHID SOCIETY MET AT A METHODIST church, leading me to wonder if all their events were held at houses of worship. This one was in the middle of a neighborhood of houses that probably went for a million or more. It resembled one of the missions, with a big tower and white adobe walls and thick wood beams all over the place. It seemed more Catholic than Methodist. Not that I knew much about Methodists.

The meeting was in a community room on the second floor. At least seventy people milled around, more than I'd ever seen at any succulent function. A typical garden club crowd, with orchid modifications. Lots of old folks, in couples and in singles of both genders. A fair dusting of sturdily built middle-aged women. Some Asian-Americans, and a couple of guys who fit the gay cliché.

To the right of the entrance, near a table full of plants, a tall skinny woman with a buzz cut was selling copious quantities of orange tickets. A raffle. We'd tried it in our cactus club and it flopped.

Speaking of the cactus club, the plant display put ours to

shame. There were well over a hundred blooming plants on the table. They were mostly in plastic nursery pots, black gallon ones and smaller green ones, with a few baskets sprinkled through. Quite unlike the cactus folks, who had a mania for presenting their show plants in bonsai pots and other fancy ceramics.

Though one guy stood at the table with clipboard in hand, it didn't look like the judging extravaganza Sam had led me to expect. I mentioned this to Gina. A voice at my shoulder said, "It's downstairs."

It was Sharon Turner. She had a sundress on, all pastel colors and soft lines. I introduced her to Gina. They swapped appraising looks. I asked Sharon about the judging.

"Do you want to see it?" she said.

"Can I?"

"If you can behave yourself."

"I will, Ma, I promise. You coming, Gi?"

Gina shook her head. "I think I'll hang around up here. Cover more territory that way." She walked off toward the raffle table.

"Territory?" Sharon said.

"She's helping me out with my helping Laura out."

Dottie Lennox cruised up. "If it isn't my new friend."

"Hi, Dottie."

"You taking good care of him, Sharon?"

"I am."

"Good. He doesn't know anything about orchids. He needs someone to teach him. You remember, dear, how it was when you joined the club. How you didn't know anyone, and how I had to take you by the hand."

"Of course, Dottie, but we have to go now. We're going to watch the judging."

"How boring," Dottie said, and rolled off.

I turned to Sharon. "Didn't you say a friend brought you to your first meeting?"

"I did. Dottie's a little bit, well, dotty. Come, let's get downstairs."

At the bottom of the steps she stopped. "Look, about yesterday—"

I shook my head. "Forget about it. I've gotten turned down before." It came out more spiteful than I'd intended.

She opened her mouth. Nothing came out. She shut it and walked down the hall, stopping at a gray metal door. When we got there she said, "Some of the judges are pretty uptight. Just follow my lead, all right? Supposedly the judging is open to anyone who can keep their mouth shut, but—"

"My lips are sealed. And look, I didn't mean to sound so nasty a minute—"

She shook her head. "Don't worry about it. I probably deserved it." She pulled the door open.

The judging took place in a utility room with cinder block walls and an unadorned concrete floor. Overhead pipes dangled from brackets, with valves and red handles here and there. A fan on a pole in one corner more or less pushed the warm air around. Four long tables sat under fluorescent fixtures, with six or eight people around each. One of the men caught my eye. Rather, his bad toupee did. Along with the thick black mustache inhabiting his lip, it made him look like Josef Stalin.

More tables along one side of the room held several dozen plants that were evidently up for judging. A handful of people walked around distributing them to the tables, all women except for one guy with a ruddy face and a shirt buttoned up to the neck. He was saying something about "a delectable paph" when we came in. One of the women was a nun, or enjoyed dressing like one.

Sharon hesitated before selecting the table in the far right corner. We stood by while the judges there considered the plant before them. All but one were men, ranging from thirtyish to wrinkle city. The one woman had gray curls piled on top of her head.

The center of attraction was a dendrobium, with a stem resembling a fat reed and seven or eight white flowers with red and purple highlights. It sat at the middle of the table, naked to the world. Every few seconds someone would reach out and turn it, knit his brows, lean back in contemplation.

"Anyone?" said the guy who seemed to be running things. He had a wide face, reddish hair, a matching beard.

There were a couple of headshakes, someone said, "Not with that color break," and suddenly the ruddy-faced guy was there, whisking the plant away, promising another momentarily.

Bearded Guy noticed us. "Hi, Sharon. What's up?"

"I wondered if we could sit in for a while."

He looked around the table. "Any objections?"

"Long as they're quiet," said a long-faced man chewing on an unlit pipe.

"Like mice," Sharon said. "This is my friend Joe. He's a novice. He's interested in judging." She told me everyone's names. I immediately forgot all but Bearded Guy's. He was Bob something.

I got us a couple of folding chairs and we squeezed in at the end of the table, with Bob on my right. The nun brought another plant, a cattleya. It sat there only a few seconds. There was a questioning look on one face, the slightest of nods on another, and the plant went off toward the staging area. Next was a cymbidium with spikes full of bronze-colored blooms. Another subtle nod, and away it went.

"This is the preliminary judging," Bob told me. "We pass the plants around, and if anyone thinks one has a chance for an award we set it aside for a good look later."

"But you look at them for only a few seconds. How do you know—"

"After you've looked at a few thousand, you know. You don't know for sure what's going to award, but you know what's not."

"Do all these people vote on a plant?"

"In the prelims it'll go to all the tables, and anyone can pick it for final judging, where it ends up with only one group."

"And at the one table you just, what, average everyone's scores?"

"Not everyone. Just the full judges and the probationaries. The other folks at the table are student judges and clerks."

Another plant arrived. "Last of the preliminaries," said the nun, standing by with a benevolent expression, like a parent indulging her children. Quick headshakes made their way around the table, and off the plant went, rejected in seconds.

They took a break. Most of the people at the table got up to stretch. I noticed some guy at one of the other tables watching me. Blue oxford shirt, brown hair combed straight back over one of the highest foreheads I'd ever seen. I vaguely recognized him from Albert's party. Our eyes met briefly.

I turned back to Bob. "Why do you need monthly judging sessions? Why not just have judging at shows?"

"If we waited for shows, a lot of the plants couldn't be judged because they wouldn't be in bloom."

"So really all you're judging is the flower."

"Pretty much. Although there are cultural awards too, where we take the whole plant into consideration."

"Something else I've been wondering about. The names of the plants. They seem way too complicated."

"Let's go through one." He picked a book up off the table and showed me a picture of several flowers, mostly white, with one or two violet spots on each petal and sepal. The pattern on the lip resembled a tiny angel with outstretched yellow and purple wings and outsized purple boots. The caption said "*Odontoglossum* Boreal 'Sunset Sunspots' HCC/AOS."

"First is the genus, *Odontoglossum.* Then Boreal is the grex, then—"

"The which?"

"It means a group of plants resulting from a crossing. Then 'Sunset Sunspots' is this particular hybrid. HCC means Highly Commended Certificate, which is the lowest award. The AOS means the award came from the American Orchid Society."

"And these awards, I understand, can mean money for the grower."

"Right. If you can propagate an awarded plant, by divisions or ideally by mericloning—tissue culture, that is—you can make a significant amount of money."

I remembered people at Albert's discussing tissue culture. I had only the vaguest idea how it worked. Something about stimulating certain cells to grow up into entire plants. *Brave New World,* here we come. "If someone were denied an award, and felt it was because of a particular judge, that person could be upset and want to take it out on the judge."

"You're talking about Albert, aren't you?"

"Yes."

"It doesn't seem likely."

"But there are politics to the judging, right? In our cactus club, there are always people marking down plants because they know they belong to someone they don't like. The entry tags are folded to hide the shower's name, but if a judge has a thing about one of the entrants, they have a knack of recognizing the handwriting. Not to mention the plants. Once a plant gets to show size, it looks pretty much the same from year to year. You look at it, you say, I remember that, it's John Doe's plant. If you hate John Doe and you're a judge you, whether consciously or not, tend to mark down his plants."

"It's not that easy to recognize an orchid from year to year. But, yeah, we have some of that."

"Sometimes," Sharon said, "the problem is that the judge doesn't like the entrant's lifestyle."

Bob glanced over at her. "There's some of that too."

"What do you mean?" I said.

It took him a few seconds to answer. "See that guy over there?"

"The one with the hair," Sharon said.

I looked. "Stalin?"

"Yes." She giggled.

"What about him?"

Bob: "He, uh . . ."

"Just say it, Bob," Sharon said. "The man's a homophobe. If he knows a plant's entered by one of the gay members, he's almost certain to downgrade it."

"It's kind of embarrassing," Bob said.

"Since we realized what was happening," Sharon said, "when some of the gay members put plants in for judging, they have someone else fill out the entry form so he doesn't recognize the handwriting."

"But can't he just read the names?"

"They go in with identification numbers." She glanced toward another table, at which the guy with the big forehead sat kneading his earlobe and staring at a plant. "And the aides generally know about judges' prejudices, and will try to keep certain plants away from them for the final judging."

"That's probably enough, Sharon," Bob said.

"You're right. He's going to think we're a bunch of bigots."

The woman judge returned to the table. "Time to get going," she called out, and the others took their places. The nun arrived with the first of the finalists.

It was a phalaenopsis called 'Pollo Loco' and it had white flowers with bright red highlights. All eyes were on it while the nun distributed score sheets and made sure everyone had a writing implement. Suddenly they were all talking about whether something was feathering or whether it was a color break. After a couple of minutes they marked their sheets. One of the guys tabulated the scores and announced that the average was 72.5. No award for this plant.

I asked Bob how one became a judge.

"There's a training program. After a while you get to be a probationary and eventually, if you play things right, a judge. And there are senior judges. Albert, for instance, though I'd heard he was on the verge of giving it up."

"How come?"

"Politics," Sharon said.

Suddenly I was aware of how close to me she was sitting, how her thigh was barely touching my own. And I was experiencing feelings I'd gotten unfamiliar with. And I was thinking, this woman certainly is intelligent, and attractive, and gee, Joe, you haven't been with anyone in a while, have you?

She saw me looking at her leg. Our eyes caught. She smiled, looked away.

"Oh, just look at this baby," Bob said.

The "baby" was, I soon found out, a member of the genus *Pleurothallis*, no more than three inches across, with flowers at most three quarters of an inch wide. These, Bob told me, were the core of a group of miniatures known as pleurothallids. They were what the woman at Albert's had been regaling us about, and now I knew why. The petals were iridescent, with green and purple predominant, the purple so dark it was almost black. Minute hairs grew from their edges.

Each person at the table wore a broad smile. There was no discussion, save for the guy with the pipe asking what the parents were. A couple of minutes later, the clerk added up the scores. 87. An Award of Merit. Someone slapped his hands together, and I thought they were going to break out into applause. Cooler heads prevailed.

I sat through a couple more plants, wanting to switch tables, maybe see Stalin in action, but not knowing how to do so politely. I decided to watch one more, then go back upstairs and compare notes with Gina.

When the next orchid was put on the table, I got a glimpse of its entry form, filled out in an unusual handwriting that slanted to the left. The plant was an oncidium called 'Nagano Snow.' It had at least a hundred flowers on a spike four feet tall. Each bloom was an inch across, with a pale yellow background and purple edges. There was red mixed in there, too, and some green, and some color I couldn't even put a name to. The inflorescence shimmered above us, luminous even in the harsh light.

"What are the parents?" Pipe Guy said.

Someone read them off, and they got out a book and looked at pictures of both. Bob leaned over to me. "A plant has to show the influence of both parents to get awarded."

They dwelled a while on the plant, kicking around this

and that aspect of it, before putting it to a vote. It got a 74. Just short of an award. Bob told me if it would have scored higher had it shown more of the pollen parent's characteristics.

I thanked everyone and excused myself. Sharon and I went out and closed the door behind us. "That last one," I said. "It belongs to a guy named Yoichi, doesn't it?"

"I wouldn't be surprised. He's been hybridizing oncidiums for years. Why did you think that?"

"I bought a plant from him yesterday. On my way out. The handwriting on the receipt matched what was on the entry form. It's very distinctive."

"How clever. You really may be cut out for this detective business."

"Is he here? I haven't seen him."

"Probably not. Someone else usually brings his plants in. He generally goes to a club down in Orange County, but they don't have judging."

"Oh, there you are." Gina came bounding down the stairs. "I thought maybe you got eaten by one of the plants. Like in *Little Shop of Horrors.*"

Sharon put a hand on my arm. "I'll see you later." She headed upstairs. I watched her go, evidently with enough interest for Gina to comment on. "You're hot for her."

"I am not."

"Of course you are. I know the signs. You did the nostril thing."

"I did not."

"You did. Flared wider than I've ever seen 'em."

I smiled guiltily. "She *is* attractive."

"I don't like her."

"You don't get a vote." Slight pause. "*Why* don't you like her?"

"General principles. And what's with the hair? Hasn't she heard of L'Oréal?"

"I'll take your disapproval under consideration. You get tired of the shenanigans upstairs?"

"They're on a break. They did a repotting demonstration. The woman doing it wore surgical gloves. Said something about 'the ever-present threat of virus.' Then they had a slide program on Madagascar. What is it with plant people and slide programs on Madagascar? If I ever see another cute picture of a lemur, I'll puke. Come back upstairs with me, before all the goodies are gone."

We returned to the meeting room, filled plates with cookies and fruit, dropped a couple of bucks in the paper cup, watched the crowd. I told Gina about the judging session. When I finished, she said, "Maybe Albert had some secret prejudice and marked someone down and they knocked him off."

"Doesn't seem likely."

"You don't know. He could have been a real Nazi."

The public address system squealed. A lanky guy in his forties, the only one in the room wearing a jacket and tie, asked for everyone to take their seats. He held the cordless microphone in a death grip. "He's the president," Gina said. "Name's Dean something, or something Dean. I think you should wear a tie when you run your cactus meetings. It's very presidential."

We found places on the aisle halfway back. Dean waited for everyone to sit. He would have waited forever if Ms. Buzz-cut hadn't stood up and shouted, "Everyone find your goddamned seats," evoking laughter from some, nervous looks from others, the requested behavior from all.

Dean positioned himself behind a podium bearing a sizable gold cross. "Ladies and gentlemen," he said. "Many, nay all of you know that our longtime member and dear friend Albert Oberg was, uh, killed last Saturday night."

"Did he say 'nay'?" Gina whispered.

"Aye, he did," I whispered back.

A diminutive woman sitting in front of us turned around and put a finger to her lips.

"Sorry," I said.

Dean went on. "Some have asked about Albert's funeral service. I'm afraid there won't be one. In accordance with Albert's wishes, he will be cremated, and the ashes spread in his greenhouse. There will be a memorial service later on. So." He seemed relieved to be done talking about the service. "Tonight we have a special guest. Tonight we have here with us someone involved in the investigation of Albert's death. He may seek you out to ask questions. I beseech you to answer these truthfully and honestly, and to give him your fullest cooperation. For only through his efforts can we determine the perpetrator of this terrible crime."

Huh? How did he know I was investigating Albert's death? What was I going to say when I got up to speak? And was the perpetrator—as the president put it—in this very room, and would he or she jump up the moment I reached the podium, shout, "Die, cactus-collecting scum," and launch a plant stake at my heart?

"Ladies and gentlemen," said Dean. "From the Los Angeles Police Department, Detective Hector Casillas!"

11

CASILLAS MARCHED UP FROM THE BACK OF THE ROOM, wearing a gray suit and a kindly smile. I hadn't seen him back there. Maybe he was hiding behind a cymbidium.

He whisked to the podium, shook hands with Dean, took the mike, waited while Dean got it that Casillas didn't want him standing there. When the president stepped away, Casillas tapped the mike, saying, "Is this thing on?" He smiled sheepishly when feedback erupted from the speakers. His ingratiating manner, admirable a year before, had been honed to a fine point.

I didn't know which was worse. That I'd nearly made a fool of myself with my self-aggrandizing image of Joe Portugal, criminal catcher, or that my nemesis Casillas was there, addressing the orchid crowd much as, the previous spring, he'd done the same at a meeting of the Culver City Cactus Club.

He went around the podium to lean against the raffle table. "First," he said, "let me express my sympathy at the loss of your friend. I understand he was a fine man."

Someone in the back began to applaud, and a few more folks picked it up, before Casillas gestured for silence.

"Like Mr. Dean said, as part of our ongoing investigation, I'd like you all to know that I may be calling on you to ask questions about Mr. Oberg and his associates. Please be assured that any questioning you undergo does not necessarily mean you are suspected of a crime."

"Notice the *necessarily,*" I said. The woman in front of me did the finger thing again.

Casillas did some PR, took a couple of questions, asked a few of his own. I sat there with my arms crossed over my chest. I didn't know why Casillas affected me so viscerally. Maybe it was because he represented authority, and ever since my days as a somewhat-out-of-control rock-and-roll kid I'd had a problem with authority. Maybe it was because authority had sent my father to prison when he should have been home teaching me to hit a curve ball.

After fifteen minutes Casillas thanked everyone profusely and walked out into the hallway. Dean regained the podium and told everyone it was their last opportunity to buy chances at the raffle, touching off a small frenzy around the buzz-cut woman and her roll of orange tickets. When they called a halt to sales, I got up. Gina didn't. She pulled out a strip of raffle tickets. Go figure.

I made it into the hallway just as they began calling numbers. Casillas was waiting for me, leaning against the wall and chewing a toothpick. "Expected you'd be here," he said.

"Who are you checking up on?"

"What makes you think I'm checking up on anyone?"

"You wouldn't waste your time here if there wasn't someone you wanted to watch."

He tossed his toothpick in a potted palm. "If that's the case, why aren't I back in there watching them?"

An excited squeal escaped the meeting room. Someone had gotten the plant of their dreams. I pointed at the door leading back inside. "That's the only way out of there. You can watch just fine from here."

"Let's just say you're right about this, and I'm watching someone. Who might that someone be?"

I shook my head. "You're not going to get me to give up my suspects so easily."

Suddenly he was in my face. He'd had something with garlic for dinner, had eaten mints since then, but they weren't quite up to the job. "Suspects? You got suspects? If you know something, you better tell me now. I'm sick and tired of you butting your ass in where it doesn't belong, but if your butting got you something useful you better tell me about it."

"Back off, Detective."

"And if I don't?"

Hmm. Good question. "There's really no one in there I suspect."

"You sure?"

"Yeah. I came up to—"

His eyes wavered. Just for an instant his glance went off me and onto whoever was in the doorway to the meeting room. Then it returned to me. But something had changed. He'd seen whoever it was he wanted to see.

I turned. The person he'd reacted to was around my age, average height, jet-black hair. Thin features, just enough makeup, tasteful jewelry. She had her arms wrapped around a potful of oncidium. Its flower stalk towered over her head.

The guy I'd seen watching me at the judging, the one with the monumental forehead, emerged from the room, proprietarily put his hand on her shoulder, guided her down the hall and onto the stairs. I turned back to Casillas. "It's that woman, isn't it?"

"You are so wrong."

"I saw your eyes flicker."

"You're going to see your head flicker if you don't get your ass out of the way of official business."

"It *is* her. Who is she?"

"I've had about enough of you. Just stay out of my way." He barged past me, and down the hall to the staircase.

Gina emerged from the meeting room, barely carrying a cymbidium I was sure had been the biggest thing on the raffle table. "What's happening?"

"Casillas suspects some woman." I considered following him outside. I decided it wasn't a good idea. I did it anyway.

The three of them were standing at the far end of the parking lot, engaged in a heated though low-volume conversation. I moved a few steps across the lot to try and hear them better. Casillas saw me. He gave me a nasty look. I beat it back inside and up the stairs.

"Who is she?" Gina asked.

"I don't know." I eyed her acquisition. "What's with the plant?"

"I thought it would look good on the patio."

"You realize how ugly those things are when they're not in bloom?"

"So I'll throw it out. I only spent a couple of dollars on tickets. It was an impulse buy. I've been doing that a lot lately. Come on, let's get out of here."

"In a minute. There's someone I want to speak to."

"That Sharon, no doubt."

"I'll meet you at the car."

"Take this. If I try to carry it down the stairs, I'll fall down them for sure."

I let her give me the plant. "Okay, shrimp."

She stamped off. I returned to the meeting room, where Sharon was winding up the fat extension cord that had powered the projector. "There's a woman," I said. "Forties, very black hair. With a guy with a high forehead who's a judge. Who is she?"

"That would be Helen Gartner. The man's David."

I thought of the night Albert was killed. What Laura had told me. *As for Helen, she has problems of her own.*

"Casillas practically chased her outside," I said.

"I wonder what for."

"Maybe those business dealings you said they had with Albert went awry."

"Maybe." She indicated the plant I was carrying. "Nice cymbidium."

"It's my friend's."

"How much of a friend is she?"

"My best friend. Why do you ask?"

"I was just curious."

Curious, my eye. I can recognize the Ten Warning Signs of Interest in the Opposite Sex.

I put down the cymbidium. "I hope to see you again soon."

"That would be . . . nice."

"Let's go out on a date."

Her eyes looked stricken. "Look," she said. "A long time ago I had a bad experience with a relationship. I'm very careful now."

"Fine. No big deal."

She took up another loop of the extension cord. "I knew you would ask again."

"I won't bite, I promise."

"I know you won't. I think you're probably a very nice

man." At least she hadn't said *sweet.* "But I need to know you a little better."

"How about this? Tomorrow afternoon I'll be at the Kawamura Conservatory at UCLA. I do volunteer work there. Why don't you come by, let me show you some of the plants *I'm* into. We can spend a little time together, but it won't really be a date."

"That sounds interesting."

"You told me *interesting* means a person hates something."

"I did, didn't I? That's not what I meant just now. I meant it literally. I meant—"

I smiled. "I knew what you meant."

She returned the smile. "This will work out well. Tomorrow's my day off. What time?"

"How about two?"

"Sounds good."

"You need directions?"

"I'll find it."

"I'll see you tomorrow then."

"Yes."

"Two o'clock."

"I won't forget."

"Good." We stood there awkwardly, not knowing how to part. Finally I held out a hand, and she took it, and I put my other one over hers, and she put her other one over mine. We gave the whole thing a shake and she went on her way. I picked up Gina's plant and went on mine.

We got back to Gina's place at ten-twenty. She put the cymbidium on her balcony and went to check her answering machines. On the business line a client insisted the color was coming off her chairlegs and staining her carpet. "And," the woman added, "I'm having the head of production at Sony over tomorrow night."

The personal line bore a message from Gina's mother. The Virgin had made an appearance in a little town in the Mojave, at a 7-Eleven, on the wall above the Slurpee machine. Mrs. Vela was making a pilgrimage in the morning and wanted to know if Gina would go with her.

"Fat chance," Gina said. She went into the kitchen. "You want some ice cream?"

"I'll pass."

She came out with a pint of Häagen-Dazs chocolate chocolate chip and a spoon and transferred a couple of slabs into her mouth. Then she said, "Have you realized you're interested in sex only when somebody gets killed?"

"I'm a man. I'm always interested in sex." Pause. "What makes you think I'm interested in sex?"

"The way you look at that Sharon woman. The only time I see you look that way anymore is when somebody gets murdered and you get involved in the investigation."

"That's the stupidest thing I ever heard."

"Is it? When was the last time you got laid? Or even had a date?"

"I don't know, let me think—"

"Of course you know. It was right after we solved Brenda's murder. That coed. And before that, the other one, *while* we were solving Brenda's murder. And before that?"

"I don't keep a scorecard."

"Well, I do. Before that it was another year. Now don't you think it's weird that you got involved with two women when Brenda was killed, and now this Albert guy's dead and you're ready to go screw this Sharon, and in between you were like a monk?"

"I'm not ready to screw her. You're making me sound like some kind of necrophiliac because I happen to meet interesting women only when someone gets killed."

"I'm just saying—"

"Drop it, okay?"

"Okay. Sheesh."

We put on the news, then watched Letterman. Julia Roberts, Madeleine Albright, Tori Amos. When they'd all done their thing, Gina got up from the sofa. "I'm going to bed."

"Okay."

"Are you coming?"

"I don't think so. Last night was one thing. We were drunk."

"You'll sleep with me only when you're drunk?"

"You know what I mean."

"Come on, Joe, do you really want to drive home at this time of night?"

"It's not that late."

She looked down at me. "Fine. I'll talk to you tomorrow." She walked out of the room. Shadows in the hallway shifted as she turned on the lamp in her bedroom. I heard her doing stuff in the bathroom. Shadows reverted when she switched off the bedroom lamp.

I sat for ten minutes, got up, turned off the TV, walked into the bathroom. Always empty your bladder before you go home, that's my motto.

As the stream diminished to a trickle, I asked myself, What the hell are you afraid of, Portugal?

Yeah, but what about Sharon?

What about her? You haven't even had a Real Date with her.

You haven't even had a pseudo-date with her.

I went into the bedroom, stripped to my Jockeys, climbed into the empty side of the bed.

Ten minutes later I was still awake. Gina wasn't. Her even breathing was the only sound I could hear.

Until a car backfired outside. Gina raised her head from her pillow. She reached out a hand, encountered my shoulder, said, "Good," withdrew her arm. Moments later she was back asleep. Sometime after that, so was I.

I awoke to the sound of Gina in the shower. When the hissing stopped, I jumped out of bed and got dressed. A few minutes later she came out, wearing the biggest terry cloth robe I'd ever seen. It dragged on the floor like a bridal gown. She saw me looking. "Mom got it at the outlet mall. Seven dollars. What a bargain."

I went into the kitchen to rustle up some tea. She came in just as the water boiled. "Are you going to infiltrate anybody's confidence today?" she asked.

"My day's pretty well laid out. I may not have any time for infiltrating."

"Oh? How so?"

"To start with, this morning I'm going to an acting class with Laura."

I expected static. Nope. "That's good. Some real acting would be good for you. What else?"

"I promised Eugene I'd work up at the Kawamura this afternoon. We're shifting euphorbias."

"Sounds like a Talking Heads album."

"And Sharon's coming up to see the collection."

"What was that? I didn't hear you."

"Why don't you want me seeing her?"

"I don't not want you seeing her. I want you to get laid. So you'll stop trying to maul me all night."

"No mauling went on last night. I would remember." I looked into her eyes. "Gi, this sleeping in the same bed is really bizarre. I think we ought to quit."

"You did too maul me. I woke up in the middle of the night with your hand on my breast."

"You did not."

"Did. I poked you with an elbow and you rolled over."

"I had a hand on a breast and I didn't even know it?"

"You snooze, you lose." She headed toward the door. "Let's have dinner at French Market tonight. Meet me there at seven." Then she was gone.

I finished my tea, thought about going home to shower and shave and change, realized I didn't have time. So I showered there and locked up. Gina and I had traded keys long before.

The sky was especially bright as I drove up Beachwood Drive and parked at Laura's. The jacaranda danced in the breeze. The same two kids were out front. The bikes had been replaced by skateboards. I said hi to them. They mumbled something back.

I went to Laura's door and knocked. No answer. I knocked again, louder, realizing how stupid that was. In that bandbox, if she didn't hear me knocking the first time, she wouldn't hear me if I used brass knuckles.

Could she have forgotten me? Doubtful. Maybe she'd run to the market and was even then turning onto Beachwood.

No. Her car was outside.

Maybe she was in the laundry room.

Or maybe—

I don't know why I took the knob and tried to turn it. I don't know why I wasn't surprised when I was successful.

I poked my head in. "Laura?"

The sofa bed was pulled out, the sheets and pillows scattered around on it. Suppressing a ridiculous urge to make and fold up the bed, I walked into the kitchen. That's where I found Laura.

She was lying on the floor, more or less on her left side. There was a gun by her side, a few inches from her outstretched hand. There was blood on her head, and on the floor. Not a huge amount. Just enough to tell me she was dead.

12

I CALLED 911 AND TOLD THEM WHAT HAD HAPPENED AND gave them the address and my name and whatever other trivia they asked for. When I hung up, I looked for something to cover Laura with. It seemed cruel to leave her there, exposed to the world. But grabbing a shroud might mess up evidence. I looked at her one more time, feeling horribly guilty about my doubts about her innocence, then let her be and went outside.

The taller of the skateboard boys knew something was up. He rolled over, with the other one close behind. I shut the door and stood in front of it. I told them nothing was happening. They didn't believe me. I suggested they go back to their previous loitering spot. They liked their new one. We made sparse small talk until authority arrived.

The paramedics came first, with a couple of uniformed officers at their heels. They hustled my new friends and me off to the sidewalk in front of the house. Another car or two showed up, and while the first pair of cops protected and served inside, their comrades strung yellow crime scene tape and kept an eye on me. Some length of time later—it might have been five minutes and might have been thirty, things were a little hazy—Casillas showed up.

He was driving a big blue Chevy sedan with an antenna farm on the roof. It looked identical to the one he'd driven a year before, prior to his promotion. He got out and saw me and rolled his eyes. "Make sure this one doesn't go anywhere," he said, and he and the lanky guy who'd been riding shotgun went inside.

A crowd, a weird midmorning mix, gathered and gawked behind the yellow tape. Some senior citizens. Some young faces who had the look of out-of-work actors. Ambition tempered with the beginning of the realization that they hadn't a chance in hell of making it in their chosen profession. They'd all have an interesting story to tell their waiter and waitress friends that evening.

There were a couple of street people too. One had a brown cardboard sign telling the world he was a Vietnam vet with diabetes. Maybe he was telling the truth about the diabetes. If he'd served in Vietnam, he was about six months old at the time.

They all stood making conjectures about what had happened. Somebody said a gas leak had killed someone. One of the old folks began a discourse on automatic earthquake shutoff valves. If there's been one, he said, no one would be dead now. The cardboard sign guy pointed out that there hadn't been an earthquake.

Finally Casillas came out. The bags under his eyes were darker than ever. He spotted me and said, "I'll take this one," like I was a burrito in the deli case at Vons. He led me under the overhang, where a skinny Filipino guy, one of ten or so crime scene types scurrying about, was poking around in Laura's Accord.

I thought the first thing out of Casillas's mouth would be

an accusation. *Tell me you did it,* I expected him to say. *Then we can all go home early.* But he simply pulled out his pad and cheesy wood pen. "Okay. Why don't you tell me exactly what happened here today?"

"How the hell do I know?"

"I mean when you came up here. I'm assuming it was after she was dead, if that's what you're worried about."

I shrugged. "The door was unlocked. I went in. I found her. I called 911."

"How come you happened to be over here?"

"Laura was going to take me to her acting class."

"You need classes for commercials?"

"I thought I might get back to the theater." Like he cared.

He wrote something on his pad, looked up at me again. "Got any idea why she did it?"

It took me a second. "What? You think she killed herself?"

"And Oberg too. It makes a nice little package, doesn't it?"

The scene in the kitchen materialized in my mind's eye. "You're assuming, just because the gun was in the general vicinity of her hand, it was suicide?"

"Sure. Felt guilty about Oberg."

"But she has an alibi for the night he was killed."

"She does, does she?"

"You know she does. She had dinner with Helen Gartner. Speaking of whom—"

"Time of death could have been after they say they went their own ways."

"Could have been?"

"You think we can come in, see a body, know the minute they died? You been watching too much *Diagnosis Murder*."

"But she has an alibi after she left Helen too. She came back here to feed her cat. She must have told *you* this."

"You believe the cat story, huh?"

"Why shouldn't I?"

"It's not much of an alibi. No one saw her doing it except the cat, and he's not talking."

"He didn't yell for his food when I took Laura back to her place. So she must have fed him when she said she did." My experience with cats was pretty much limited to *Garfield,* but the yelling thing seemed reasonable.

"You an authority on cats?"

"No, but you know how animals are when they haven't been fed."

He pursed his lips. I got the impression he agreed with me but didn't want to admit it. "If she didn't do it," he said, "who do you think did?"

"You're asking for my opinion?"

A small shrug. "Can't hurt."

"How about Helen Gartner?"

"What do you know about her?"

"I know you chased her into the parking lot last night. Why was that?"

"Let's say I hadn't. Why'd you think of her?"

Good question. One with no answer, other than some tenuous business association. "If you tell me what you talked to her about last night, I might be able to give you an answer."

"Fat chance. Anyway, it doesn't matter. She can account for her whereabouts."

I jerked a thumb toward Laura's apartment. "Her alibi's lying in the kitchen in there."

"So you're willing to think the story of them being together could be bull if we're talking about the Gartner woman, but not if we're talking about—" His turn to hook a thumb at Laura's place. "Her."

He had a point. But it got me thinking. What if the dinner story was an invention? What if Helen Gartner had killed Albert, and somehow gotten Laura to cover up for her? And then, when she thought Laura might crack and blow her alibi, she did away with her too.

Casillas snapped his pad shut and called over a young uniformed officer. "Take Mr. Portugal here into the station for a statement."

"This way," she said.

"Wait," I said.

"What?" Casillas said.

"I have questions."

"You're not allowed to have questions," he said. "You're the civilian, I'm the cop." He turned away to speak with the guy going over the Accord.

"This way, sir," the officer said.

Another cop, a robust guy with a walrus mustache, came out of the building carrying Monty the cat at arm's length. "I found this in the closet," he told the world at large. "What should I do with it?"

The two kids burst from the crowd. "We'll take him," said the bigger one. "We take care of him sometimes."

Casillas looked them over. "Why not?" he said.

The cop dropped the cat into the shorter kid's arms. He took it and gently cradled it. The other one petted Monty's head. It was funny. They'd seemed surly little boys, but you could tell from their faces they loved animals. Maybe there was hope.

Casillas saw me. "You still here?" he said.

"I'm going, I'm going."

I had to wait around at the station for a while. Once they

got to me, the statement took just fifteen minutes. I basically dictated what I'd told Casillas. I signed what they shoved in my face and was on my merry way.

I stopped at home, changed clothes, got up to the Kawamura at a quarter to two. Eugene insisted on telling me more about his ice-skating adventure with Sybil two nights before. "I kept falling down," he said. "And she would help me up, and I wasn't embarrassed about falling down. Isn't that wonderful?"

"It sure is. Listen, I've got a visitor coming up in a little bit, that I'm going to show around. Hope you don't mind. It won't take long, and then I'll get to the euphorbias." I didn't say anything about Laura. It would invite a conversation I didn't want to have.

He was miffed that I didn't want to continue reviewing his date. "Yes," he said. "The euphorbias." He stalked off.

Sharon showed up precisely at two. She was back to black jeans, along with a lightweight knit top that clung nicely to her breasts.

"There's some bad news," I said.

"I heard it on the radio."

"It's on the radio already?"

"Yes."

"Did the radio say I discovered her body?"

She registered the appropriate degree of surprise. "No. How did that come about?"

I told her.

"If you don't want to play tour guide now," she said, "I'll understand."

I shook my head. "It'll be good for me. Get my mind off Laura."

"Should we get started, then?"

"Yes." I swept an arm around the conservatory. "This is it. Second-biggest succulent collection in the greater Los Angeles area."

"It's very impressive," she said.

Actually, it was. Eugene and a cadre of CCCC volunteers had dumped most of the dead plants, cleaned up the live ones, and generally spiffed up the place. We'd ripped out a bench against the east wall, amended the soil, and put a bunch of specimen plants in the ground. Three big agaves—century plants—one against the far wall, two at the near corners of the plot. A dozen columnar cacti, a mix of North and South American species, formed a border in the back. Big mounds of mammillarias, cacti with tiny tubercles instead of ribs, were more or less artfully arranged among some rocks liberated from someone's yard. A few of the mams were in bloom, with rings of white or purple flowers around each of their many heads. An assortment of leafy succulents filled in the gaps. *Echeveria setosa,* for example, a pale green rosette of furry leaves, whose blooms mimicked pieces of candy corn.

Another major improvement: The plants on the benches were now arranged by families. Cacti had been segregated to the west end. The aloes and other lily relatives congregated in one area, the ice plant family in another. The euphorbias, the so-called succulent spurges, were jammed in on the ground in a corner, awaiting transfer to a new bench Eugene had built to replace one that had rotted.

"Are all of these cacti?" Sharon said.

That's where it usually starts when you're showing non-succulentophiles around the conservatory. "No," I said, pointing. "Just the ones down at that end. And some of the ones in the ground."

She picked up a pachypodium seedling. "This looks like a cactus to me."

"It's not. It's actually in the oleander family."

"That's a bit hard to believe."

"If it were in bloom, you'd see the flowers are very similar to an oleander's. It's all in the flowers. And the areoles, or lack thereof."

"Areoles?"

I grabbed a notocactus, a big ball of not-too-sticky yellow spines. "See how the spines come out of the white spots on the stem?"

"Sort of."

"The spots are called areoles. Only cacti have them. The flowers come from them too, and new stems." I put down the notocactus and took the pachypodium from her. "If you look at the spines on this, they're just an outgrowth of the skin. So it's not a cactus."

"Where's it from?"

"Madagascar. An awful lot of succulents are from Madagascar."

"Orchids too."

"Not cacti, though. They're New World plants. Except there are a couple of species of rhipsalis, which are epiphytic cacti, in Madagascar, and in Sri Lanka too, but they think birds brought them there."

" 'They'?"

"The cactus gurus." I grinned. "The succulent equivalent of orchid judges."

She wandered down the bench, stopping here and there to inspect a flower or lightly touch the surface of a plant. There's a big sign near the entrance that says not to do that, but it's there mostly for kids. I could steer her away from the occasional plant with white powder on the leaves that you really could mess up by handling. I didn't want her to think I was an anal personality whining "Don't touch that," at the slightest provocation.

After a while I got the feeling she was wandering aimlessly. "You don't have to look at any more," I said. "It's like me with the orchids. You don't hate looking at the plants, but you don't really—"

My words degenerated into a shriek. My arms windmilled around my head. Two definite signs that Joe Portugal has encountered a wasp.

It was a yellow jacket, the first one of the spring in the greenhouse, and it had picked a hell of a time to show up. It buzzed by my head once, twice, and zoomed off to bang itself against the roof.

"It was just a bee," Sharon said.

"Actually, it was a yellow jacket," I said, trying to gather my dignity. "Bees I don't have trouble with. Bees are our friends. I just have this thing about wasps." I not-so-subtly checked up above to see if it was going to make another run at me.

She shrugged, came to me, put a hand on my shoulder. "We all have our fears." Even through my shirt, my skin felt tingly where her fingers lay.

"Still, it's embarrassing."

"Don't worry about it." Her hand gave a little squeeze and departed.

This was good, I told myself. She'd seen me at my worst. Anything else had to be an improvement. "Where were we? Oh, yeah, you were about to tell me you'd seen enough."

She smiled. "They *are* interesting, and I mean that literally. And beautiful. It's just that—"

"Once you've seen one, you've seen them all."

"Maybe not one. But after a couple of dozen, they all look alike to me."

"I understand."

"I haven't hurt your feelings?"

"Of course not. I appreciate your coming up here to see them."

"Though you know that's not the only reason I came up."

"Oh?"

She paused, seeming embarrassed, glancing up as if inspiration floated somewhere above. Then she looked right at me. "There does seem to be something going on here, doesn't there? Some sort of . . . attraction?"

"Well, yes, now that you mention it." I cracked a smile. "Yes, Sharon, I'm attracted to you. That's why I've already asked you out twice. Let's go on a Real Date."

She sucked in her cheeks. "Yes. Let's do that."

"You seem uncertain."

"I'm certain."

She wasn't. There was something going on, some doubt about the advisability of going out with me. "How about tomorrow night?" I said. I wanted it to be that very night, but I already had plans with Gina. Besides, I didn't want to seem too eager. Great. I hadn't even gone out with her, and already I was playing games.

"Tomorrow?" she said.

"Yes. Tomorrow. Wednesday."

"Tomorrow will be fine."

"We'll have dinner. A time-honored first-date tradition."

"All right."

"It's set, then."

"Yes. All set."

I had a Real Date. What a concept.

We got the details out of the way, and Sharon said she had some errands to get to. I walked her to her car, a Ford Tempo, which she'd parked in a handicapped spot. She saw me looking at the blue marking on the pavement. "I couldn't find another spot anywhere that wasn't a mile away."

"It's all right."

"You think less of me now."

"Stop it. That's ridiculous."

One of the Ten Warning Signs of Infatuation: not caring if the other party exhibits behavior you customarily hate. Ordinarily, normally abled people who park in handicapped spots piss me off. But I was willing to overlook Sharon's transgression. Because when you're just getting into someone, you hide their faults, put them away in a little silk purse in the back of your head, to be opened only when the affair has ended disastrously and you're looking for things to make you say, "I should have known."

She got in her car, rolled down the window, leaned on the door. "Are you okay to talk about Albert for a minute?"

"Did you think of something?"

She nodded. "It has to do with Yoichi."

"Yoichi Nakatani?"

"How many Yoichis do you know?"

"Good point."

"He had a phragmipedium hybrid. Like paphiopedilum, the slipper orchids that made you uncomfortable, but the petals hang down two feet."

"No way."

She nodded. "He was very proud of it. He brought it to the judging a year or so ago. Albert was one of the judges, and his score was considerably lower than anyone else's. Enough to bring the average down to an HCC."

"Remind me again."

"Between seventy-five and eighty. The lowest award. Yoichi thought it deserved more. He confronted Albert."

"Sounds terribly déclassé."

"It's definitely not done. But Yoichi is a bit of an enfant terrible of the orchid world."

I tried to think of some more French, but the only thing that came to mind was *soixante-neuf.* "So what happened?"

"There was some yelling in the hallway. Yoichi said some very bad things to Albert."

"Like what?"

"He said he had the eyes of a newt."

"He didn't."

"And the judgment of an ass. It was awful. It was like listening to a train wreck, if I can mix a metaphor."

"Did Albert get mad too?"

"No, he just said that Yoichi would do better next time. Yoichi kept saying it was a glorious plant and Albert said, yes, it was, but it didn't show enough of one parent's influence. And it was clear that Yoichi placed the whole blame for the score on Albert."

I remembered Sam mentioning such behavior to me, though not with any particular grower's name attached. "But how could he know? Aren't the scores secret?"

Her look said, Boy are you dumb, Joe. "They let *you* in to watch."

"But I didn't have an interest in any of the plants. Surely they don't let the entrants watch their plants being judged."

"They do. For instance, the judges are growers too. Sometimes they have plants in."

"They get to vote on their own plants?"

"During the preliminaries they'll just keep quiet. If a plant of theirs comes to their table for final judging, they'll step away, or not turn in a sheet. But generally the aides know enough to keep the plants away from the table where the submitter is."

"Wait. I thought you said Yoichi didn't come to your club. That he went to one in Orange County."

"I said usually. That night, he brought his own plant in."

"It's a little hard to believe Yoichi held a grudge since then, enough of one to shoot Albert. And it doesn't say anything about Laura's death."

She fastened her seat belt, started the engine. "You're probably right. It's not much."

"It may not be much, but it's one of the better leads I've come across." *Leads?* Who was I, Joe Friday? "I'll follow up on it."

She reached out and gave my hand a squeeze. "Be careful if you do," she said, and drove off.

Eugene and I had gotten all the euphorbias nicely arranged. The Madagascar ones were together, with the shade-loving dwarves getting some cover in the shadow of a big yucca. The medusa-heads were grouped, as well as the tall ones, the shrubby ones, the leafy ones. Eugene seemed satisfied.

He walked me to my truck. He seemed reluctant to let me leave, commenting on trivial things, inventing questions for me to answer. Finally I said, "You want to talk about something?"

"How could you tell?"

"You're acting weirder than—you're acting weird."

"Oh. Yes. I want you to tell me how not to lose Sybil."

"What makes you think you're going to lose her?"

"Isn't that what happens with boyfriends and girlfriends? Don't most people go through a bunch of them before they find the right one?"

"Sometimes."

"It's taken me so long to find the first one. If I lose her I'll be alone forever."

"That's ridiculous."

"I don't know what to do to keep her."

"Just be yourself. That's what attracted her in the first place."

"But—"

"What makes you think I'm such an authority? Have you ever seen *me* with a girlfriend?"

"You know your way around women."

"Like I know my way around Watts."

He stared at me, not knowing what to make of such a stupid analogy. Frankly, neither did I.

"Look," I said, "whatever you're doing is working. It's no good to try to change it, because if there's one thing I *have* learned about women, it's that they want you to be yourself. But stop worrying about this stuff. You'll drive yourself crazy. Just enjoy the thing while it lasts."

"While it lasts? Does that mean you think it won't last?"

"Eugene, get a grip. She likes you a lot. Anyone could see that the other night. Go with the flow. And, speaking of going, I've got to." I slipped into the truck and escaped, leaving him standing there, baffled and inept when it came to women and their whole unfathomable world. Just like I was.

13

I DROVE DOWN WESTWOOD BOULEVARD, UNWILLING TO dare the freeway. I finally let my mind deal with what it had been unable to tackle for the last couple of hours: the gun by Laura's hand.

Had she really killed Albert, and then herself? Hard to believe. Somehow, even if she had murdered her boyfriend, the Laura I knew, the one who had lived through two or three decades of scrabbling to make it as an actress, didn't seem like the kind of person to take her own life if things got rough.

And if she had indeed knocked off Albert, why on earth would she ask me to look for the murderer? She would have enough trouble with the cops; why bring a wild card like me into the picture?

Now my agreement—and there was another est word for you, *agreement,* they tossed it around like confetti—to investigate Albert's murder loomed larger. With Laura dead I felt a responsibility to do what I'd said I would, try to track down Albert's killer, even if it turned out to be Laura herself.

And there was another thing. If the culprit was somebody

else, I was probably the only one around with the slightest interest in clearing Laura's name.

I needed to get my mind back into an investigative set. I'd been distracted by my attraction to Sharon. And while I could rationalize and say my time with her was useful because she had lots of insights into the orchid people, I knew it was time to talk to someone else. But who?

There was Bob from the meeting, but I didn't remember his last name and hadn't the slightest idea how to get in touch with him. I supposed I could—

Of course. Dottie Lennox. *If it has to do with orchids around here, I know about it,* she'd said.

She'd also said, *Come anytime.* I dug in my wallet for the scrap of paper she'd given me. I consulted my *Thomas Guide* and braved the freeway after all.

Hawthorne Boulevard had a small-town feel, a sense that two or three blocks to either side of the main drag the houses petered out and woods sprang up. Virtually nothing was more than two stories. The signs in and above the front windows had a certain quaintness. The taco stands and discount furniture places and used-car emporia emanated the aura of another era. The hard, crass edge of the nineties hadn't reached the area yet. It was still steeped in the not so hard, not so crass edge of the seventies.

Dave Leeper's Baseball Academy marked the intersection of 138th and Hawthorne. I turned right, then left onto Grevillea Avenue. The trees were sporadic, the streets clean. Few of the vehicles were new. Not many sport utility vehicles, a definite plus.

I found the house number and pulled up in front. Next

door a couple of kids were playing something involving a soccer ball and a laundry basket. Across the street a little terrier yapped at me.

The house needed a coat of paint but was otherwise well kept up. It was small and spare and simple, just a white stucco box with green trim, with a driveway along the side leading to a smaller white box, in front of which sat a green Econoline van. In the front, a couple of potted geraniums decorated the top of the ramp that had replaced the front steps.

Great patches of the lawn had been removed to make room for neat rows of rosebushes. Floribundas, grandifloras, hybrid teas, many with big, gnarled stem bases that attested to how long they'd been there. They displayed hundreds of flowers in a grand range of colors. More roses lined the south side of the house, and two climbers lay claim to the front walls, each abundantly abloom, the one to the left of the door red, the right-hand one peach with splashes of yellow.

Dottie's daughter was out front, wearing a sunbonnet and a long summery dress with pale flowers on it. She held an oval basket. Six or seven roses lay in it.

She saw me get out of the truck and came down the walk. "You were at Albert's Saturday."

"Yes." I introduced myself.

"I'm Maureen Lennox."

"Also known as Mo."

"Only to my mother."

"Then Maureen it is. She said to drop in anytime."

"Yes." Slight pause. "Have you heard about Laura Astaire?"

"Yes. On the radio." A small lie, to make things simpler.

"A pity." She sighed, put down her basket, removed her bonnet, inspected it. A ladybug crawled around its perimeter.

She blew softly on it and it took to the air. "Ladybug, ladybug, fly away home." She put the hat back on. "How much time did you spend with Mother?"

"Not much. A few minutes."

"I must warn you of something."

"What's that?"

"She's a bit of a case."

"What kind of a case?"

"A nutcase, as they say." She picked up her basket and moved to a bush full of gorgeous orange flowers. "I like this one, don't you? It's called Brandy." Snip, snip. Two more roses joined their fellows in the basket. "Mother has always been a bit odd. It's gotten worse over the last few years." She smiled sweetly and moved toward the front door. "See for yourself. She's in the back. In her conservatory. You can go through the house."

The living room was a wonderland of glass cabinets. A half dozen lined the walls, filling every available space between the rose-patterned slipcovered sofa and side chairs and the wide-screen TV. Each cabinet displayed a different kind of collectible. One had Hummel figurines, another some Oriental-looking porcelain. The largest, almost as tall as I was, held the nicest group of Wedgwood I'd ever seen. Not that I'd seen much Wedgwood.

The hall was lined with photos. One showed an aviator about to climb into the cockpit of a World War II–vintage plane. Another man, in coveralls, stood at the nose of the plane, giving the thumb's-up sign.

The back door was open. I went through it, stopped, and stared.

I'd thought when Maureen had said "conservatory" it was a figure of speech. I pictured a hobbyist's greenhouse, more or less like mine, with fiberglass walls and a wood frame and shade cloth tacked around wherever it would do some good. I wasn't prepared for the little piece of the Royal Botanic Gardens in the midst of this suburban backyard. It was fifteen feet across, shaped like an octagon, with white-painted walls up to bench level, glass above. Real glass, not some space-age plastic, some clear, some neatly whitewashed to minimize the sun streaming through. The vertical structural elements were painted white, too, leading up to a glass roof, with its eight faces sloping up to a point, atop which sat a miniature cupola with a red, green, and yellow pennant flying in the breeze.

I walked down a gravel path to the doorway, pushed it open, peered through. Benches full of orchids lined the periphery. The flowers' colorful shapes stood out boldly against the white of the wood. Unlike Albert's greenhouse, or my own, or any other hobbyist's I'd ever been in, each plant had a bit of breathing room, its own little domain. Like they were being displayed, rather than just grown.

Dottie sat in her wheelchair in the open area in the center of the conservatory, clad in a sweater and a dark blue dress. The chair rested on a small rug, octagonal like the structure, patterned with yellow whirls and loops on a forest-green background. Next to Dottie was a tiny table, no more than a foot across, with a china teapot, two dainty cups, and accessories.

Dottie's attention was focused on her lap; she seemed to be reading. She looked up when I knocked. "Oh, goodie. Well, don't just stand there. Come in."

I swung the door wide and entered. I heard a faint voice. I realized what was in Dottie's lap wasn't a book, but rather one of those tiny TVs from Casio or whoever. I heard the words *your boyfriend and your own sister* before she snapped the device off.

A large fan was mounted in one of the walls, and opposite it a set of louvers let the outside in, but it was still ten or fifteen degrees warmer inside. How Dottie sat there in a sweater was a mystery. I'd been in the place ten seconds and already wanted to take my shirt off.

She watched me approach. When I stopped a couple of feet away, she said, "Have a seat."

I looked around. "There isn't one."

Her brow furrowed. "Right. I keep meaning to get a guest chair, but I keep forgetting."

I'd noticed a couple of cheap plastic chairs outside. I ran back out and retrieved one, placed it on the redwood planking just beyond the edge of the rug, sat down.

"You'll be wanting some tea," said Dottie. She reached for the pot.

"Oh, that won't—" At the raise of her eyebrows, I said, "Yes, that would be lovely."

"Nothing like a nice cup of tea on a spring afternoon." She poured one for me. "Milk? Sugar? I'm afraid I haven't any lemon, though you could pick one from the neighbors' tree. They won't mind."

"Straight, please."

She handed over the cup. I took a sip. It was good tea, though it had been in the pot too long.

"Nice setup you've got here," I said.

"It is lovely, isn't it? Charles knew his way around a toolshed."

"Charles was Mr. Lennox?"

"Oh, yes. He's gone now, but he certainly knew his way around a toolshed."

"A good thing to know."

"He was good with wood, but better with metal. From working on the airplanes."

"He was an airplane mechanic?"

"And a damned fine one. When the war was over, Hughes Aircraft hired him, and over the pond we came."

She looked into her cup, brought it a few inches from her face as if making sure there was nothing left in the bottom. She poured some more tea, added milk, stirred, sipped. "Testicles," she said.

"Excuse me?"

"Testicles. That's where the word *orchid* comes from. The Greek word for testicles. Because the first orchids that were discovered came from Greece and their tubers look like testicles. Oh, those Greeks."

"I didn't know that."

"Some orchids, the ophrys come to mind, look like bees."

True enough. I'd seen one in Albert's greenhouse.

"Some resemble wasps."

How nice. "I didn't know that."

"It's to fool the insects into pollinating them. Insects aren't very bright. It was the Communists, you know."

Whoa, Dottie. Slow down, there. "What was the Communists?"

"That killed Albert."

It was bound to happen sooner or later. Eventually, if I was going to go around poking into homicides, I had to run across a total wacko. "How do you know I'm interested in who killed Albert?"

"I know these things."

"I see." I tried to look thoughtful. "I hadn't thought of that possibility. The Communists."

Maureen had been right. The woman was a nutcase. I wanted to just get up and leave. Some semblance of manners kept me there. "How did you find out about this?"

"Albert told me. It was at his house one night. He'd invited us up, Mo and me, for dinner and to see some of his new orchids."

"How long ago was this?"

"Last autumn. Albert had some new miniatures that he was very excited about. From one of those countries in Asia, Vietnam or one of those. There was one in particular he liked very much. It was such a dark purple, with a little beard and hairs that came off the sides. And it was scented with nutmeg. He held it out and said, 'It's so hard to get things from there because the Communists are in power.' " She shrugged. "Communists, that's who it was. Trying to keep their orchids in their country."

She leaned forward and adopted a conspiratorial tone. "I had Mo take me to the library, and I did some research on the World Wide Web." You could hear her pronounce the initial capitals. "Soon I knew everything."

So that was her inspiration. The Internet. A place where any crackpot could share his or her delusions with the world. Sometimes, when there was nothing watchable on TV and the video store was out of Jackie Chan, Gina would take me on surfing expeditions. We would drop in on the flat-earthers, the moon-landing-was-fake crew, the Bert-Parks-was-Jesus crowd. It was a perfect place for little old ladies to have their brains messed with.

Again I thought to leave. But as long as I was there already . . . "Have you heard about Laura Astaire?"

"Breaking news."

"Excuse me?"

"I was viewing Jerry Springer, and they came in and said, 'Breaking news.' They said she was dead. I wouldn't be surprised if she was a Communist." She reached out and took my wrist with a bony, yet strong grip. "I think she killed Albert."

"Why?"

"I see it all now. Her Communist superiors had her do it."

"Because of the orchids from Southeast Asia."

She nodded furiously. "It makes perfect sense, don't you think? Then they had her killed as well. To cover their trail." She still had her hand on my wrist. It was cutting off my circulation. The old lady was surprisingly strong. Maybe she'd killed Albert. The wheelchair was a front.

"Who else is a Communist?" I said. "How about Helen and David Gartner?" I didn't feel right encouraging her, yet I couldn't help myself. It was as if she'd injected some of her daftness when she wrapped her hand around my wrist.

She let go her death grip, wheeled to a bench, plucked off a small pot, began worrying the bark at the surface with her fingers. "Do you like my mix?"

I cast a glance around the conservatory. "It seems to work."

"Of course it works. I've been using it for thirty years. Some people have funny ideas about orchid mix."

I like free association as much as the next guy. But this was getting ridiculous. It was time to escape. I drained my tea and got to my feet.

She put down the plant and wheeled back onto her rug. "I know everything about the orchid society," she said. "And if I don't know, well, it's all in the archives. You'd be amazed at what goes on. A couple of the members are drug addicts. And there's a Japanese fellow who's a smuggler. And of course several of them are homosexuals. But you know what I say."

"What's that?"

"Live and let live, that's what I say." She picked up her tea, sipped, made a face. "Well. I'm tired now, but come back again, young man. Anytime. I have many stories to tell. I've been in the orchid society longer than anyone. I'm the club historian, you know."

"I'll try."

"See that you do," she said. "It will be worth your while." She looked down into her lap, moved a pale finger. Tinny voices came from the Casio.

I went outside, shut the door behind me. The beginnings of an overcast had come in from the west. As I stood there, a cloud drifted over the sun and threw everything into dull shadow.

Maureen was in the kitchen, putting together a meal. "How was she?"

"She thinks Communists killed Albert."

"Oh, that again. She hasn't been on Communists for a month or two."

"How do you deal with it?"

She smiled and spread her hands apart, as if to say, what can I do. "Her health is good, except for her hips. And her delusions aren't harmful. She's my mother. I have to take care her. It's really not a burden. You were thinking it was a burden, weren't you?"

"No."

"Of course you were, and please don't. I'm fine. Don't worry about me."

"I won't." I said goodbye and left.

More clouds were coming in. As I drove toward the freeway, the late afternoon sky turned gloomy. Appropriate to my mood. I could see from street level that the 405 north was jammed, so I continued west and picked up Sepulveda. By the time I approached LAX, the clouds had given the day a surrealistic cast. In the middle distance I could see the old control tower, undergoing renovations, swathed in white plastic like a Christo project.

There's a piece of Sepulveda that dips to travel under one of the runways. Just as I entered the underground section, a 747 rumbled over, from some airline I'd never heard of, from Malaysia or Indonesia or one of those places, all filled with Malaysians or Indonesians or whoever come to America for streets paved with something good.

The behemoth overhead evoked some primal fear of being crushed under tons of concrete. I shrank down into my seat and stayed that way until, thirty endless seconds later, I exited the tunnel.

14

ELAINE HAD PHONED. I HAD A CALLBACK AT THREE-THIRTY the next afternoon for the toilet bowl cleaner commercial. I took down the pertinent info and called her back to confirm. She said I sounded funny. I said it was allergies. She reminded me I didn't have any. I said I must be developing some.

French Market Place is a funky complex on Santa Monica Boulevard in West Hollywood. It's two stories, with the central area, where the restaurant is, going all the way to the roof. There's a horseshoe of offices on the second floor; on the first a variety of shops surrounds the restaurant. A card place, a swimsuit store, stuff like that.

The restaurant has a New Orleans theme, with low brick walls, and vegetation hanging over the tables. It sounds like it should be tacky, but it's not. Somehow it works. Or it *is* tacky and it works anyway.

Gina was waiting up front when I ran in from the rain

that had erupted from the cloud cover. She was wearing a yellow slicker and reading a copy of the *L.A. Weekly* from a stack near the door. When she saw me she snapped it closed, started to put it under her arm, instead threw it back on the pile. "I have enough crap to read already," she said.

A guy in a black apron, with a shaved head and nine, count 'em, nine earrings in his left ear, escorted us to a table in the corner, under a ficus that was standing in for a magnolia. A waiter came over half a minute later to ask what we wanted to drink. Gina told him she was ready to order. I said I hadn't quite decided yet. Gina glared at me. I ordered a hamburger. Gina had a Denver omelet.

"I suppose you know about Laura," I said.

"What about her?"

"She's dead. Someone shot her. I figured you knew because everyone in the world seems to have heard about it."

"I've been out of touch." She stared at me. "You're not kidding, are you?"

"I don't kid about stuff like that."

"Then that's it."

"Then what's what?"

"That's it. No more looking into murders."

"But I promised Laura, and now that she's dead—"

"Fuck Laura. You don't owe her anything. There's someone dangerous out there and I don't want them killing you too."

I watched her, tried to think of a clever response. I couldn't. Because she was perfectly correct.

"You won't back off, will you?" she said.

"Probably not."

She nodded. "All right. I've played the voice of reason. Tell me about Laura."

I told her everything. When that got too depressing, I moved on to my upcoming date with Sharon.

Later when we got back to her place, Gina asked if I wanted to come up. I said no. She didn't put up any resistance. I drove home in a continuing drizzle, listening to the Beatles. "All you need is love," they told me. It sounded so simple.

I awoke Wednesday morning a little after seven. The rain had stopped, but the sky was still low. I switched on the TV to check the weather and found all the stations were running live coverage of some guy who'd stopped his pickup on the freeway, gotten out, and begun taking potshots at passing motorists with a shotgun. They'd blocked off the freeway—causing a traffic jam more massive than usual—and had hostage negotiators talking to him, even though there wasn't a hostage.

Finally, after an hour, just when it looked like the guy was about to give himself up, he pointed the shotgun at his head and blew his brains to smithereens. The Channel 6 traffic chopper got a fine shot of it. One second his head was there, the next it wasn't. The anchor apologized for letting us see such graphic footage. Then they showed it again. I turned off the TV.

I made tea and went outside for greenhouse rounds, wearing old Nikes instead of my usual karate slippers as a concession to the weather. My *Gymnocalycium ragonesii,* a South

American cactus resembling a round gray rock, had bloomed. As I was inspecting it the sun broke through. The gymno's white flower caught the first rays with that peculiar sheen cactus flowers have. A tiny bee or fly was busy gathering pollen among its stamens. I watched as it withdrew from the petals, waited while it had found its way outside, closed up the greenhouse.

Over by the garage I spotted a golden polistes wasp. First one of the spring in the garden. I shivered and gave it a wide berth. Someday I was going to get therapy for my fear of the damned things. Sure. Right after I won my Emmy and raised a family.

I went inside and took a shower. While I was in there I reviewed the conversation where Sharon and I arranged our date, wondering if she really wasn't sure she wanted to go out with me. Or if maybe she was already involved with someone and was merely setting me up as a backup plan. That had happened before. Right in the middle of passionate sex, the woman pulled away and said she wasn't really into it because she was waiting for her true love to return from visiting his family in Samoa. Because I'm a masochist when it comes to women, we continued seeing each other. A month later she said she was getting married. To the Samoan, I said, and she said no, to some guy she met at work. It was the nearest I've ever come to striking a woman, although it really wasn't close at all.

But the Samoan was history. He had nothing to do with my current situation. Why did I always have to view a date with apprehension? Maybe things would be great. Maybe there'd be a magic moment or two, a time when our eyes caught and held and we knew each other better than we had a right to. And maybe there'd be sex.

Alberta Burns was the LAPD homicide detective I'd gotten to know during the Brenda business. She'd been Casillas's partner before he got promoted to Robbery–Homicide, and had been much more receptive to my poking around than he had. I'd developed a small crush on her, but never pursued it, partially because I didn't want to go out with a woman who could beat me up.

She worked out of the Pacific Division, at Centinela and Culver, about two miles from my house. I got her on the line. "Burns."

"Joe Portugal here."

"I thought I might hear from you."

"You talked to Casillas."

"Yes."

"You're still in touch, then."

"What can I do for you?"

"It's what I can do for you. I'm going to buy you breakfast."

"And pick my brain?"

"If you'll let me."

I expected to be turned down. Surprise, surprise. "Pick me up in front of the station. Ten minutes."

"Yes, ma'am."

I stepped outside into full sunlight. The front walk was nearly dry already. The truck was plastered with leaves that the rain had brought down from the weirdos' elm. I ran the wipers to clear the windshield and hit the road.

Burns was waiting out front when I got to the station. She jaywalked across Culver and hopped in the truck. Five minutes later we were at Western Bagel. Burns ordered a blueberry with cream cheese and a large black coffee. I had a pumpernickel with cream cheese and tea. I paid. We picked a table outside, under a green plastic umbrella. A few renegade raindrops dotted our chairs. I wiped them with a napkin and we sat down. As we were getting ourselves arranged, Burns caught me staring at her bagel. "What?"

I shrugged. "There are rules about what kinds of bagels should have cream cheese on them. Blueberry is not one of those kinds. Not that blueberries should be in a bagel in the first place. Mind you, I love blueberries, but—this is an inane way to begin a conversation. How've you been?"

"All right."

"Just all right?"

"Things are going okay."

"You're looking good. I like the hair."

"Thanks. I like it too." She picked up her bagel. "It was time for a change."

My compliments were more than idle chatter. Burns had had her hair straightened when I'd known her before. Now she'd let the curl come out, and had it cut short so that it formed a black halo around her head. She'd also softened her look in clothing. The lines were less severe, a bit more feminine than before. Not enough to detract from her image as an all-business cop, but conspicuous to Joe Portugal, fashion authority.

"This change," I said. "Was it around the time Casillas got promoted?"

She looked pretty silly, sitting there motionless with the bagel inches from her mouth. After a couple of seconds she took a bite, chewed, swallowed. Then: "You're pretty perceptive."

"I try. You wanted a promotion too."

She put down the bagel and picked up her coffee. "Let's not go there, all right?"

"No, let's."

She glared, sipping her coffee without taking her eyes off me. "All right, then," she said. "Yes, I wanted a promotion too. He got one. He's been on the job longer than I have. End of story."

"Your time will come." Jeez, Portugal, can't you come up with anything better than that?

A misplaced sesame seed clung to my bagel. I carefully picked it off and put it on my plate. Finally I came up with something semi-intelligent. "You have a new partner, then?"

"Uh-huh."

"Are you, like, mentoring him?"

"Her. Like, I am."

We talked about work for a while, her new partner, my bug events at the malls. When we'd finished off our bagels, she said, "Casillas says you're digging around in Albert Oberg's murder. And that you discovered Laura Astaire's body. You went, what, a year, without finding anyone dead. Not bad."

"Night before last," I said, "Casillas came to an orchid society meeting because of a woman named Helen Gartner. The woman Laura was with the night Albert was killed."

"The woman she *said* she was with."

"Fine, whatever you say. He talked to Helen when she left. I want to find out what about."

"You do, do you?"

"Yes."

She just stared at me.

"What?" I said. "I have cream cheese on my nose?" Her deep brown eyes wouldn't let me go. Finally I turned away. I spied the sesame seed on my plate, licked a finger, picked up the seed, ate it.

We sat there silently for half a minute. "You don't get it, do you, Joe?" she said at last. She'd never called me by my first name before.

"Don't get what?"

"Criminals are bad people. You get mixed up with them, you put yourself—and those you love—in danger."

"I'm being careful."

"Are you? Tell me just how you're being careful."

"I—" Of course, I couldn't come up with anything. Because I wasn't being careful at all. Disregarding the admonitions of my father, ones now repeated by someone who should know, I was blithely careening around among a bunch of possibly dangerous characters.

"Look," she said, "I have to get back. Regardless of what you might think, I've got cases of my own to worry about."

"Can you find out from Casillas why he was after Helen Gartner?"

"Why should I?"

"For old times' sake."

She sighed. "I just know this is a bad idea, but . . . I'll see what I can dig up."

"There's one more thing I'd like you to dig up."

"Don't push your luck."

"I'd like to know whether Laura killed herself."

"Now how on God's green earth am I supposed to find that out?"

"Ask Casillas."

"And what makes you think he knows?"

"The police can always tell. Powder burns, bullet trajectories, stuff like that. Like on *Homicide*. Come on, don't tell me they haven't been trying to figure that out already."

Next to the word *baleful* in the dictionary, they have a picture of the look Burns was giving me. "I'll see what I can find out," she said.

I took her back, dropped her off, watched as she strode back into the station. I liked the way she walked. Powerful and womanly. Nice ass.

Jesus. Why was I thinking about Burns's ass? Gina was right. Investigating homicides made me horny.

15

ORANGE COUNTY IS ALIEN. THAT'S THE ONLY WORD THAT seems to do it justice. When I pass one of the big green freeway signs that say I'm entering it, I immediately feel like an interloper, and like everyone who sees me will know it and treat me appropriately.

O.C. is a hugely conservative area, one of the last bastions of the Reagan dream. But my discomfort is more than just political. The women with their frosted blond heads might as well be of another species. The men, perfectly coiffed with caterpillar mustaches, could be from another planet. I have nothing in common with them. They are interested in phenomena I have no knowledge of.

Even the traffic lights in Orange County are weird. They travel to the beat of a different electronic drum, so when you're driving one of the long straight streets you end up waiting for two or three minutes at a time, while cars go in every direction but yours, and turn left from places you didn't know existed. Then you move on a couple of blocks to do the whole thing all over again.

At a little before noon Wednesday, I found myself on one

such stretch. Beach Boulevard, in Stanton, a small city I knew only because there's a cactus nursery there that I used to go to once a year, until I realized I was buying something only because I was embarrassed to leave empty-handed. I passed a lot of ugly apartment buildings and uglier shopping centers, spending the interminable traffic-light intervals listening to Moby Grape's third album, a ninety-nine-cent Tower Records find.

Finally I found the avenue the *Thomas Guide* told me to turn left at. I made another left onto the street on the receipt Yoichi Nakatani had given me and found the long rutted driveway that led to his place. I bounced down it on shocks that were new when Jimmy Carter was in the White House, taking in the colorful cymbidiums planted in tubs alongside, and pulled to a stop in front of a greenhouse. It was typical of those at specialty plant dealers. Sections poked off at odd angles. Saggy benches were haphazardly propped up. At least four kinds of shade cloth drooped over various areas. The electrical wiring would meet no building code on the planet. Plants sat on every horizontal surface and hung from most of the vertical ones.

Yoichi emerged from a house trailer across the driveway from the greenhouse. Its undercarriage was covered with plywood sheets that were nailed in and painted to match the trailer. A variety of plant benches surrounded it: planks on cinder blocks, constructions cobbled together from fiberboard and two-by-fours, metal racks from Home Depot. All were loaded with orchids. Most of them were shaded by the big sycamores and eucalyptus that dotted the lot, though they would have gotten some direct sun in the morning.

I left the truck behind and picked my way through the plant gauntlet to him. His olive-green shorts reached below his knees. He wore the same orchid T-shirt Sharon'd had on at the show, but his was beat up, with a ripped seam on one shoulder. On his feet were rubber gardening shoes, the kind they sell for exorbitant prices at Smith and Hawken.

His hand was clammy, his handshake weak. "I thought I would see you again," he said. "The lure of the orchid is very strong. You must have more."

"Something like that."

He had a giant plastic cup of iced tea, and asked if I wanted some before we hit the greenhouse. I told him it was an excellent idea. He led me into the trailer.

The door opened on the kitchen. Yoichi pointed me to a tiny table accompanied by seats consisting of benchlike wall projections with cushions. He poured me some tea from a pitcher he got out of a refrigerator that seemed way too big for the space, and sat down at right angles to me. Our knees banged. "Sorry," I said, even though he was the one who'd clobbered me.

"No problem," he said.

He watched as I took several swallows of iced tea. It was good, freshly brewed, unsweetened. I waited for him to say something. He didn't, so I did. "Quite a spread you've got here." Quite a wordsmith, that Portugal.

He nodded and took a long draught of tea. While he still had the glass up to his mouth, I said, "I saw the judging at the Palisades Orchid Society the other night."

There was a slight hitch to his swallow. He finished off his tea, put the glass down. "You said you were a newcomer to orchids."

"So?"

"Why were you at the judging?"

"Call me precocious. Did your plant do as well as you expected?"

"No, it didn't. More tea?"

"Your glass is empty, not mine."

He looked down at it. "Ah, yes." He got up, refilled it, sat down again. "I did expect a higher score. At least an HCC."

"Why do you think you didn't get it?"

He shrugged. "Who can tell with orchid judges? They get things in their heads. They don't like a genus, they don't like a grower. They didn't get what they needed the night before from their wives." He smiled. His teeth were too even, too perfect. "Or, in a few cases, their husbands. Or whoever."

"Doesn't it bother you, putting months and years into a plant, then having it judged down in a matter of minutes?"

Another shrug. "That's the rule of the game. What about Olympic sprinters? They train for four years, and some of them, the ones eliminated in the heats, are out of the competition in ten seconds."

"You weren't there Monday night."

"No, I wasn't. Would you like to see my lab?"

"Where were—"

"Of course you would. Come. Please leave your tea behind. And . . ."

"Yes?"

He pointed to the minuscule sink. "Would you mind washing your hands?"

"Not at all."

I scrubbed up using soap from a push-button dispenser and wiped my hands on paper towels. Yoichi produced a trash can, took the towels, made the can disappear again. He went through a door and I followed.

The room I found myself in was perhaps thirty feet long, filling that whole end of the trailer. It was chock-full of scientific apparatus. Test tubes, beakers, pipettes, and a load of other stuff vaguely remembered from high school chemistry class. Cases with meters on the front, some with dials, some digital.

Racks of flasks filled with something green lined a ten-foot section of the wall. Strong fluorescent fixtures lit the place clearly. Over in a corner, a security camera on a bracket gave everything the once-over.

"This is pretty amazing," I said.

"Yes."

I walked over to the racks with their dozens of flasks. The green things within were little plants, a couple of dozen in each. They didn't really resemble orchids. There wasn't any soil; instead, the plants were stuck into some goopy substance lining the insides of the flasks, each of which had a computer-printed label bearing plant names and dates. "What's all this?"

"These are some of my creations."

Great. I'd tracked down Dr. Frankenstein. "Creations?"

"My hybrids." He pulled a flask from the rack, jogged over to a workbench, shuffled some papers, came back with a couple of photos. "The plants in this flask, for instance, are a cross between these two angraecums."

They had long stems up which pairs of leaves climbed like a ladder, and big white star-shaped flowers. "I don't know angraecums."

"A very interesting genus. You see the nectar spurs?"

"Those long pointy things dangling from the flowers?"

"Yes. They're designed for one pollinator and one pollinator only."

"Nature. Isn't it wonderful? Where are they from?"

"Madagascar."

I nodded. "Madagascar has a lot of wonderful plants. Too bad they're destroying so many of them."

He gave me a funny look. "Who is?"

"The locals. With their deforestation."

"Oh. Them. Yes, it is too bad."

I pointed to the flask. "Did you sprout them yourself?"

"What do you mean?"

"I've heard that orchid seed is really small and hard to get going." What else had Albert told me? "And that a lot of people send it out for germination."

"Ah. I germinate my own. All the best growers do."

I took the flask from his hand. He gave it up grudgingly. "So you just grow them in these flasks until they get big enough to pot up themselves?"

"Oh, no. This is how I sell them."

"Why do people buy them like this?"

"They grow them on. They want to see what will develop. You never know what two parents will come up with. Like humans, hmm?" He took the flask back, placed it on the rack, dropped the photos on the workbench. "So tell me, Mr. Portugal. What is the real reason for your visit today?"

"I thought I might learn some more about—"

"Do you think I'm an idiot?"

"No."

"Then tell me why you're here."

I drew in a big breath, let it out slowly. "I'm investigating Albert Oberg's death. And, now, Laura Astaire's as well."

"And what gives you the right to do that?"

"The right?"

"I don't have to talk to you, you know."

"But why wouldn't you, if you have nothing to hide?"

"Did someone imply I had something to hide?"

"Everyone has something to hide."

"Yes." He sat in a leather desk chair, decided he didn't like it, got back up. "Go ahead with your questions."

"You had an argument with Albert some time ago. About judging."

"I did?"

"You said, among other things, that he had the eyes of a newt."

He smiled. "And so you came down here expecting to find out I put a bullet into him."

"Not really. If it were as simple as that, I expect the police would have carted you away long ago."

"I don't think I can help you."

"Why not?"

"For one thing, the argument never happened."

"I have it on good authority that it did."

"Your authority is mistaken."

"You're sure?"

"Of course I'm sure. I would remember if I ever had an argument with Albert. I did not. We got along well. And if I did have an argument with someone, I would never say he had the eyes of a newt."

"Maybe I've been misinformed. Let's say I have. But perhaps, as a grower, you might have seen or heard something that would give me an idea of where to go next. For instance, have you heard anything about business dealings between Albert and the Gartners?"

He frowned, looked away, back at me. "The Gartners?"

"Yes. David and Helen."

"Business dealings? What kind?"

"I'm not exactly sure. That's why I asked you."

He shook his head. Too fast? Hard to tell. "Nothing. I've heard nothing like that. I really don't know the Gartners very well."

"You seem nervous."

"Having a virtual stranger question me in my home does that to me."

"I'm just trying to—" To what? To see justice done? That was way beyond my limited moral scope. "To help clear Laura's name. Would you mind telling me where you were Saturday night?"

"Yes, I would."

"Tell me anyway."

He looked toward the heavens, then back at me. "Very well. I was at a board meeting of the Anaheim Orchid Society."

"Saturday night seems an odd time for a board meeting."

"It was a dinner as well. Orchidists enjoy each other's company. Why not spend Saturday evening together?"

"I suppose people saw you there."

"I suppose they did. Come, let's go look in the greenhouse. You might find something you want to buy."

"I might want to buy one of the flasks."

"I don't think I would sell you one. They're for people who know more than you do."

We went out to the greenhouse. Suddenly he was the same happy-go-lucky guy I'd met at the show. I looked for something to take home. Like I said, I always feel funny about visiting a nursery and not buying anything. I almost got one of the angraecums, but the ones that were significantly sized were too much money, and the ones I could afford were, according to Yoichi, a couple of years from blooming. So I picked out an *Isabelia virginalis,* a string of tiny pseudobulbs attached to a stick, with a single needlelike leaf poking out from each, the whole affair covered with a webby shroud. Twenty-two dollars. It would have gotten me a massive cactus.

16

I MADE IT BACK UP TO HOLLYWOOD IN PLENTY OF TIME FOR my three-thirty callback. I parked at Pep Boys again, did my stint in front of the camera, cut through the store on the way back to the truck. A guy in a short-sleeved white shirt and Daffy Duck tie gave me the eye. "You were all out of fuzzy dice," I said, and hustled out to the lot.

I drove up to Franklin, cut over to Beachwood, continued north. I parked in front of Laura's place, stared at it, willed something important to come into view.

It worked, though I didn't know it at the time. The two neighbor boys came skateboarding down the street. The smaller, blond one had Monty the cat draped over his shoulder like a big orange muffler. They were yelling at each other, calling each other "butthole." When they saw me sitting there, they screeched the skateboards to a halt and stood looking moderately sheepish.

I gestured them over. I probably looked like a drug dealer.

"How you kids doing?" I asked.

"Fine," said the taller, dark-haired one. Blondie said nothing.

"That's Monty, right?"

"Uh-huh," said the shorter one.

"My name's Joe. What are your names?"

They exchanged looks, like their mother had told them not to talk to strangers. But we weren't exactly strangers.

"I'm Sonny," said the tall one. He had a stud in his ear with a peace sign on it. "My brother's Crock."

What a lousy thing to do. Naming a kid Crock. A Crock boy, like the one who'd dropped the pot and uncovered the secret of the stanhopeas and their hidden flowers. "I was a friend of Laura's. You remember? You saw me the other day."

"She was nice," said Crock. No earring, but a tattoo of a lightning bolt on his upper arm. It was smudged. Had to be fake. Good thing.

"She hung out with us when our mom wasn't home," said Sonny. " 'Cause she was home a lot in the afternoons. She was nice."

"Real nice," said Crock.

Okay, we were making progress. We'd established that Laura was nice. "You guys like cats?"

"We like Monty," said Sonny. Knowing his cue, the cat picked his head up from Crock's shoulder, looked at me, and yawned.

"You said to the policeman yesterday that you took care of him sometimes."

"Sometimes, before she got killed," said Crock. "Now he's ours."

Sonny punched him in the arm. Crock flinched away. "Sorry," he said. "I forgot."

Interesting behavior. "Did you guys ever feed Monty for Laura?"

They exchanged anxious looks before turning back to me. "You mean like when she wasn't home?" said Crock.

"Yes."

Another swapping of glances.

"Yeah," said Crock.

"No," said Sonny. He went to sock Crock's arm again, but the smaller boy danced away.

I smiled. "Which is it, guys?"

"Yeah," Sonny said, though he wasn't happy about it. "We fed him sometimes when she wasn't home in the afternoons. At night our mom did sometimes."

"Is your mom home?"

"Yes," said Crock.

"No," said Sonny.

"Which is it, guys?"

"She's home," said Crock. "She just is kind of tired."

"Can I talk to her? I promise it'll only be for a minute."

His eyes darted around. "Yeah, I guess it's okay. Come on."

The two of them skateboarded a couple of apartment buildings up the street. I locked up the truck and followed. Their building was similar to Laura's, but pale green and without any dangling house number digits.

They led me upstairs. Crock had a key on a chain around his neck. He pulled the chain over his head, approached the apartment door, stopped. He looked at his brother, then at me. "When our mom found out we told the cops we took care of Monty, she told us not to talk about it with anybody."

"I won't say anything."

He looked at me, evaluated me, evidently decided I was telling the truth. He opened the door and took a step inside. "Ma!"

"Yeah?"

"There's a man here to see you. He says he's Laura's friend."

"The place is a mess."

"I don't care," I yelled. "My place is a mess too." That got a little smile out of Sonny. He and his brother and their new cat vanished into the apartment.

A few seconds later she appeared. She was short and a little heavy and wore worn denim cutoffs and a sweatshirt. Her hair was some kind of blond. "Hi," she said. I might have smelled alcohol.

I held out a hand. "Joe Portugal. I used to hang out with Laura."

She took my fingertips in hers, let go. "Nice girl." That made it unanimous.

"Yes, she was. I understand you fed Monty sometimes."

She threw a glance back into the house, turned back to me. "Where did you hear that?"

"Laura told me."

I didn't know if she believed me or not. I hoped I hadn't gotten the kids in trouble.

"She said that?"

"Uh-huh."

She looked at me as if realizing for the first time that some stranger was at her door asking her questions. "Why should I tell you anything?"

"Like I said, I'm a friend of Laura's. I'm trying to prove her innocent of killing her boyfriend. And herself, I guess."

"The fat guy."

"Yeah, the fat guy."

She heaved a big sigh. "You wanna come in?"

"Sure."

She opened the door all the way, and I entered the apartment. I'd expected a pit, but the place was relatively neat. Maybe the kids liked housework.

I could hear the boys being boys somewhere in the back. In the living room, the TV had one of those talk show people on, some redhead I didn't recognize. The volume was way down. A bottle of vodka and one of Cranapple juice and a glass decorated the beat-up coffee table.

She slumped onto the Herculon couch, pointed vaguely at the matching chair. "Have a seat. Want a drink?"

"No, thanks."

She nodded, as if I'd explained a mystery of the universe. "Yeah, I fed the cat sometimes."

"You had a key?"

She frowned. "Sure I did. Something wrong with that?"

"Of course not."

"She had mine too. So she could give the kids snacks when I wasn't home from work yet."

"Why aren't you at work now?"

She tried to give me a dirty look, didn't quite make it. "I wasn't feeling well today."

I wondered if the kids really did go to a year-round school. There was another explanation for their being on the street so much. Mom's drunk again. Let's skip class. She won't care. "Feeling better now?"

"Yeah."

"So if Laura was away, sometimes you'd go down the block and feed Monty."

"Yeah."

"Do you remember if you fed him Saturday night?"

"You're not going to tell the cops any of this, are you?"

"Not if you tell me the truth."

"I just don't want to get involved with the cops."

"I promise. Go ahead."

"She called while *Nash Bridges* was on. I wouldn't have answered the phone, but the commercial was on." She scratched her chin. "It's such a good show. They haven't made a show like that in a long time. They haven't made a show like that since—"

"Since *Miami Vice*."

Bingo. She smiled for the first time. Sometime long ago she probably had a nice smile. "Wasn't that a great show? I love that Don Johnson."

"You must really love him to name your kids after his character." Sonny. Crock, whose full first name, I suspected, was Crockett.

"I was gonna name the next one James. That was Sonny's real name on the show. Or Jamie if it was a girl. But I never had a next one."

"So last Saturday night, when Laura called, did she ask you to go over and feed Monty?"

"She sure did. And as soon as *Nash Bridges* was over I did. Minute I walk in the door he starts hollering at me, like he does when he's hungry. I gave him a Sheba and some kibble and some water."

So I'd been right about Monty. He liked to yell when he hadn't gotten his food on time. And I'd been right when I told Casillas about him seeming like he'd been fed before Laura and Gina and I arrived at Laura's place early Sunday morning.

I'd just been wrong about who fed him.

We talked a few minutes more, but nothing came of it, except for my acquisition of a finer appreciation of the films of Don Johnson. *A Boy and His Dog* was playing at the New Beverly in a couple of weeks, and I promised to see it.

As I unlocked the truck, I realized I didn't know Sonny and Crock's mother's name. I decided it didn't matter.

17

I SPENT THE RIDE HOME IN A FUNK. LAURA HAD LIED TO US. It should have been upsetting, but not as upsetting as it was. Maybe that was because I'd set her up in my mind as a mistress of integrity, and she'd shown she wasn't.

I called Gina as soon as I got back. "Guess what. Laura didn't feed Monty Saturday night. I found the neighbor who did."

"Oops. There goes the old alibi."

"I still don't think she did it."

"So why did she lie about feeding the cat?"

"Maybe she went somewhere else after she left Helen, somewhere she didn't want us knowing she went."

"Like where?"

"I don't know. Damn it."

"What?"

"What if she was playing me for an idiot? What if she really did it and sent me off to find some fake killer?"

"Why would she do that? You never would have gotten mixed up in the whole thing if she hadn't gotten you involved."

"I don't know. As a smoke screen?"

"Doesn't seem likely. You find out anything else today?"

I told her about Burns and about Yoichi. She said Yoichi sounded suspicious. I asked why. She said, "Oh, you know those Orientals," trying to get my goat and failing.

When we were done with my day, we went on to hers. "I went to the Beverly Hills Gun Club," she said.

"What for?"

"I hadn't practiced in months."

"And now you had a sudden urge to? You're not going to begin carrying your gun, are you?"

"I'm not sure yet."

"Please don't."

"We'll see."

"Gina—"

"I'm a big girl."

"Yeah, okay, whatever. Just don't shoot your toe off." I glanced at my watch. "I'd better go."

"To get ready for your big date."

"Uh-huh."

"Talk to you tomorrow, then."

"You want to have breakfast?"

"Okay." She didn't sound very enthusiastic.

"How about I come up and we do French Market again? How's nine sound?"

"You sure you can make it?"

"What do you mean?"

"You might get lucky."

"I'm not going to get lucky. It's only a first date."

Suddenly I felt awkward. Gina and I had had this kind of conversation a million times. Talking about our lovers. Sometimes including what we did with them after the lights went out. Sometimes in explicit detail. It had always felt totally comfortable before. Now it was different. Not quite right.

I'd wanted to pick Sharon up, make it as much of a Real Date as I could manage, but when we'd set things up she said she might have to come straight from work, and why didn't she just come to my place? I spent the time before she showed up straightening the house as best I could. I even vacuumed the living room. Half of it, anyway. Somewhere to the left of the coffee table the vacuum began gargling. Shortly thereafter, all suction ceased. My guess was that a belt had broken, but I didn't want to dig around to find out.

At six-thirty, the appointed time, Sharon was nowhere in sight. Five minutes later I started to worry that she'd decided going out with me was a stupid idea and she'd blown me off. After five more I was sure. By a quarter to seven I was ready to call Gina and say, Let's get married.

I hadn't always been so distrusting of women. Only since I was twenty, when somebody I was dating said she'd come by, and I waited two hours before getting on the telephone and finding out she'd gotten hold of some acid and was blowing her mind in my bass player's water bed.

I was pacing the living room, making up stories about what had happened to Sharon, when the half-used package of condoms in my nightstand somehow jumped to mind. It dated back to Iris, the UCLA coed I'd had a ridiculous couple of weeks with a year or so before. I found myself wondering if the damned things had an expiration date. Would pinholes develop if you kept them too long? Or would the nonoxynol turn sour and emit an evil odor when you tore the foil packs open?

I dashed into the bedroom and grabbed the little cardboard package from my nightstand. Durex Extra Sensitive. *Super thin for more feeling.* There was indeed an expiration date on the box, as if they were cough syrup or Tylenol, but it was a year away. I was opening the box to check the integrity of the foil packs when the doorbell rang.

I threw the box into its drawer and flung the drawer closed. I ran to the front door and opened it. Sharon stood there, wearing a pale yellow Izod shirt and khaki pants. Not her traditional black jeans. She apologized for being late, saying there was some last-minute stuff at work. We stood there awkwardly until I comprehended that the civil thing to do would be to invite her in. She slipped through the door and into the living room.

I gave her the thirty-cent tour. Most people give a fifty-cent tour, but at my place you get a discount because there's not much to see, except the greenhouse, and it was too dark for that. "This is the living room. This is the kitchen. This is the, uh, bedroom." She smiled and nodded and seemed genuinely interested. Then we got to the canaries' room. "Oh, how cute," she said, and insisted on being introduced to them all. So I named off Muck and Mire, and Groucho, Chico, Harpo, Zeppo, Gummo, and Brillo, more or less at random, since the only person who really knew which was which had left this mortal coil some months before.

I took her to Akbar, an Indian restaurant on Washington Boulevard a mile or so from the ocean. It's more pricey than my usual Indian places, but it's fun and neighborhoodish. They put tiny slivers of edible silver foil in some of the dishes, which is always good for conversation. The first time I'd gone there, with Gina, the waiter had told us he had a "photogenic memory," and he always remembered my name, even though I showed up no more than three times a year. Always with Gina, too, and the waiter remembered that as well, giving me a quizzical look when he saw me with Sharon.

We ordered some *somosas* to start, and a couple of the dinners. I had tandoori chicken. After considering the lamb, Sharon went for chicken too. I was glad she'd forgone the lamb. I had trouble with people who ate baby animals. Eating grown-up ones probably wasn't all that much better, but I hadn't gotten around to facing that moral dilemma yet.

The waiter departed. I said, "Want to hear about my big investigation?"

She gave me an indulgent smile. "Sure."

I gave myself two dramatic seconds. Then I said, "Laura's alibi doesn't hold up."

"She didn't have dinner with Helen?"

"No, not that part. I mean after, when she supposedly went home to feed her cat."

"How'd you find that out?"

I told her about my encounter with Laura's feline day-care providers. Halfway through the story our *somosas* came. They'd made special ones, with just a bit of cauliflower mixed in with the potato, and they were excellent.

I brought Sharon up to date on my visit with Yoichi. When I told her he said the argument with Albert never happened, she shook her head. "He must be practicing selective memory. I heard it with my own ears."

"I'm not doubting you. I'm just reporting what he said. You know, I'm getting the opinion everyone in the orchid club is hiding something."

She gave me a look.

"Present company excepted, of course."

We shelved the talk of murder when our entrees came. We discussed plants and movies, El Niño and the president's tribulations. She told me she lived in Westchester, near the airport, and I asked if the noise bothered her, and she said you got used to it. I told her about how I'd somehow stopped using my NordicTrack during the past year, and how I felt I was turning into a stack of flab.

Somehow we got onto the subject of her hair. She said it had all gone gray when she was in her late twenties, and she'd colored it until she'd come to L.A. eight years before. She couldn't find her regular color, kept putting off locating a substitute, finally decided she was fine with the natural shade. I told her I liked how it looked, and she thanked me, and we had Meaningful Eye Contact until I developed a sudden interest in the chutneys.

We got into my theater days. She wanted to know if I'd ever gone to New York to try to make it in the big time. Then we went further back, to my childhood. I came close to telling her about my father's prison stint. But I didn't. I knew infatuation was taking its toll on my judgment. I suspected if I told her such things, I'd regret it later.

She told me about her kid days too. She'd grown up near St. Louis, gone to Yale, then moved around the country for ten years chasing a career. I asked what kind of career and she said, "Oh, you know. High finance stuff." She burned out on that and settled in Los Angeles because she was sick of cold weather. She worked at Kasparian's, an electronics repair place on Pico Boulevard, doing the books and helping customers and performing some of the simpler repairs.

"Quite a comedown from the world of high finance," I said.

"Oh, I don't know. I feel like I'm doing something useful now. Working with real people. I really wasn't cut out for a high-pressure field like the one I was in."

"And when did you join the orchid club?"

"Shortly after I moved here."

"The friend that brought you in, have I met her?"

"No, she moved away a few months later."

Eventually I looked down at my plate and discovered all the food was gone. I hardly remembered eating any of it. We ordered dessert. Sharon wouldn't eat the foil on her *kheer*, which is a rice pudding-like concoction, so I ate it as well as my own. When the waiter came to clear the table and discovered I'd absorbed two doses of foil, he gave me a big impressed look. I asked him why. He said the foil gave you great sexual prowess.

He walked away. Sharon looked me straight in the eye. "Interesting stuff, that foil," she said. "Maybe I should try some."

"Maybe."

She took my hand. Hers was nice and warm. "But that comes later, doesn't it?"

"What does?"

"Sex, silly. We don't know each other well enough for that, do we?"

Was this a test? Did she want me to play big macho man, jump up and say, Yes, we do, come home and do it to me now? "No. We don't. Not yet."

She smiled and nodded. Yes, it had been a test, and, yes, I'd passed. Richard Dawson was yelling in my head. "Good answer, family. Show us, 'No. We don't. Not yet.' " I got a hundred points and the audience was screaming, "Joe, Joe, Joe."

Sharon withdrew her hand and pulled out a mirror and touched up her lipstick. Usually it bugs me when women check their makeup at the dinner table, but this time it didn't. If the romance went sour, I'd look back on that moment as another one of those I-should-have-knowns.

With just the slightest of arguments—"All right, but I get the next one"—she let me pay the check. We went outside. I was ecstatic that she was already thinking in terms of the next one.

We walked on Washington, toward the beach. After a couple of blocks I thought it might be appropriate to hold hands. Or even put my arm around her. But I couldn't quite bring myself to do either. I felt fifteen again, not knowing what was appropriate, not wanting to screw things up by asking for too much too soon. This from a guy who had been checking condom viability earlier.

We reached the beach, but it was too cold to walk on it, so we turned back. We got into the truck, drove home, got out, stood there awkwardly. "Do you want to come in?" I asked.

"What for?" Not the expected answer.

"I could make some tea, or coffee if you like. We could sit around and chat some more."

She just stared at me with that same peculiar half-smile she'd had on the first time we met.

"We could watch reruns of *Seinfeld* on Channel 5. Look, I don't know the answer to the question. You go out with someone, when you get back to whoever's house you started at, you invite them in."

"Are you sure tea and TV are all you were thinking of?"

"What do you want me to say?"

"Say what you're thinking."

"What I'm thinking? What I'm thinking is I'm very attracted to you and, much as I know how stupid it is to rush into physical stuff, part of me wants to get you in there and jump your bones."

The other half of the smile was gone. I'd blown it. Whatever made her think she wanted to be with me had been as ephemeral as a discocactus flower. Richard Dawson yelled,

"Show us, 'Jump your bones,'" and the big red *X* appeared and Dawson said, "Bad answer, family," and the studio audience moaned, "Awwwwww."

It was like it had always been, all the way back to my teens, seeing a date go wonderfully until one thing went awry, and suddenly things turned mushy and I ended the evening alone, wondering if I'd ever see the person again. I felt like someone was playing a cosmic joke on me.

"I can't come in tonight," she said. "I have to be up early."

"Does not tonight mean maybe some other night?"

"Let's just play it by ear." I knew what that meant. It meant she was trying to get rid of me as quickly and with as little fuss as possible.

She walked to her car and unlocked the door. I could hear the bubbling sound as the whole evening went down the drain. She slipped in and fastened her seat belt. "Are you free tomorrow night?" she said.

"Tomorrow?"

"The day after today."

"Yes, I'm free tomorrow."

"Do you want to go out again?"

"Sure."

"Good. But this time I pick the place. I'll come by for you at seven." She blew me a kiss, started the engine, pulled away from the curb, and left me standing in the gutter like a bewildered adolescent.

18

MORNING. THE CRAZY PEOPLE NEXT DOOR WOKE ME. They'd moved on from Iron Butterfly to African drums. Loud ones, played with no discernible sense of rhythm. I dragged myself out of bed, did my bathroom stuff, went in the kitchen for tea. The ants were back, eight or ten of them in a ragged trail originating somewhere behind the refrigerator. I considered dealing with them, decided to give them one more chance to leave the premises of their own accord.

Out in the greenhouse, every cactus bud I looked at was infested with aphids. Some of the ants' handiwork, perhaps; they liked to tend the aphids, protecting them from predators in exchange for tiny bubbles of honeydew. The aphids didn't seem be doing any damage; their wee green bodies merely performed that peculiar little dance aphids do. "Call Olsen's," I said. "Get ladybugs." I amused myself greatly.

Before I could split my sides too much, the phone rang inside. It was Elaine. "You got it."

"The toilet bowl commercial?"

"The toilet bowl *cleaner* commercial."

"That's what I meant." I grabbed a pencil and paper. "All right, when does it shoot?"

"Tomorrow. At Riverrun Studio in Sunland." Way up in the foothills.

"I have to go to Sunland to shoot a toilet bowl commercial?"

"Twice. You have to go up today for a costume fitting."

"Costume? What costume? Why can't I wear my nice suburban dad clothes?"

"They didn't tell me. Is there a problem?"

"No."

She gave me the details of where I had to be and when I had to be there. Then, "I've got a million calls to make. See you Saturday night."

"You will? Where?"

"At your father's. Our big family gathering."

"What big family gathering?"

"He's having us over. He hasn't told you about this?"

"No. He's getting forgetful."

We ended the conversation. I put the handpiece down. Something occurred to me. If I was with my family, it would preclude having a Real Saturday Night Date with Sharon. If a Real Date was a big deal, a Real Saturday Night Date was an order of magnitude bigger. No work that day, so you're not worn out. No work the day after, so you can stay out as late as you want. Then, if you get lucky, sleep in the next morning. Or, at least, stay in bed. With the person you were with Saturday night.

I glossed over the fact that since I had no real job, I didn't have to worry about being anywhere most any morning. And that Sharon had mentioned she worked Saturdays, thereby negating the not-worn-out factor. She'd switched her day off the week before to attend the orchid bash.

Didn't matter. The principle held.

I took stock. It was Thursday already. What made me assume Sharon would be free Saturday?

And, if she were, why would I let being with her interfere with plans with my loved ones?

Of course, I could make the family thing part of my big date, the one that hadn't been arranged. But I didn't want to do that. I hated when the family met someone I was seeing. Because then, when the inevitable breakup happened, they delighted in telling me how much they liked her and how sad they were that I wasn't seeing her anymore.

Gina and I were back at French Market for breakfast. In celebration of my latest commercial triumph, I was buying. Gina began quizzing me the minute we sat down. "So how was your big date last night?"

"Pretty good. Though I nearly screwed things up at the end."

"What, you tried to score and she didn't like it?"

"No."

"*Did* you score?"

"What is this, the boys' locker room?"

"Did you?"

"No. I really didn't try very hard."

"When are you seeing her again?"

"Tonight."

"Really?"

"Really." I took a sip of water. "Gi?"

"Yeah?"

"You know your theory?"

"Which one?"

"That when I get mixed up in a murder I get horny."

"Oh. That theory."

"Yes, that theory. I think you're right."

"Of course I'm right."

"It's not only Sharon. Yesterday I was viewing Burns's butt with lust in my heart."

"It's a nice butt, all right."

"You remember her butt?"

"Bisexual Woman remembers all butts. Boy butts, girl butts—all fodder for my libido."

"Fodder for your libido?"

"It has a certain ring, doesn't it?"

"No."

The waiter came and took our order. When he left, Gina said, "Do you think Laura did it?"

"I've been thinking about that a lot. And I keep coming back to, if she didn't do it, why would she lie about being at her place feeding the cat? Damn it, I wish I knew if the police had decided whether she killed herself. Because if she did . . ." I plucked a sugar packet from the dispenser. It had a picture of Grauman's Chinese on it. Sorry, Mann's Chinese. Part of a chain now. "I kind of want to drop the whole thing. I want to go back to my orderly life."

"Then why don't you?"

"Because I promised Laura."

She picked up her purse and pulled out a tissue. There was something odd about the way she was handling the purse.

"You've got your gun in there, don't you."

"Yes, and now the whole restaurant knows, thank you very much."

"Given that you've armed us, it doesn't sound like *you* think I should give up my detective work."

"Considering the orderly life that's the alternative, I'd say the murder thing's a lot more exciting."

"But is that reason enough to keep doing it?"

"That's a decision only you can make."

But, of course, I'd already made it.

Gartner's Tires was on a depressing strip of Reseda Boulevard. The mix of businesses was similar to the one in Hawthorne, but here everything was more tawdry, more used-up, more sad. Car dealerships, new and used, with tattered colored flags snapping in the breeze. Fast-food joints, both chains and locals. Nail parlors. Property managers. Martial arts places. It was at least ten degrees hotter than it had been in West Hollywood. The air was motionless.

Gartner's was on a corner, an L-shaped building that surrounded a parking lot in which a half-dozen cars waited with numbered magnetic hats on their roofs. A big sign announced WE CARRY ALL BRANDS. Hundreds of old tires were piled into mountains in the empty lot next door.

As I pulled up, a fat guy wearing a light gray shirt and pants strolled out to the parking lot. He squinted at his clipboard, using a finger as a reading aid, got into a giant Mercedes with ridiculous mag wheels, and squeezed it into one of the stalls inside the building. He got out, spotted me, grabbed a car hat, came over. The embroidery on his shirt told me he was Ronnie and that he was the assistant manager. "Those front tires look pretty bad," he said. He knelt beside the Datsun. His knees cracked. He face registered concern, whether for my tires or his knees I couldn't tell. He whipped out a tiny ruler, measured my tread, shook his head. "Only two-thirty-seconds."

"Or one-sixteenth, as we say on my planet."

"We got a special today, Pirellis, special purchase, special price. Two for fifty-three fifty, plus balancing, of course. And valves, of course."

"And tax, of course."

"Of course."

"Sounds like a good deal, Ronnie, but the tire money in my budget doesn't break loose until around the Fourth of July. I'm really here to see Helen. Or David. Or both."

"The cops stop you with tires like that, they'll—"

"Look, I'll think about the tires, okay? I really need to see the owners."

He stood back up, emitting a groan, and shrugged. "It's your truck. Helen's in the office. David's somewhere." His customer radar sensed the VW Cabriolet turning into the lot. He rushed off to push Pirellis.

I shouldered open one of the twin glass doors and went in. Tire paraphernalia surrounded me. On one wall hung a tire that had been cut through to show its interior construction. Next to it a display proclaimed one tire was GOOD and another was BETTER and another was BEST. A fourth was FOR RV'S, as if this were some measure of quality better than BEST. Across the way a poster showed the horrible things that could happen to your tires if they weren't properly balanced. Another, a decade old, informed me Goodrich was the one without the blimp.

A couple of customers sat on low black couches. The vinyl seating surface was about a foot off the ground, making it easy for them to select from the pile of *Tire Retailer Gazettes* and out-of-date *People* magazines on the chipped wood-grain table before them.

The office area was visible through an interior window. I cruised by the displays to the adjoining door, knocked, heard a woman's voice say, "Come in." I opened the door and stepped through.

The walls inside bore minimum wage statements and OSHA reminders. A calendar from some tool jobber featured a pneumatic babe in a 50s-style two-piece bathing suit, a porkpie hat that said Snap-on, and a big fake smile.

There was a desk clad in the same phony wood laminate as the table in the lobby. A red-flowered phalaenopsis sat on it, and Helen Gartner sat behind it. A Y-shaped necklace with purple stones rested on her nicely filled white blouse. Whatever else she had on was hidden behind the desk.

I walked over and offered a hand. "Joe Portugal. I'm an old friend of Laura Astaire's."

She took my hand. "Yes. I saw you at the orchid club the other night. Well, any friend of Laura's, et cetera, et cetera. I'm Helen Gartner. But you must know that."

I nodded. "Sad about Laura."

"Yes. I can't believe she's gone."

"You were close?"

"Fairly." She gestured toward one of the olive-green leatherette chairs across the desk from her. "Have a seat." After I had, she said, "Now that we've gotten the clever banter out of the way, what can I do for you? I'm guessing you're not here to talk the price down on a set of tires."

I shook my head. "I'm looking into Albert Oberg's murder," I said. "And now, Laura's too."

"I see." She made a notation on a yellow legal pad, tapped the pen against the fingertips of the opposite hand. "And why don't you just leave that to the police?"

"I promised Laura."

"Ah," she said. And again, "Ah."

"I hate to see her under suspicion, and—"

"And now that she's dead you feel someone needs to protect her name. Is that it?"

"Something like that."

"Do you think she had something to do with it? I can assure you she didn't. I was with her when Albert was killed."

"Actually, the time of death could have been after you two said good night."

"Do you have any reason to think she left my house and ran over to Albert's and shot him?"

Something was wrong here. *She* was asking *me* the questions. "No. Of course not. I'm trying to clear Laura, not convict her." I caught her eye. "You knew, I suppose, that she was involved with Albert."

She blinked five or six times. "Of course I did."

"And how was that going?"

"You were such close friends with her." Her voice had picked up a harsh note. "Going out of your way to preserve her innocence. You should know."

What I'd been asking shouldn't have brought on such hostility. But as long as she was getting antagonistic, I thought I'd try pushing some buttons. "I understand you had some sort of business dealings with Albert."

"Oh? Where did you hear that?"

"Around."

She stood, revealing teal-blue pants of some fine material that looked like silk but that I suspected was a fashion phenomenon I wasn't up on. She walked to the window that looked out on the sales floor. "We started out with two stalls leased from a gas station that didn't do mechanical work."

"And now you have six. A two hundred percent increase in stall capacity. And as many magnetic car hats as you could imagine."

"Are you mocking my business?"

"Of course not. I just don't see why you're telling me this."

She turned from the window and came to sit in the other green chair. "Whatever you heard, it's wrong."

"You've had no business with Albert?"

"You've been misled."

"Was Detective Casillas misled about whatever brought him to the orchid society meeting?"

Her eyes went to the door. Mine followed. Her husband, David, stood there. He had on a nondescript striped shirt and brown slacks. His hairline was as high as ever. I wanted to tell him, Do something about that forehead, man. Comb your hair down. Or shave the whole thing. It's very in these days.

Helen said, "David, this is Joe Portugal. He's a friend of Laura's. He's trying to make sure her name isn't besmirched."

David came in and held out his hand to be shaken. "It'll blow over," he said.

"I'm sure it will." The belt between my brain and my mouth broke. "I hear you went to the hockey game last Saturday night. Anybody see you there?"

His lips went rigid. "Yeah. About fifteen thousand people. And the four buddies I sat with."

"Sorry. Asking you that was probably out of line."

He forced a smile. "Don't worry about it."

"I was just asking Helen about the two of you being in some sort of business arrangement with Albert. I've been told there was one, but Helen says it's not true."

"You expect me to say she's wrong?"

"Of course not. I just thought—"

"Look, we're respectable businesspeople."

"I'm sure you are."

"So why are you—"

I threw up my hands, both literally and figuratively. "I'll drop it, okay?" I got out of my chair. "Forget I said anything." I took a deep breath, looked from David to Helen and back. "But look, as long as I'm here . . . do either of you know anyone that might have had anything against Albert? Or Laura, for that matter?"

"No," they said simultaneously.

"How about Yoichi Nakatani?"

"What about him?" David said. His voice was too loud and too nasty. "I don't have time for this. I've got a business to run. And if you're not going to buy anything—"

"Would you stick around if I bought some tires? Okay, fine. How about a nice set of Bridgestones? Ronnie out there said I'm about due."

"We don't carry them."

"Your sign says you carry all brands."

"The sign's wrong."

"How come you don't have Bridgestones?"

"Just don't like them." He seemed about to say something else, thought better of it. "I've got to go check on some stock." He turned and walked out.

I looked at Helen. "Was it something I said?"

"No. David's sometimes a little lacking in the social graces. Don't take it personally."

"I won't, if you answer my last question. Yoichi Nakatani."

"I know him from the club. I've bought a couple of plants from him. That's all."

"I heard he got mad at Albert because of some judging a while back."

"I hadn't heard that. I doubt it happened. Yoichi doesn't care that much about judging."

"I've heard the scores can go a long way toward determining how a plant sells."

"Yoichi thinks if a plant is good it doesn't matter how it's been judged. Collectors will find it anyway."

I'd reached the point of diminishing returns. I thanked her for her time and headed for the door. I opened it, turned, said, "Another answer I never got. What about Casillas? What did he want from you the other night?"

"Nothing. It was a case of mistaken identity."

No, it wasn't. There was something there. I didn't think I had much chance of her telling me what it was. Not yet. "See you around," I said.

Outside, someone had turned the temperature up another ten degrees. I got to the truck without Ronnie or anyone else trying to sell me tires, and headed up to the 118 Freeway and my date with a costume fitter.

19

All thoughts of murder tucked themselves away when I reached Riverrun Studio and walked into the room where my costume awaited. It was a dog suit.

"Whose idea was this?" I asked the guy from the production company.

"We thought it would be clever if you and your wife were a dog couple."

"Dogs don't use toilet bowls. Dogs shit in the street."

"These dogs don't."

"This is humiliating."

"Nonsense. You'll make a great dog."

The suit weighed a ton and looked hotter than hell. I struggled into it and checked myself out in the mirror. I didn't look like a dog. I looked like a person in a dog suit.

The actress playing my wife showed up five minutes later. It was Diane. I hadn't seen her at the audition, hadn't even known she was up for the toilet bowl cleaner spot.

Shortly after she put on her costume, the director bubbled into the room. He took one look at the two of us and pronounced us "The perfect dogs." Then he told us the powers-that-be had deliberately cast us together because "Everyone is used to you as a couple now, because of the bug spots, and they'll buy the relationship even if you're dogs."

I turned to Diane. "Maybe we should audition for everything together. We could do cats and birds and fish next."

"What would our agents think of that?"

"They don't get a vote." I scowled at the director. "They don't have to dress up as basset hounds."

Some costume guy looked us over for three seconds each and pronounced the dog suits a perfect fit. For this we schlepped all the way to Sunland?

We ditched the suits and went out to our cars. Diane told me she was nervous about the preview for her play that night. After I made the proper calming comments, I told her I was apprehensive about my evening too. "I have a date," I said.

"A Real Date?"

"Uh-huh. Second night in a row with the same person."

"That's something. I do feel for you. I'm glad I don't have to deal with dating anymore. What's her name?"

"Sharon. Sharon Turner."

"Hmm. I knew someone by that name once. Let me think . . ."

"It couldn't be that uncommon a name."

"I guess not." She unlocked her car. "Do you still want to come to the play?"

"Of course I do."

"We talked about Saturday."

"That won't work. A family thing. How about Sunday?" It was important to show my support for Diane early in the run. With L.A.'s theater scene, you never knew if early in the run might end up being the whole run.

"Sunday's good," she said.

The director came running out. He'd gotten a bright idea. Maybe Diane should be a cat. "A mixed marriage kind of thing, like the interracial couple in the IKEA spots."

"Maybe you should make us both the same sex," I said. "Like the gay couple in the IKEA spots."

"America isn't ready for that," he said.

"America's ready for a mixed animal couple, but not a gay animal couple?"

"But of course." He grabbed Diane's arm and tried to herd her inside.

She shrugged him off. "I'll have your comps waiting at the box office."

"Great. Just one thing."

"What?"

"Where's the box office?"

"I didn't tell you? I thought I told you. It's the John Diamante Theatre."

I'd heard the name before. "Didn't that used to be—"

She was nodding. "Yes. It used to be the Altair. Where we first met, all those years ago." She let the director drag her inside.

I first got involved in theater in 1974, at twenty-one, when a band I was in was hired to work in one of the many rock musicals flooding the stages of L.A.'s smaller theaters. The play lasted only a couple of weeks, but it opened my eyes to a new creative outlet. Over the next few years I got more and more into theater work—both acting and behind the scenes—while finding less and less time for my guitar. Then, in '78, I was working at the Altair when the guy who ran the place found some leftover acid from his hippie days, had a life-changing trip, and went off to join the Hare Krishnas. I found myself in charge, right in the middle of a production of *Equus*. I guess things went okay, because when the run was over the board of directors offered me the job full-time. It didn't pay a whole lot, but it paid enough.

I did the serious theater guy thing, putting on shows and occasionally acting in them, dealing with lighting people and program printers and a myriad of others. Then, after seven years, it got old. I pictured myself at sixty, still painting sets and fixing toilets, and hearing the conversations between the ingenues. "Oh, that's Joe," one would stage-whisper. "He's been here forever. It's his whole life." I didn't want the theater to be my whole life, at least not a little ninety-nine-seat house like the Altair.

Two years later I left the place. I traded it in for my "career" as a TV commercial actor, and I'd been rolling along with that ever since, associating with other actors only at auditions and shoots. Now, suddenly, after talking with Diane about her play—and Laura about her class—I was feeling an urge to tread the boards again. And being reminded of the Altair threw me into a funk. What had I done with the last decade?

I went home and called my father. "I hear you're planning a family thing Saturday night. When were you going to get around to telling me?"

"Today maybe. Or tomorrow. I knew you could come."

"Why do you assume I have nothing better to do on a Saturday night than hang out with my family?"

"Do you?"

"Don't rub it in."

"Do you want to bring the girl?"

"What girl?"

"You sound funny. There has to be a girl."

"As a matter of fact, I am seeing someone."

"Seeing? What's that mean?"

"Dating. Going out with."

"Do you like her?"

"No, I hate her. I just go out with her because she gives green stamps. Of course I like her."

"My son, the comedian. You should bring her Saturday."

"Oh, right. That'd be the end of the relationship for sure."

"Relationship? This is a relationship already?"

"No. Not yet. Which is why I'm not ready to have her meet my family. Too much pressure. We've only been going out for—" Hmm. We'd only been going out for one day. "For a little while."

"Makes sense. You don't want to burden the girl. You tell me when you want us to meet her."

"I will, Dad. I will," I said, and signed off.

I sat on the couch, thought about Albert and Laura and all the supporting players, found myself getting nowhere but sleepy. I took off my shoes and lay down. My eyes kept fluttering shut. I tried to keep them open, couldn't, said the hell with it and let myself nap.

My eyes opened. They focused on the VCR. It was blinking 12:00. In many households this is a normal state of affairs; in mine it isn't. I looked at my watch. Just past six. I got up off the couch, checked in the kitchen. The clock on the stove said twenty till. There'd been a power failure. Not that uncommon in my part of Culver City. I fixed all the clocks and went out to the Jungle.

I felt like crap, worse than just the dry mouth and general sweaty feeling I always experience when I wake up from a nap. And the crappiness wasn't just physical. I was undergoing depression and dread and a bunch of other negative emotions I couldn't put names to. I knew it was time to confront something I hadn't been ready to deal with: the fact that I felt responsible for Laura's death.

The thought had come inching into my consciousness at various times over the last two days, and I'd always pushed it away. But while I was asleep on the couch, it had worked its way to the forefront. I had the inescapable feeling that if I hadn't agreed to look into Albert's killing, Laura would still be alive. Someone knew I was sticking my nose in, knew who I'd been seeing, and felt if such contact continued they might be exposed. So they took care of that possibility.

And there was more. Maybe the killer suspected I now knew something he or she didn't want me to, and was going to deal with me as well. They just hadn't gotten around to it yet.

Monica Shriver, the little girl from two houses down, yanked me from my contemplation. She drove by on her Big Wheel, headed directly for a VW Thing in the wackos' driveway. I jumped up and dashed to the rescue. As I grabbed the Big Wheel a car pulled up. I half expected someone to jump out with a tommy gun and mow me down. Little Monica too. Or maybe just Monica. I'd be guilt-ridden forever.

Then I recognized the car, and someone did get out. "I'm early," Sharon said.

I pointed Monica in the right direction and she pedaled toward home. I looked at Sharon. "I know."

"I got free earlier than I expected, and I was looking

forward to seeing you, and—well, here I am. I hope I'm not intruding."

"Of course not."

She walked up and kissed me on the cheek. "You're sure I'm not too early? I can go wait at a coffeehouse."

"Come up on the patio with me."

"All right." She passed in front of me, and I put my hand to my cheek and held it there, as if some trace of magic had been deposited and I didn't want to let it get away.

I followed her and brushed off a wicker chair. A daddy longlegs fled down its side, scurried across the planking, dropped over the edge into the shrubbery below. "Here," I said. "Have a seat."

She did, and I regained mine. She was wearing a sleeveless top like the one she'd had on the first time I met her, this one pale green. Her legs—at least, all I could see of them between the hem of her cotton skirt and her white canvas tennies—were slim and nicely tanned.

"I call this the Jungle," I said. "I keep a lot of epiphytic plants here, stuff that needs a fair amount of shade. It's a south exposure, which you've probably figured out already, but that big elm shades it most of the day. Maybe I could grow some orchids here."

"Maybe. You know, you don't look very good. Your face is pale."

"It's nothing."

"Don't tell me it's nothing. It's something. Tell me."

"I hardly know you. I don't want to lay heavy stuff on you so soon."

"Go ahead and lay."

"You're sure?"

"Yes."

"All right. Here goes. I feel responsible for Laura's death."

"How so?"

"I have a feeling the killer thought she either told me or was going to tell me something incriminating. So they offed her. And if I hadn't been sniffing around, no one would have been threatened, and she'd still be alive."

"You're still thinking it wasn't suicide."

"No one's said for sure one way or the other."

"I see. All right, then consider this. What are the chances she told you something she didn't tell the police?"

"I'm not sure where you're leading."

"Where I'm leading is, if she was murdered because the killer thought she would say something incriminating, it would have happened whether you were around or not. Because who would expect her to reveal something to you that she hadn't told the police? No offense meant, but you're not exactly a professional detective."

"Maybe you have a point." I shook my head. "Do you know anything about her funeral?"

"I was talking to one of the other people in the club this morning and found out she's being cremated, just like Albert. After the police are done with her body, I suppose. That sounds so macabre. 'Her body.' There's no service. I think Albert must have convinced her that was the way to go."

We were silent. There was a light scent in the air, something very springtime, floral but not cloying. "I like your perfume," I said.

"You do? I don't often wear any, but tonight I—oh, I should just shut up."

More silence. Once or twice she looked over and smiled, before turning back to watch the sycamores across Madison waving in the breeze.

Finally I said, "Where are we going tonight?"

She turned her chair a few degrees toward mine. "I worried about that all day. After the nice place you came up with last night I wanted something special. But nothing seemed right."

"We don't have to go to a restaurant."

"We don't?"

"We can order in. We can stay out here and then have someone bring food."

"Let's do that. Let's stay here." She inched her chair closer, reached out a hand. Nicely manicured, no nail polish. "Are you feeling better?" she said.

I took her hand. "Yes, thanks." We were still too far apart for efficient hand-holding, so I shuffled my chair toward hers until they were a few inches apart. I looked over and smiled. She smiled back. Suddenly the world was very smiley.

20

WE TALKED ABOUT MY NEW COMMERCIAL. WE TALKED about plant shows, sharing stories of paying too much for plants at auctions, of finally getting specimens we'd nurtured for years to bloom. We managed not to mention Albert or Laura, though they hung over the conversation like the alien spaceship in *Independence Day* over New York.

At seven-thirty we went inside, consulted the menu for the local Thai place, called, and ordered. They said the food would arrive in thirty to forty minutes, which was what they always said, whether it was the middle of a weekday afternoon or eight o'clock on a busy Saturday night.

Thirty-five minutes later, a Hyundai pulled into the driveway. Sharon paid the driver. We took the food inside and I dished it out. "I've got a couple of trays," I said. "We could use them in the Jungle. Or we could eat inside."

"Do you have a blanket? Like a beach blanket?"

"I believe I do."

"Let's have a picnic."

"It's a little dark in the park. It's a good neighborhood, but, still—"

She was shaking her head. "In your backyard. Wouldn't it be nice to eat our dinner under the stars?"

"I'll get the blanket."

I didn't really have a beach blanket, but when she suggested it I didn't want to put the kibosh on whatever groovy idea she was working on. So we sat outside on the extra blanket from my bed, the one I hadn't used since the weather started improving. The night was a fair amount warmer than the one before; the ground still retained the day's heat. I found us a couple of sweatshirts, and they were enough to keep us comfortable.

We agreed that the *pad thai* was the best of the three dishes. We sat there eating prodigious quantities of it and the *rad na* and the stuffed chicken wings. When we were done, I ran inside, put the scant leftovers in the fridge, and came out with some fruit for dessert. We knocked that off too, and sat around moaning about how full we were.

After a while she pointed at my greenhouse and said, "So that's where your cacti live."

"Yeah. And my other succulents too. I should have shown you around it while it was still light. Maybe you can see it in the morning."

She cocked her head and gave me a funny look.

"Wait," I said. "That came out wrong. I wasn't assuming anything. I meant, maybe you could come back in the morning and see it."

"Is that what you meant?"

"I'm not sure."

She lay back on the blanket. "Let's just see what happens."

Promising. Something could happen. Good thing I'd inspected my condoms.

I stretched out on the blanket next to her. The sky was

clear, light pollution at a minimum. I could see a fair number of stars. Lustful thoughts ran through my head. Maybe Gina was right. Maybe I did think about sex only when I was investigating a murder. Maybe it was because getting laid made me deduct better.

Or maybe, after nearly a year of celibacy, I was just getting horny.

As we lay there quietly contemplating the heavens, I tried and failed to envision what Sharon would look like without clothes on. I'd never been able to picture a woman naked, at least one I'd never actually seen that way. It would have been nice to be like the guys in the Virgil Partch cartoons in the *True* magazines my father had when I was growing up, and have a thought balloon appear above my head with a nude representation of whatever female specimen I was interested in. But I just couldn't make it happen.

I continued watching the stars and the planes and the blimps. It was a two-blimp night.

"I'm worried about something," Sharon said.

Uh-oh. Here it came. Here was the part where she told me about the Samoan.

"Maybe this is selfish," she said. "But I feel we might have something between us, and I don't want to invest a lot of emotion in someone who's going to get himself killed." She raised herself on her elbow, looked down at me. "Do you really need to be nosing around after some murderer?"

I considered telling her, You're right, I should butt out. That was what she wanted to hear. But I'd made a career out of screwing up relationships by molding myself to what I thought the woman wanted me to be. This time, I thought, honesty was the best policy. "Yes," I said. "I do."

"I guess I knew you would say that." She let out a tiny sigh. "As long as you feel that way, why don't you bring me up-to-date? Maybe I can be sort of a sounding board. Another set of ears. Everyone needs a sounding board."

I felt a flush of guilt. I had a sounding board. I'd had one for years.

But Gina wasn't there just then. I wondered what she was up to. Then I sat up, put my arms around my knees, and started talking.

I started with Yoichi, and Sharon offered suggestions here and there, pointing out places where what Yoichi had said was questionable. She reconfirmed that she'd heard him arguing with Albert.

I told her about my visit with Helen and David as well, then asked if she could remember any more about their connection to Albert.

"Maybe I've made something out of nothing," she said. "I just heard them say something about contracts once."

"It's not nothing. Everybody's acting too much like it's something for it to be nothing."

"Maybe we do have to seriously consider the possibility a robber murdered Albert. Or some transient."

"Do you really believe that?"

"I don't *believe* it, but you have to admit it's possible. And if that's the case, I don't think you're ever going to find them."

"You think the same transient killed Laura?"

A wry smile. "Same transient, different transient. You're still feeling it's your fault, aren't you?"

"A little."

"Don't. It's not."

After a while I reached out and began to stroke her hair.

I'd never stroked gray hair before. It felt just like any other woman's hair. Soft.

I saw her smile in the moonlight. "You're sweet," she said.

"That's what all the girls say."

"No, you are, I mean it. Not pushing. I like that."

"It's hard for me not to."

"Me too. And that's why I'd better go now."

"But the night's still young."

"Joe, if I stay here any longer we may sleep together."

"The possibility had crossed my mind."

"And I'm just not ready. And I feel that if I'm not ready and we do it anyway, it will make things wrong between us." She eased to her feet. "So I'm going to go."

I stood as well. Things were too weird. Was she really going to go because we were too hot for each other too soon? Or was there a Samoan lurking? "But you'll be back in the morning," I said.

"I will?"

"To see the greenhouse."

"It would have to be early. Seven or so. I have to be at work by eight."

"That's fine. That's perfect, as a matter of fact, because I have to leave for my commercial at eight."

"I'll bring bagels."

"Real bagels? Like water and egg and pumpernickel? Or frou-frou bagels, with blueberries and the like?"

"Real bagels."

"It's a date."

We walked out to her car. I kissed her good night, very lightly, no more than a touching of lips. She got in and started the engine.

It just slipped out. I hadn't been planning it and I really didn't want to say it, but out it came. "My family's having a little get-together Saturday night. I know it's a really high-pressure situation, so if you say no I'll understand, but you're welcome to come."

She took a second to think about it. "I can't. I have other plans Saturday night."

"Oh?"

"But how about tomorrow? I'll cook you dinner."

"Then you'll have to tell me where you live."

"I'll come here. I like it here. How about I come at seven? Seven in the morning, seven at night."

"Huh?"

"The greenhouse, remember?"

"Oh. Right."

"You're upset I can't see you Saturday."

"No," I said. "It's fine."

She reached out, grabbed my hand and kissed it. "Don't get too clingy," she said, and sped away.

I went inside and called Gina. "It's me," I said.

"Hi, you."

"What's happening?"

"My girlfriend's moving to San Francisco. What should be happening?"

"I thought you were over that."

"I thought so too."

"Well, like they say, easy come, easy go."

Silence from the other end.

"Gi? You still there?"

"It's early yet," she said. "Did it go badly with the orchid woman?"

"Is that from a Broadway show? *Kiss of the Orchid Woman.*"

"Did it?"

"No," I said. "Actually, it went pretty well. She left because she didn't want to sleep with me. No, wait. She left because she did want to sleep with me, and she wasn't ready yet. Or something. Right, she left because she was too hot for me and wanted to wait before we got it on."

" 'Got it on'?"

"But I'm seeing her tomorrow night. She's cooking for me. And she's coming over in the morning for a greenhouse viewing."

"How nice for her."

"Don't be snide. Hey, listen. Dad's having the whole family over Saturday night. You want to come?"

"Okay. But are you sure you don't want to bring your new girlfriend instead?"

"She's tied up Saturday."

"So I was your second choice."

"Well," I said. "If you must put it in such simple terms. Yes."

"And you're probably upset that she's not free."

"No, not at all, I—"

"People have lives, Joe. Some of them aren't able to make Saturday night available just to suit your dating regimen."

"I don't need you to berate me now."

"I'm not berating you. You need company?"

"No."

"You sure?"

"Sounds like you want me to say yes."

"Well, the truth of the matter is . . . I'm lonely."

"I don't think I've ever heard you say that before."

"There's a first time for everything."

Silence. Then I said, "Okay. I'll come on up."

"No, my place depresses me. I'll come down there. Half an hour." She hung up.

We sat on the couch, trading two pints of Ben and Jerry's back and forth. I brought her up-to-date on Sharon and on the orchid people. When I was all talked out, I turned on Letterman. Drew Barrymore was one of the guests. The little girl from *E.T.* was all grown up. Something was wrong there. Maybe it was that I was getting old.

Gina got up and put the ice cream away. When she came back, she lay down on the couch with her head in my lap.

I flicked a few channels, spaced out. When I returned I found I was stroking Gina's hair. Two women's hair in one night. A new Joe Portugal record.

I moved one hand down to her shoulders. She shifted around to improve my access. I continued down her back.

"God," she said. "I haven't had a good back rub in such a long time."

"We should remedy that."

She lay on her stomach. I threw some of the cushions on the floor and straddled her. I revisited her shoulders first, then moved down to her back, working out from her spine.

I recalled other women I'd given back rubs, some on that very couch. Back in my heavy-dating days, it had been a good way to get into someone's pants. You both knew you wanted each other, but no one would admit it. So one would say, "My back is sore," and the other would say, "Do you want a massage? I'm pretty good," and you'd look at each other meaningfully, and both would know where it would lead. The massager would work their way down the back and, seeming tentative, onto the buttocks. The massagee would turn over with open arms, and carnal activities would ensue. In the morning you could say you got carried away.

My reverie had carried me down to where Gina's hips flared. Nice hips. Baby-making hips, Gina's mother called them, and Gina would roll her eyes and say, "Not in this lifetime, Ma."

I took up a holding pattern. Any further and we'd be in new territory, or at least territory we hadn't visited in seventeen years. Was this a good idea? Our judgment was impaired. Gina's from her breakup with Jill, me from my neurotic worry about what would happen with Sharon.

I took another look at Gina's hips. I sucked in a deep breath. I let it out. I patted her butt once, twice. "All done."

She moved to a sitting position, looked in my eyes. Spent a few seconds like that. Then she said, "That was great. I feel a lot better."

We sat side by side watching TV. After a few minutes I realized she was asleep. I went in for my extra blanket. It wasn't there. It was still on my back lawn, gathering dew. I dragged the other one off my bed. When I got back, she was stretched out on the couch. Which had a mattress inside. Like Laura's. "You want me to pull the bed out?"

She didn't even open her eyes. "Too much trouble. This is fine."

I draped the blanket over her.

"Take off my shoes," she said.

I did.

She opened her eyes. "And my jeans."

I gave her a look.

"You don't expect me to sleep with my jeans on."

"Of course not."

She undid them and raised her hips. I reached under the

blanket, grabbed the hems, pulled. I folded the jeans neatly and set them on a chair. When I left the room, she was back asleep.

I went into my bedroom, set the clock for six-fifteen. That would give me time to get cleaned up and get Gina the hell out of there before Sharon showed up. I reclaimed an old blanket I'd been planning on giving to the Boys and Girls Club, and went to bed.

21

THE ALARM CLOCK WENT OFF. I REACHED OUT AND smashed down on the button. The clock went off again.

I leapt out of bed. "Aha," I said. The ringing wasn't the alarm. It was the doorbell. But, if the alarm hadn't gone off yet, it had to be before six-fifteen in the morning. Who was ringing my doorbell so early?

And why was it so light out so early?

I looked for my pants. Couldn't find them. I pulled on my Jockeys and stumbled into the hallway, yelling, "I'm coming." But when I got to the living room, the front door was already open. There were two people there.

The one outside the door was Sharon. She had on a T-shirt and jeans. She carried a brown paper bag.

The one inside was Gina. She had on a T-shirt as well. No jeans.

I saw Sharon take in Gina's bare legs, then stare at her face. "Nice seeing you again," she said.

Then she looked across the room at me. "I think I'll forgo the greenhouse tour," she said, and turned and disappeared from sight.

"Wait," I yelled. I ran across the living room and out the door. The paper bag was on my lawn. A couple of bagels had spilled out. An egg and a pumpernickel. Sharon was already at her car, with the door open.

"It's not what it looks like," I said.

She got in and slammed the door. I made it to the car before she pulled away. "It's not what it looks like."

"A cliché like that's bad enough once. Don't insult me by repeating it."

"She slept on the couch."

"Do I look like an imbecile?"

"It's true."

"I was all upset because I was late and all it did was give you more time to be screwing your so-called friend." She shook her head. "I can't deal with this." She sped away from the curb.

Old lady Thompson across the street was watching me intently. Only when I saw her did I realize the state of my attire. I ran inside. Gina hadn't moved. "Why'd you have to open the door?" I said.

"It wasn't exactly a conscious decision. The doorbell rang, I got up, I answered it."

I said something like, "Argh," and stomped off to my bedroom. I sat on the edge of the bed. I looked at the clock. It was blinking 12:00. Another goddamned power failure. I picked up my watch. Just past seven-thirty.

I tried to figure out how to convince Sharon that Gina's lack of pants was perfectly innocent. Somewhat hypocritical, given where I'd been headed with the back rub the night before.

Gina came in. She'd put her jeans on. She sat beside me on the bed and put an arm around me. "Sorry," she said.

I reached up and patted the hand on my shoulder. "Not

your fault." I looked at the clock. "Got to get going. Got a commercial to shoot." I went into the bathroom, stripped off my underwear, turned on the shower, got in.

I brooded while I washed my hair and soaped up. At some point I realized I wasn't alone in the bathroom. I could see Gina's blurred outline through the translucent shower curtain. "You could blow off the commercial and go after her," she said.

"You don't really think I'm that irresponsible."

"No."

I stewed for a few seconds more. "Screw her. If she's not going to believe me, what do I want to be with her for anyway?"

"That's the spirit."

I began rinsing off. "Why waste my energy on her?" Even as I was saying these things, I knew I was deluding myself.

"No reason I can think of," Gina said.

I finished my shower, stuck my head out. "I'm ready to get out."

"So? Oh, sorry." She walked into the hallway, closing the door partway behind her. I stepped out of the shower and began drying off. "Can we talk about the Albert and Laura business?" she said.

"Sure."

"Because I had a thought. Didn't Sam tell you that Albert was into conservation?"

"Uh-huh."

"And you told me Yoichi acted kind of flaky when you started mentioning habitat destruction and that kind of stuff."

"So you're thinking—"

"Maybe Yoichi's into something not quite kosher. Maybe

some of his plants came from somewhere they shouldn't have."

"He has an alibi."

"Oh, right. Some orchid club's Saturday night extravaganza."

"But, still, why don't you give Sam a call? See if Albert ever mentioned anything about Yoichi to him." I gave her the number.

I finished drying, wrapped the towel around my waist, lathered up my face. Muffled conversation came from the bedroom. Sharon kept swimming into my mind. I kept pushing her back.

From outside the bathroom, Gina said, "Are you decent?"

"Uh-huh."

The door swung open. "Sam definitely heard Yoichi's name from Albert. But he can't remember in what context. I asked if it was Yoichi being pissed off about having his plant marked down. Sam couldn't remember for sure. He said it was months ago that Albert mentioned Yoichi to him. Then I asked if it had something to do with conservation. He wasn't sure of that, either."

We kicked it around while I finished shaving. I went into the bedroom and put on shorts and a T-shirt. No sense wearing good clothes under a dog suit. I slipped on my watch, picked up my wallet and keys. "Okay," I told Gina. "Here's what I want you to do while I'm at the shoot. I want you to call Sam back."

"And what do I say?"

"We need to find someone."

"Who?"

I told her. She said it was a good plan. I went off to shoot my commercial.

The animal miscegenation scheme had been scotched by the higher-ups, and Diane remained a dog. Regardless of my show of bravado in the shower, I still very much wanted to patch things up with Sharon, and during one of the breaks I slipped over to a phone and tried to reach her at work. They said she wasn't there. I was sure she'd told everyone there to blow me off.

We were done about two-thirty. I corralled Diane out in the hallway. She was still in costume, with her dog head under her arm, like a football player with her helmet on the sidelines.

"Ready for your opening tonight?" I said.

"I am, but I don't know if the play is. The preview was a fiasco. They missed a bunch of lighting cues and the lead had a big blowout with the director during intermission." She shook her head. "Actors. You still coming Sunday?"

"Sure am. I wouldn't miss it for anything."

We went our separate ways. I wasn't quite sure what I would do with my comps on Sunday. If I ever got Sharon to talk to me again, I could ask her. If not, there was Gina. There was always Gina.

I checked my machine, in case Elaine had another audition for me. Instead, there was a message from Alberta Burns. I called her back. "Did you get anything out of Casillas?"

"We certainly are pushy, aren't we?"

"Did you?"

"Yes. Evidently Helen Gartner has a bit of a past."

"Oh?"

"She did a little time."

"What for?"

"She was a con artist. Pigeon drop, dead man's curse, that kind of thing. Almost twenty years ago, when she lived in Denver."

"She wouldn't admit it when I saw her yesterday."

"You went up to her house and bothered her about this?"

"Her store, actually. You're sure that's what Casillas was after her about?"

"Yes. And to answer your other question, no, it wasn't suicide."

"You sure?"

"Will you stop asking me if I'm sure?"

"Sorry."

"Whoever did it did a fair job of making it look that way, but it's damned difficult, if not impossible, to fake a suicide."

"So—"

"Enough."

"Huh?"

"It's enough. Don't ask me any more questions."

"How come you answered these?"

"I've been asking myself the same thing. Maybe it's because I like you. Hard to figure out why, isn't it?" She hung up.

I phoned the tire shop. Helen answered. I didn't want her to know I was checking if she was there. I said, "Otto?" in a fair approximation of a Teutonic voice. She said, "Sorry, no Otto here," and I said I was sorry and hung up.

I drove to Reseda and rounded her up and said, "I know about Denver."

She got up, closed the office door, sat back down. "I suppose it was bound to come out."

"Tell me about it. Tell me about when you were a crook."

"Do you really want to know all the details? I was much younger then. I thought the easy way to make a dollar was the best way." She looked down at her hands, inspected a finger. "Detective Casillas found out about that and thought it worth questioning me when Albert was killed."

"Did he accuse you of having something to do with Albert's death?"

"Not in so many words."

"And you convinced him otherwise."

"Probably not."

"*Did* you have something to do with Albert's death?"

"Of course not. I was with Laura."

"Who is conveniently dead, and therefore unable to confirm that anymore."

"You're suggesting I killed Laura?"

"Maybe."

"Why would I kill my own alibi?"

"Because it was phony, and you thought she was going to crack and tell the police the truth."

"Do I really look that diabolical?"

She didn't, but I wasn't going to tell her that. "I suppose you're still denying you had any sort of business arrangement with Albert."

"I suppose I am. Who told you that, anyway?"

"It doesn't matter."

"I think I have the right to know."

"You admit something was going on, I'll tell you who told me."

"There's nothing to admit." Again she checked out her finger. "What are you going to do with what you've found out?"

"Nothing, if you'll come clean with me." I was getting good with those cop movie clichés.

"I am coming clean. I would tell you if I knew anything about Albert."

This was getting me nowhere. I let her dismiss me and went outside. There I found David, kneeling by the jacked-up front end of a big Ford pickup. He was tightening a lug nut with an air wrench. His boring shirt was soaked with sweat under the arms and along the center of his back. Judging from his expression, something wasn't going right. He put down the tool, picked up a torque wrench, tried it too. No go. He began kneading his earlobe with his fingers.

I'd seen that ear thing before. At the orchid society meeting. When Sharon was telling me about the Stalin surrogate and his homophobia. I hadn't known who David was then, so it didn't make an impression. Now it did.

I approached and stood over him. "David."

He looked up, shaded his eyes. "Yes, sir, may I—oh, it's you."

"Yes," I said. "Me. With a question."

He climbed to his feet. "All right," he said. "Ask your question. And then get out of here and let me get some work done."

I let him stand there sweating. Then I said, "Why do you hate the Japanese?"

He took a second too long to answer. "I don't know what you're talking about."

"You don't sell Bridgestones, though you say you carry everything. I didn't see any Yokohamas, either. You got all bent out of shape when I mentioned Yoichi Nakatani."

"So?"

"And everyone at the orchid society knows you like to downgrade Japanese members' plants."

His hand tightened on the wrench. "Come with me."

I followed him around the building, into the vacant lot next door. A winding path led through five or six piles of tires, each ten or fifteen feet high. There was a lot of rubber on that lot.

David stopped. Some of the hair he normally kept combed straight back had fallen down over his expansive forehead. It was an improvement.

I cut short the tonsorial critique when I realized he still had the torque wrench. He held the handle in one hand and kept flexing the other around the attached socket, a big one, three inches or so long, an inch in diameter, heavy steel. The sun reflected off its chrome finish.

"The Japs killed my father," he said.

It sounded bogus, like he'd said his father was spirited off by Dottie Lennox's Communists or something. But when I looked at his face, I knew it was true. "In the war?"

"Of course in the war. What kind of a stupid question is that?"

"Sorry."

"He was captured. He was in a prison camp. He died."

"They killed him?"

"He broke a leg. They let it get infected. He died."

"David, that was war. Lots of things like that happened, on both sides. You can't blame a whole nationality for your father's death. We've been at peace with Japan for over fifty years."

"They didn't follow the Geneva Convention."

"You mean the so-called rules of war? The term's an oxymoron. You think countries are going to follow a bunch of rules made up in peacetime when they're trying to beat the crap out of each other?"

"They should have fixed up his leg. They just let him die. Frigging Japs."

He was slapping the wrench into his palm. This had me a little concerned. It wasn't as good a weapon as, say, a crescent wrench would have been—the socket messed up the balance a little—but I had little doubt that, if wielded correctly, it could brain me nicely.

"How do you know this?" I said.

"One of his buddies got out. He told me. He said when my father screamed in pain they just laughed at him."

"Maybe he didn't remember correctly. Maybe—"

I shut up because his face was suddenly six inches from mine. His tone was reasonable. Too reasonable. Very quietly, he said, "You defending them?"

"No. Not at all. I'm sure very bad things happened during the war, on both sides. Hell, look at what we did to all those thousands of loyal Japanese-Americans, herding them into internment camps."

His eyes bored into mine. "You comparing throwing a bunch of Japs in a camp to them killing my father?"

I stole a glance back toward the street. Because of the way the path wound through the piles of tires, I couldn't see it. My father's admonitions about being careful swam into my head. And Burns's. I took a step back.

He was smiling. "No one can see us here," he said, waving the torque wrench in front of my face. "I'm sure none of your Jap friends would see if something happened to you."

"David, be reasonable." I glanced around for something to defend myself with. My only option was stacking tires around my body and playing Michelin Man. "Adding another killing to the score won't help you any."

Suddenly the wrench was over his head. Before it could come back down, I rushed him. I wasn't very good at it. The first step I took, I stumbled. My shoulder, which I'd had aimed toward his upper chest, sunk into his stomach. He fell backward, flat on his back, and I joined him on the ground. The wrench went flying, landing inside a tire that had fallen from one of the piles. We both scrambled after it on hands and knees. He got there first. I caught up and smashed my fist down on his hand just as he grabbed the wrench. He managed to hold on to it, but the socket snapped off the handle. One of us jostled the pile. Tires rained down upon us. Concrete scraped my knee.

He muttered, "Frigging Jap-lover," made his way to a standing position, raised the handle. I snatched up the socket, lurched to my feet, and backed away, eyeing him warily, with my arm drawn back, ready to hurl the socket if he came any closer. He looked at me, up at the wrench handle, back at me.

I didn't really have much confidence in my aim. But he didn't have to know that. "Drop the wrench," I said.

"What?"

"I said drop it." I drew the socket back behind my head. "Or I'll throw this thing at you."

He took in my ridiculous posture, took one more look at the handle, carefully placed it on the ground. "There. You happy?"

"More or less." I glanced at the socket poised near my ear. I wasn't ready to let go of it yet, but I brought it down to my side. My knee stung. I took a quick look. Blood dripped down my calf.

David took in the dozen or so tires that had slipped off the pile. He began to round them up. "You really think I killed Albert?"

"I didn't, until just now."

"I didn't do it. I was at the hockey game that night. I told you that. The cops have already interviewed all my buddies."

"Then why the big display?"

"I don't know. Sometimes things touch me off."

"You ever hit Helen?"

The look he gave me made me glad he wasn't holding the wrench anymore. "No. I've never laid a hand on her. And I never will."

I gave him a few more seconds to calm down. Then I said, "Ever had any run-ins with Yoichi Nakatani?"

"The people who run the judging know enough not to let me judge a Jap's plants. Look, are you done yet?"

I didn't want to be. I was sure there was more there, some big secret or two that I wasn't picking up on. But I knew I wasn't going to uncover any more secrets that afternoon. "I guess so."

"Good. Because I've got a business to run." He picked up the wrench, slapped his palm with it, turned, walked away. After a while I followed. I was back in the truck before I realized I still had the socket in my hand. I thought to give it back, said screw it, stuck it in my pocket. They could get a new one from the Snap-on truck next time it came by. Maybe there'd be a new calendar too.

22

I STOPPED AT A MARIE CALLENDER'S, CLEANED UP MY KNEE IN the rest room, had a piece of cherry pie. It didn't make me feel any better. I found the pay phone, called my father, told him where I was. "I could pick up a pie for dessert tomorrow if you want."

"That's a good boy, Joseph, but we don't need. Catherine's making three desserts. Just bring yourself. And, since you don't want to bring the girl, bring Gina."

"She's already coming. I'll see you, Dad."

"Wait."

"What's the matter?"

"I should be asking you, what's the matter."

"Why should anything be the matter?"

"I've known you forty-five years," he said. "I should know when something's the matter. It's the girl, isn't it."

"Well . . ."

"I know when my son's having trouble with a girl. What is it this time?"

This time. Like every time I got involved with a "girl," there was some kind of trouble. "Gina slept on my couch last night, and she answered the door in her underwear when Sharon came over to see the greenhouse, and Sharon ran off."

"You like this Sharon."

"I told you I do."

"Is she Jewish?"

"I don't think so. Does it matter?"

"It would be nice it she was Jewish."

"Mom wasn't Jewish."

"Shiksa or not, you should go after this girl."

"I don't know where she is. I tried at work, where she ought to be, but they told me she wasn't there."

"You think she is."

"I think there's a good chance she is."

"Then go there."

"What, just burst in like a lovesick puppy and say, Where is she?"

"What's wrong with that?"

I took a moment to consider it. Other than possible embarrassment, nothing was wrong was that. And what was a little embarrassment to a man who was about to appear on millions of television screens as a toilet-cleaning dog? "You're right. That's what I ought to do."

"Then do it. You make up with this girl. You want, you bring her tomorrow night."

"You just told me to bring Gina. Anyway, Sharon's busy tomorrow."

"Too bad. You could have brought both. Gina could be for me."

Racks of electrical appliances jammed every dim corner of Kasparian's. Big racks, small ones, metal racks, wooden ones, all loaded with TVs and VCRs, toasters and toaster ovens and Mixmasters, some bright and shiny, some layered with dust.

An array of used vacuums with manila price tags guarded the floor to my right. Belts and switches and who-knew-whats dangled from cords suspended from the ceiling, each attached to a paper clip jammed right into the plaster. How they stayed there was an electrical repairman's secret.

Two guys wielding soldering irons sat at a workbench. One had an indeterminate ethnic look. He could have been Hispanic and he could have been Middle Eastern. He was short and round and had a paper breathing mask pushed up onto the top of his head. The other, a black man about a hundred and fifty years old, wore a T-shirt from a Robert Cray tour.

Maybe, I thought, I could buy a belt for my vacuum. It would make them think I was there for a legitimate reason, let me win them over before I asked where Sharon was.

But I didn't know the model number. I wasn't even sure I remembered the brand.

"Yes?" Sitting at a service desk adorned with an incongruous orchid was a guy with a big nose and big eyebrows and a Steven Seagal ponytail.

"I'm looking for Sharon," I said.

"She's not here."

"Then where is she?"

"Beats me. You think I got time to keep track of the bookkeeper? Hey guys, you seen Sharon lately?"

The short one made a vague gesture with his soldering iron. "Nope."

The other one caught my eye. "You're the guy that called."

"Yes."

"She's not here. Go home." He was smiling. Damn him. He was enjoying this.

I turned and stalked out of the place. I headed home. I couldn't think of anywhere else to go.

It took me fifteen minutes to get there. When I did, a familiar Ford Tempo was parked out front, and Sharon was sitting on my doorstep.

I sat down beside her. "Hi," I said. "Been here long?"

"No."

"How come you came?"

She shrugged. "When I thought about things, I believed you. It took me most of the day to think about things."

"Gina is my best friend. Sometimes we stay over at each other's places. On each other's couches." Yeah, and lately in each other's beds too sometimes, but I wasn't dumb enough to say that part aloud.

She smiled and took my hand. "It was the naked legs that did it. When I saw her naked legs I just flew off the handle."

"Don't most people sleep with their legs naked? At least in L.A. in springtime? Don't you?"

Her smile turned mischievous. "Maybe. What happened to your knee?"

"I fell down."

She released my hand, stood, started out to the curb. "I have dinner fixings in the car. Come help me with them."

She had several bags full of "fixings." She also had a present for me, an orchid with two little round leaves atop each of its three spindle-like pseudobulbs. "It's a schomburgkia," she said. "The ant plant."

"I like it," I said. When we went inside, I put it in the kitchen window.

She'd brought some fish and vegetables and ingredients for some kind of Middle Eastern pilaf thing. Also a bottle of white wine. I knew white went with fish, but the label meant nothing to me. It never does.

I volunteered to help, but she said she had everything under control, so I went to take a shower. As I was getting undressed I discovered the socket from Gartner's in my pocket. Stupid thoughts ran rampant. "Is that a socket in your pocket, or are you just glad to see me?" I stood the thing up like a little monument on my nightstand.

I lingered under the shower spray, letting the jets of water pulse the dog costume sweat and the tire graveyard grit from me. I thought of Sharon, bustling around, being domestic. When I was done, I bandaged my knee, put on jeans and my Hawaiian shirt, and returned to the kitchen.

Sharon smiled when she saw me. "There was a phone call while you were in the shower. I almost picked it up, but I thought it would be presumptuous."

"Who was it?"

"Gina, I think." She giggled. "Look at your face. It's all right. I'm fine with her now. Why don't you go listen to it? It's about Yoichi."

I played back the message. "Hi, it's me. Sam hasn't heard anything back yet. But listen to this. Yoichi's alibi. It sucks. Call me."

I looked over at Sharon. "Go ahead," she said. "Call. If it will help find out who's been going around killing people . . ."

Gina picked up on the first ring. "It's me," I said.

"How are you doing?"

I smiled, looked over at Sharon. "Much better. What's this about Yoichi?"

"You know that meeting he was supposed to have been at last Saturday? It was canceled at the last minute. The host got food poisoning."

"How'd you find that out?"

"I got some names from Sam and made some calls and like that. Legwork, I think they call it." She gave me some of the details.

"Wow." I flung Sharon a glance. She was chopping vegetables. Something came over me. "So, about Dad's tomorrow," I said into the phone.

"I wanted to talk to you about that. My mother called. She wants to hang out with me tomorrow night."

"Yes, it does sound like a great time."

"No, hanging out with my mother does not sound like a great time."

"He's looking forward to seeing you too."

"Oh. Orchid Woman is listening, isn't she?"

"Yes, I think so."

"You're trying to make her jealous, aren't you?"

"Yes."

"You are a very bad boy."

"I feel that way too."

"Call me tomorrow."

"I will. Good night."

"Night."

Sharon had her head cocked. "What's this about Yoichi's alibi?"

"Like the lady said, it doesn't hold up." I filled her in, then went to the stereo and put Neil Young on the turntable. *After the Gold Rush.*

Sharon held out a glass of wine. "Here. Try some of this."

I came back over and took a taste. Pretty good, not too sweet. With nothing in my stomach but a piece of pie, it went right to my head. I nodded my approval.

Sharon took a sip from her own glass. "I just wish it were a little colder."

"You could put an ice cube in it."

"I wanted to do that, but I thought you would think I was gauche if I put an ice cube in my wine."

"You've seen my house. You think I care about gauche?"

She smiled and held out her glass. "Will you get me one?"

I took the glass, went to the freezer, opened it. It was filled with ants.

Hundreds of ants. Thousands.

They were scattered among the long-forgotten half-loaves of bread and the frozen goodies from Trader Joe's and the ice-cream dregs. Most of them weren't moving. They were dead. Or at least in suspended animation.

Usually, when whatever group consciousness runs an ant colony realizes none of the ones streaming off somewhere are coming back, they stop sending them. You spray pyrethrum around a potful of cacti, for instance, and soon the column of tiny six-legged bodies ceases. But this time was different. Some hymenopteran Jim Jones was at work, pushing them forward, convincing them curling up and being still was the way to ant nirvana. On they came, hustling up the side of the refrigerator, ignoring the relatively warm interior where jelly jars and rotting kiwi fruit beckoned, boldly stepping into the freezer, blithely riding like an ant Light Brigade, half an ant league onward into the Valley of Death.

"Stupid ants" was my clever reaction to all this.

Sharon came up beside me and took a look. "How awful," she said.

"Fuck," I said. Then, "Excuse my French." I hate when people say, "Excuse my French." Especially when it's me.

"I think a 'fuck' is called for, under the circumstances. Can I help?"

"Please."

We unloaded the freezer, filling the trash with anything unidentifiable or more than a year old, dumping anything conceivably worth saving in the sink. I wet a couple of paper towels and began mopping the little guys up, an operation that was inefficient at best. Sharon shook her head. "You have a Dustbuster?" she said.

"Under the sink." The woman was a genius.

She came back with it shortly, crevice tool at the ready. Before long she had the bulk of the ants sucked up. I imagined them coming back to life among the compressed dust bunnies, trying to figure out where their nest was.

We rounded up the stragglers, tracking them back to their source. It seemed to be behind the refrigerator. I muscled it out from the wall and discovered they were emerging from a tiny crack along the baseboard. I wielded the pyrethrum spray. Within a couple of minutes the onslaught ended. Sharon went out to empty the Dustbuster, while I pushed the fridge back in place.

When I finished, she was right behind me. "If only you'd had your schomburgkia sooner. Maybe they would have colonized it and left your freezer alone."

I turned. It seemed as good a time as any. I took her in my arms and kissed her. I hadn't realized how much I'd wanted to, until I actually did.

She put one hand behind my back and the other in my hair. I felt stirrings that had been absent for too long. Mostly absent, except for the other night at Gina's.

Finally we drew away from each other. "That was pleasant," Sharon said. We looked at each other for a few seconds more, until she swatted my butt and said, "Out. I have to finish making dinner."

She made me sit in the living room with my wine and a plate of cheese and crackers. I picked up the *Times* and scanned the comics. Mary Worth was as insufferable as ever. The women who lived in apartment 3-G still hadn't aged, and *Baby Blues* still made me laugh, even though I knew less about babies than I did about, well, wine.

After a couple of minutes Sharon sat down beside me. "Another half hour," she said.

"Smells delicious."

"It will be."

She leaned against me and I put my arm around her. We sat like that for a minute or two. Then I said, "Why didn't you tell me about David Gartner's attitude toward the Japanese?"

Her shoulders tensed. I thought I'd upset her by letting my investigation intrude on our romantic moment. Then I felt her shrug. "I started to, remember? And then I never got around to it again. It didn't really seem that significant."

"He sort of attacked me with a torque wrench today."

"Sort of?"

"I made the actual first move." I pointed to the Band-Aid on my knee. "That's how this happened."

She drew away, almost violently. A drop of wine splashed from her glass, fell on my couch. No one would ever notice the stain. "That does it. I want you to stop playing detective."

"Why the big reaction?"

"I told you—I don't want to invest a lot of emotional energy in someone who's going to get himself killed."

"All right, I'll try to stay alive. Come back here."

It took her a few seconds, but she laid her head back on my shoulder, and we forgot about murder for a while.

Two hours later. We'd had a delicious dinner, I'd stacked the dishes in the sink, and we'd taken a walk around the neighborhood to work off our meal. We held hands the whole time. It had been years since I'd held anybody's hand as much as I did that evening. We'd sat in the Jungle for a while, but the night got nippy and we went inside.

Now we were back on the couch. I felt a growing urge to make a move. I hated that I was being so calculating about the whole thing. I wished I were free enough to just be organic, get physical when our bodies wanted to, without making everything into a head trip. But not me. I had to make a production.

Finally she said, "Why haven't you tried anything yet?"

"I don't know. I love being with you, but the fact that I keep having to think about whether to try something tells me that it isn't time yet. Don't get me wrong, I'd love to make love to you, but . . . it wouldn't be making love yet. It would still be just having sex."

"Good."

I wasn't quite sure what this terse answer to my emotional unveiling meant. But I didn't want to ask. I didn't want to seem stupid.

Shortly after that she said, "I can't keep my eyes open."

"You need to go to bed."

"I do. I'm going to go home."

I walked her out to the car. "I have tickets to a play Sunday night. You want to go?"

"A play?"

"Yes, you know, where people get up on the stage and make believe they're other people."

She smiled, but her mind was elsewhere. "Let me think about it, all right?"

Okay. I'd sort of come to terms with Saturday night. But now she was wishy-washy about Sunday too. Had I, in my illimitable wisdom, somehow blown it?

"Here's the thing," she said. "I'd love to see you Sunday, but I'm not much for plays."

"Oh." I hate roller coasters. So do my emotions. "We could do something else."

"Call me at the shop after lunch."

"I have one of my Olsen's things at the mall. I'm not sure I can get to a phone."

"Then call me later on. Or Sunday." She frowned. "What do you think, if we don't have any contact for a day I'm going to disappear? I'm not going to disappear."

I pulled her to me and kissed her again. It was nice. It was exciting. But why did I get the feeling she wasn't totally into it? Why was I getting all these conflicting signals?

23

THE BIGGEST EXCITEMENT OF SATURDAY MORNING'S GREENhouse rounds came when I went to pluck a renegade particle of pumice off one of my mammillarias. When I touched the multiheaded spiny mass, it moved. This is not supposed to happen. I nudged it again. The whole thing collapsed. It was nothing but a skeleton of spines surrounding a heinous mess of orange goo.

This wasn't that unusual; cacti are very susceptible to invasion by various agents of fungal and bacterial rot. Overwatering is usually a factor, but if anything I'd been too conservative with the water lately. And sometimes the infection will get in when the pot is dry as a bone, and turn your prizewinning plant into a pile of mush overnight.

I took the thing to the garbage can. I saw the food scraps from the night before. Usually when I see food remnants in the garbage, I feel guilty for not composting. But on this particular sunny spring morning, I just felt a little sad. Sharon and I had had a lovely evening, and I was certain I would find a way to screw things up. I felt like a character in a Greek tragedy; the gods were conspiring to dole me out little scraps of love, leaving me pining for more.

I went inside, called my father, and asked him if Mrs. Vela could come to the family gathering. He said that since he considered Gina a member of the family, her mother must be one too, and of course she could come. Then I called Gina, briefed her on my date, and told her what I'd arranged about that evening. She said it sounded like a great idea. All the extra people would make being with her mom less stressful.

I went in to shower. I found myself fantasizing about Sharon. She was in the shower with me, the water coursing down her body, her nipples erect from the cold spray. Why the spray would be cold I had no idea, but it seemed a good way to get her nipples erect. Then I realized it was my fantasy and they could be erect for any damned reason I pleased. Like maybe because being with me turned her on. So I granted us some warm water.

Just a couple of days before, I hadn't been able to picture Sharon naked. What fine progress I was making.

I was about to leave for my Olsen's gig when the phone rang. "Hello?"

"Is that Joe Portugal?" said Hermann Schoeppe.

He was a plant smuggler. I didn't like what he did, but I liked him. He was charming, he was helpful, he was practical. We'd become acquainted during the Brenda business.

I wasn't surprised to hear from him. After all, I'd set Gina and Sam to tracking him down. "How are you, Mr. Schoeppe."

"Fine," he said. "And you?"

"Just fine."

"And your friend Ms. Vela?"

"She's fine too." Everyone was fine. How nice for us.

"Where are you calling from?"

"The Gambia. But please, enough small talk. Transatlantic rates are high. I understand you have been trying to reach me."

"I have. I need to ask you something."

"Has someone been murdered? Do you suspect me?"

I laughed. Feebly. "Yes to the first question. No to the second." I gave him the *Reader's Digest Condensed Books* version of the past week's events. Then I said, "Do you do orchids?"

"Do?"

"Do, as in smuggle. Do you deal in orchids?"

"Occasionally."

"But not a lot."

"No. I work in succulents. Only if something shares a site and is too charming to ignore do I take orchids. Otherwise I leave them for others. I do not infringe on their territory, nor they on mine."

Honor among plant smugglers. What a concept. "So you know some of the, uh, orchid men."

"Yes. We meet sometimes, talk about business. You know how it is."

I pictured them sitting around at the Plant Smugglers' Benevolent Society, reviewing species they'd ravaged, habitats they'd plundered. "In your contact with these gentlemen, has the name Yoichi Nakatani ever come up?"

"I don't believe so," Schoeppe said. "Should it have?"

"Possibly. I believe he might be involved in your profession."

"Involved?"

"Goddamn it, do we have to be so damned polite? I think

he's a plant smuggler. I don't care if he's a plant smuggler—well, I do, but it's significant to me right now only if it has something to do with the murders. I just need to know. I'm not going to do anything about it unless he's involved with the killings. Do you think you can find out anything about him?"

"I can try."

"I'd appreciate it." I gave him Gina's cell phone number as a backup and rang off.

My Olsen's gig at Fashion Square in Sherman Oaks went smoothly. I quizzed Diane on her opening. She said everything had gone well. There'd been three or four reviewers in the house and audience response was good. But since the place was papered with the cast's loved ones, that didn't necessarily mean anything.

A couple of times I was on the verge of calling Sharon. Just to check in, to not let a day go by without contact. But each time, I gathered a shred of self-respect and found something else to do instead.

I was done at four. I pulled up at a traffic light on Ventura Boulevard, next to a bus that had stopped to let off passengers. There was an advertising placard on the side. I was supposed to watch *Buffy the Vampire Slayer* on Channel 5 on Tuesdays. Good thing we had buses in L.A. Otherwise I wouldn't know what was on TV. What had that other sign been for, on Melrose, on the bus that nearly ran me over? Oh, yeah. *Nash Bridges*. Friday nights on CBS.

Friday nights?

Was that what it had said? I closed my eyes, tried to picture the words emblazoned between the smiling faces of Cheech Marin and Don Johnson.

Somebody honked. My eyes snapped open. The light was green. I cut in front of the bus and pulled up by a magazine stand a block ahead. I hopped out, grabbed a *TV Guide,* shuffled pages.

Yup. *Nash Bridges* was on Fridays.

I drove to Hollywood. Up Beachwood Drive to Laura's neighbor's place. I took the stairs two at a time and rang the doorbell. Rustling sounds inside. Eventually, "Who is it?"

"Joe Portugal."

"Who?"

"Laura's friend."

"Oh, yeah."

She opened the door just enough to peer out. Her face looked older and her hair was dirty. I could hear the boys hollering somewhere inside.

"I hate to bother you again, but something's not making sense. You told me that the night Laura's boyfriend Albert was killed you fed Monty. That Laura called and she asked you to feed him and you did."

"So?"

"So are you sure?"

"I guess."

"Because you told me she called during *Nash Bridges.*"

"So?"

"So *Nash Bridges* is on Friday night, not Saturday. He was killed on Saturday."

Confusion reigned on the other side of the door. "Yeah, I guess that's right."

"So she must have called you to feed the cat Friday night. Not Saturday."

"I guess."

"And are you sure you didn't feed the cat last Saturday night also?"

"I don't think so. Wait. Wasn't that the night they ran *Harley Davidson & the Marlboro Man* on Channel 13?"

"I don't know."

"Let me look." She disappeared, returning shortly with the previous week's *TV Guide*. "Yeah, that was the night. The phone never rang."

"You sure?"

"I took it off the hook. Don Johnson and Mickey Rourke both. I didn't want to be interrupted."

"Thanks. You've been a big help."

She smiled. "I have?"

"Yes. What's your name, by the way?"

"Donna."

It seemed to fit. "Thanks, Donna."

"You're welcome. Come back sometime when I'm feeling better, okay?"

"I'll see what I can do." I turned from the door. I didn't hear it close until I'd reached the bottom of the stairs.

The fact that Donna hadn't fed Monty the cat Saturday night didn't necessarily mean Laura did. But, judging from his not yowling at Laura and Gina and me when we came in early Sunday morning, somebody had. He certainly hadn't fed himself. Maybe Laura had called Donna from Helen's, gotten a busy signal because the phone was off the hook, come home to dish out the food before heading up to Albert's. I could ask Helen about that. Though who knew if she'd tell me the truth. Maybe I could get Burns to check the phone records. But were there records of calls that didn't go through? It seemed unlikely.

There was another possibility: a second cat-feeding neighbor. But that was a can of worms I didn't even want to consider.

I hadn't seen Mrs. Vela in two or three months. She'd had Gina while still in her teens, and, with a new shorter hairdo and the loss of ten pounds . . . "You look like Gina's sister, Mrs. V. Not her mother."

"You are so nice, Joey," she told me. "You are a wonderful boy. You will make someone a good husband someday." She directed a pointed look at Gina. "Someone with a brain in her head."

"Ma," Gina said. "Can we go through just one evening without someone suggesting how perfect Joe and I are for each other?"

Mrs. Vela shrugged. "Fine. But when you're old and alone like I am, don't go crying to me."

We piled into Gina's Volvo and headed over to Dad's. Mrs. Vela joined Catherine and Elaine in the kitchen. Elaine was carting around two-year-old Miles. His teenage sister, Lauren, was in the living room, playing gin with my father. She informed me that Dad already owed her eleven thousand dollars. I couldn't help staring. When I wasn't looking, she'd turned into a beautiful young woman.

I stuck my head into the backyard to say hi to Leonard

and Wayne, Elaine's husband. They were arguing about Israel. "You're Chinese," I heard Leonard say. "What do you know about the Middle East?"

After an hour we sat down to eat. I'd managed to keep the conversation away from Albert and Laura, but halfway through the soup Catherine asked me what was going on with the investigation. Immediately, everyone bombarded me with questions. It was clear they'd all been saving them up. I told them as little as I could get away with.

Then they all went off on dead people they'd seen. Catherine shared how one of her childhood friends got run over by a steamroller. Mrs. Vela told of some guy who'd been shot by the police in the East L.A. neighborhood she grew up in, inserting the phrase "leaking blood like a stuck pig" several times. Leonard recounted the epic saga of shooting "some Jap" during World War II. He looked over at Wayne and said, "Sorry," to which Wayne said his ancestry was Chinese, not Japanese, and Leonard said, "Same thing."

Only Dad was silent during this activity. He didn't want to discuss any dead bodies he'd seen.

Almost midnight. Leonard had gone to bed. Catherine and Mrs. Vela had driven off in search of swing music. Elaine and her family had gone back to their home in El Segundo.

I was in my father's bedroom. He'd asked me to come in while he got ready for bed. While he took care of his bathroom activities, I wandered around, looking at all the pictures of my mother and of me and of Elaine's kids, the closest to grandchildren Dad was ever going to get.

The room was a mess, with clothes and papers scattered

everywhere. I absently began straightening up. I was experiencing the role reversal psychologists talk about, where I was the parent and my father had slipped into the child's position. I hadn't been prepared for it to include picking up his room.

I hung some things in the closet and sat on a chair with a row of tacks up each arm. Its leather was cracked but incredibly soft. I remembered it sitting in my parents' bedroom, right about where the canaries now lived.

The toilet flushed. Dad came out of the bathroom. He had on a white T-shirt and boxers, and carried his pants and shirt in his hand. He gave the closet a cursory look and dropped his clothes on a huge stack of issues of *Modern Maturity*.

"How many times have I told you to keep your room neat?" I said.

"You never told me that."

"It was a joke. Because when I was a kid—never mind."

He shook his head, as if wondering why God had given him such a lunatic for a son. He turned off the overhead light, leaving the room lit by the lamp on his nightstand. It had a wood base, carved into the shape of a Chinese man with a huge vase on his shoulder. Or maybe he was Japanese. Same thing, if Leonard was to be believed. The lamp had been beside Dad's bed since I was old enough to know what a lamp was. Its mate, a woman hoisting some gardening implement, had graced my mother's nightstand. Now it stood on mine.

Dad plumped up a couple of pillows, climbed under the covers, sat up against the headboard. He reached over to his nightstand and picked up something by Isaac Bashevis Singer. He read a line or two, seemingly oblivious of my presence, then looked up and patted the bed beside him. "Come, sit."

I sat.

"So tell me about your new girlfriend."

I felt like a teenager. Susie's okay, Dad, but we just go out in big groups. Of course, I'd never had that kind of conversation with my father when I was a teenager, because he was in prison. "She's nice."

"Nice? All you can say is nice?"

"I don't want to spoil it. I don't want everyone to get all excited about her, because then if it doesn't work out you'll all feel sorry for me, and that'll make things worse."

He put down Isaac Bashevis Singer and took my hand in his. "I want you to be happy. To be married." He left the *and give me grandchildren* unspoken.

"Someday, Dad."

"I worry about you and women, Joseph."

Uh-oh. Secret code phrase. "I thought we put this to bed a long time ago."

"I worry."

"Dad, I'm not gay."

"No one said you were."

"You were thinking it."

"Get married, I'll stop thinking it."

"Is this what you dragged me in here for?"

"No." He let go my hand, picked up his Singer again, leafed through as if unsure of his place, put it down. "You're in danger. I can feel it."

"I'm not in danger, Dad."

"You don't understand." A long sigh. "People who kill will kill again. You are like nothing to them."

"I'll be careful. That's all I can do."

"You could stop your playing detective."

"I can't. I gave Laura my word."

Another sigh. "That's what I thought you'd say." He shook his head. "Don't give me any heartache. Okay?"

"Okay, Dad." I got up to go. When I reached the door I turned, but he was already buried in his book. I found Gina and we went out into the night.

24

WE'D DRIVEN A BLOCK OR TWO WHEN GINA'S CELL PHONE rang. We both reached to pick up her purse. "Keep your hands on the wheel, Gi," I said.

The phone shrilled again. I grabbed the purse. I had to dig around under her gun to get to the phone. I pressed the button. "Hello?"

"Joe?"

"Hermann?" Great. Now I was on a first name basis with a plant smuggler.

"Yes. I have the information you want."

"And?"

"Your suspicions are correct. Mr. Nakatani is indeed involved in my profession."

Gina was making a "who?" face. I mouthed Schoeppe's name and motioned for her to keep her eyes on the road.

"How so?" I asked Schoeppe. Make that Hermann.

"He serves as a conduit to the United States for one of the orchid men."

"Is there a name?"

"There is, but I cannot provide it. I can, however, tell you that he is from the Czech Republic and he does most of his work in Madagascar. Will there be anything else?"

"No."

"I had to call in favors to find out this information. I hope you are properly appreciative."

"I am," I said. "I owe you one."

"As you promised, you will not use this information against him. It would put me in very bad stead with my colleagues."

"Only if it turns out to be a motive for murder."

"That seems appropriate. And now, I must go. The rates, you know. Be careful. There are many bad people about."

We said our goodbyes and I slid the phone back in Gina's purse. My hand brushed up against the gun again. I couldn't suppress a shiver.

I noticed something else in there too. A little square cardboard box. I frowned and closed the snap.

"So?" Gina said.

I filled in the side of the conversation she hadn't heard.

"So he's a smuggler," she said. "That doesn't mean he killed anybody."

"But Albert was involved in plant conservation. So there's a motive right there. And you found out Yoichi's alibi for last Saturday was lousy. So there you are."

"Where I are?"

"He's a bad guy. We should go down there and tell him what we know."

She pulled the car to the curb and switched off the ignition. "Why don't we tell the cops what we know?"

"Because I promised Schoeppe that if Yoichi wasn't mixed up in the murders, I wouldn't expose him. So we have to do it ourselves."

"What if he's not there?"

"Then we'll sneak around his place in the dark. Remember how much fun we had at Brenda's last year?"

"Yeah, but we had a key then. And you still nearly got busted and I had to hide in the bathroom with Brenda's ghost." She shook her head. "I'll go down there, but only if he's there. No breaking and entering."

"Fine." I got the phone back out, found Yoichi's number in my wallet, dialed.

"Hello?" He sounded wide-awake.

"Is Otto there?" My German accent had improved. Must have been the exposure to Schoeppe.

"You have the wrong number."

"I'm very sorry." I hung up. "He's there."

"So I gathered." She started the car again and pulled into the flow of traffic.

We found him in the greenhouse, under weak fluorescent lighting, watering some gallon-size angraecums, the Madagascar orchids with the long nectar spurs. I'd always thought you weren't supposed to water at night. It promotes fungus growth. But maybe things were different with orchids. There was so much about them I didn't know.

He saw us and nodded, like our showing up wasn't any surprise. I introduced Gina. He regarded us quietly, then said, "Darwin."

"The naturalist, or the city in Australia?"

"Yes," he said, inscrutably, like the mysterious scientist in an old Republic serial. He turned and indicated the plants with an open hand. "When Darwin found these angraecums, he postulated the existence of some insect with a long proboscis. A very long proboscis. One that would be inserted all the way into the nectar spur to ensure pollination and the continuation of the species."

"The Continuation of Species," I said. "The sequel to *The Origin of Species.*"

He eyed me. "Enough jokes." He touched one of the nectar spurs almost lovingly. "No such insect was known. None was found until forty years later, when *Xanthopan morgani praedicta* was discovered. A moth, with a proboscis twelve inches long. Long enough to reach the end of the spur."

He watered one more angraecum, passed the hose over a trayful of tiny plants with marble-like pseudobulbs, laid its end on a bench. It sat there a moment; then water pressure twisted it up and snapped it to the ground like a rubbery green snake. He stepped to the faucet and turned it off. "Darwin knew sooner or later the moth would appear. I am no Darwin. But I knew sooner or later you would appear. Although I did not expect the lovely companion." He headed for the door. "Come into the trailer with me."

We crossed the orchid-strewn yard. He stopped with one hand on the trailer door. "By the way," he said, "Otto stopped by. He was sorry to have missed you." He shook his head and went in.

We followed and took seats. He shuffled around for a minute or two, offered us iced tea. We declined. He poured himself a glass, conjured up a stool, sat across from us. "So," he said. "What have you found out?"

"About you and the Czech."

"The Czech?"

"The biggest orchid smuggler in Madagascar," Gina said. Schoeppe hadn't said he was the biggest. Sometimes Gina's given to hyperbole.

Yoichi's smile was rueful. "Indeed."

"Why?" I asked.

"Why? I don't actually know."

"You don't make enough with the stuff you propagate yourself?"

"It's not a matter of money." He inspected his tea glass, found an invisible spot to wipe off. "It started almost by accident. A shipment of *Aerangis* became available. Some rare species, seldom seen. I bought it. I knew there was a possibility its provenance wasn't quite legal. But the plants . . . oh, the plants. The people in the clubs love those plants. I don't think they know they were collected illegally. Or perhaps they don't care. Many of them don't, you know. Many of them don't even know about CITES. Many are content to grow their plants and not worry about the environment." He shrugged. "I help make those people happy."

His attitude matched that of Hermann Schoeppe exactly. People want the plants, I provide them. The environment can look out for itself. End of story.

"And after that shipment?" Gina said.

"I bought more from the person who sold me the *Aerangis*." He shrugged. "It continued from there. You don't need to know the details, do you?"

"Not really," I said.

He rubbed his lower lip with a fingertip, asked, oh so casually, "Now that you know, what are you going to do with this information?"

"That depends."

"On what?"

"On whether or not you killed Albert Oberg, Laura Astaire, or both."

"You still think some imaginary altercation upset me so much that I exacted revenge?"

It was interesting that he was still denying the argument.

At this juncture it seemed pointless to do so. "No. Not anymore. But Albert was a big CITES supporter. Always working to stop illegal trafficking in plants. Maybe he found out about you and—"

"And what? I killed him for it?" He smiled indulgently, shook his head. "I am not a violent man. I assure you, I did not kill Albert. Nor Laura. I barely knew the woman. Only through—" A tiny head shake.

I stood and leaned against the stove, such as it was. "See, here's the thing. Gina checked into your alibi for the night Albert died. It doesn't stand up."

"Oh," Yoichi said. "You did, did you?" It seemed he'd been prepared for me to figure out his smuggling connection, but not for me to find out his whereabouts the previous Saturday were imaginary.

"Yes," Gina said. "The board meeting, dinner, whatever, got canceled. So where were you really?"

"I can't say."

"You have to say," I told him. "If you don't, I'm going to do two things. First, I'm going to send the cops down here to question you. This will be a big pain in the ass and not very good for business. And they might find out about your smuggling connection, except they won't have to do that because the second thing I'm going to do is contact the customs service and turn you in."

"And, if I tell you where I was that night, you won't do any of this?"

It had sounded good up to then. But what if he did tell me? Should I go ahead and turn him in anyway? An interesting moral question.

"No," I said, glancing at Gina, then back at Yoichi. "What we've learned won't go beyond this trailer."

He nodded, sighed, slumped on his stool. "I was with someone."

"That's good," I said. "That's the best kind of alibi. Who were you with?"

He squeezed the words out. "My lover."

"Who is she?"

"Is this absolutely necessary?"

"Yes."

He looked me in the eye. "Very well. My lover is Helen Gartner."

25

I RECALLED HOW HELEN HADN'T SEEMED AS UP-TO-DATE ON Laura's relationship with Albert as I thought she ought to. Probably because while they were supposedly chatting over dinner, Helen was actually slinking around with Yoichi. And I remembered how, when I was talking to Casillas, I'd wondered if the story of the two of them being together was Laura covering up something Helen had done. I'd had the principle right. I'd just gotten the subject of the cover-up wrong.

I stared across the miniature kitchen at Yoichi. I didn't quite know where to go next. Yoichi and Helen. Helen, whose husband held a passionate dislike for the Japanese. And who had, I knew well, a violent streak. No wonder Yoichi didn't want anyone to know. "How long?"

"Almost a year."

"Does David suspect?"

"Helen doesn't believe so. We have taken the greatest pains to keep our relationship secret. Laura was a great help in that effort. Several times she covered our trail, as it were, by saying she had spent the evening with Helen."

"So Laura wasn't with Helen last Saturday night."

"No. As I said, I was."

"Do you know where she was?"

"I do not."

Super. I'd finally managed to convince myself Laura's alibi for the latter part of the evening was good, just in time to blow the one for the rest of it to hell.

If she wasn't with Helen, who was she with? And what was she doing?

Maybe she *had* shot Albert. Some sort of lovers' quarrel.

But then who'd killed her?

"Now that you know," Yoichi said, "what are you going to do with this information?"

Good question. There didn't seem to be any reason for anyone else to know about it. If it were true.

"I'm going to have to confirm what you told me."

"Confirm? What do you mean, confirm?"

"I'm going to have to ask Helen about it."

He jumped up and slapped his hands down on the table. "No! You will not do that!"

"But I have to. How do I know what you're telling me now is any more the truth than what you told me before?"

"Would I invent something like this? Would I invent a story that could bring the wrath of an angry racist husband down upon me? Be reasonable."

"Goddamn it, I am being reasonable. I'm not turning you in to the Feds. But I can't just accept your story without corroboration."

He frowned, sat back down. "When will you speak with her?"

"Tomorrow, I guess. Why?"

"No particular reason. I guess I just want to prepare myself."

"For what?"

"In case David finds out."

"Why should David find out?"

"You might tell him."

"Why would I tell him? I'm just trying to find out who killed a couple of very nice people, not rid the world of adultery."

I nodded to Gina. She got up, opened the door, navigated the steps, looked back in at us.

"Helen doesn't know about the activities we've discussed," Yoichi said. "You won't tell her, will you?"

I stood and looked down at him. "No. That's up to you. But if you love her, you shouldn't keep any secrets from her."

Joe Portugal, expert on affairs of the heart, stepped out of the trailer. We got in the car and headed out of Orange County and back to somewhere we belonged.

"Maybe they're both in on it," I said.

We were on the Santa Ana Freeway, almost to downtown L.A. We'd discussed our visit with Yoichi when we first got into the car, but had driven in virtual silence for the last twenty minutes.

"Both?" Gina said.

"Yoichi and Helen. That touching bit about her not knowing could have been a sham."

"But for what reason?"

"I don't know. I just wish I could figure out what this business connection between Albert and the Gartners was. Maybe if I knew that—"

"Where'd you hear about that again?"

"Sharon."

"Could she have been mistaken?"

"Maybe."

More silence. I reached behind the seat, grabbed Gina's purse, pulled out the little cardboard box. A pack of Trojans. "What's this about?" I said.

She took her eyes off the road long enough to see what I was referring to. "Best to be prepared," she said.

"Prepared for what?"

"I just thought it would be good to have them. In case—"

"In case what?"

"Damn it, Joe. Just, in case."

I shut up. Five minutes passed. Gina negotiated the interchange weirdness around downtown and got on the Hollywood Freeway.

"Even if I weren't scared of what it would do to you and me," I said, "I couldn't. I mean, there's Sharon."

Strained silence.

"And anyway, I've got some."

"I thought you might, but I wasn't sure. It was kind of an impulse buy. I told you I was doing that a lot lately. I went to Rite-Aid for shampoo, and there they were by the checkout."

"And anyway, if we did, do you really think I might be infected with something?"

Even in the dark I could make out the Joe-you're-an-idiot look. "Remember before AIDS? They sold condoms then too. For birth control."

"Birth control? I thought you had that taken care of."

"I've been seeing a woman for the last four months. Why would I be dealing with birth control?"

"Oh, yeah." I was still sitting there like a fool with the pack of Trojans in my hand. I replaced them in her purse, put it back down. I tried to think of something to say, but nothing sounded good. When we got back to Gina's place I went right to my truck. She didn't provide any argument.

The phone woke me Sunday morning. It was Sharon. When I'd gathered about sixty percent of my wits, I told her what I'd found out about Laura's activities the latter part of the night Albert was killed, and Casillas's take on it. I didn't say anything about Yoichi. I felt it would be betraying a confidence. I was developing a high degree of consideration for plant smugglers.

"I agree with your policeman friend," she said. "Even if Laura fed her cat, it doesn't clear her." There was silence. Then she said, "Um, Joe . . ." and I knew, I just knew, I was about to hear the four worst words known to modern man.

She didn't disappoint me. "We need to talk," she said.

26

We need to talk. Womanspeak for "I've thought it over and I just want to be friends." Or "I've decided to join a biker gang and move to Montana." Or "The Samoan's back in town." It's usually followed by a somber discussion guaranteed to destroy the guy's self-esteem. Then come a chaste hug, a parting of the ways, and a night spent staring at the ceiling.

The cotton in my mouth parted enough for me to speak. "This is bad, isn't it?"

"You know, as soon as the words left my mouth I realized how ominous it sounded."

"And how ominous *is* it?"

"I'd rather talk face-to-face."

"Oy."

"Can we? Do you have a little time?"

I could always make time to be dumped. "Sure I do. Are you going to come over? Or do I get to see your place at last?"

"How about we meet on neutral ground?"

Neutral ground? What was this, the Paris peace talks? "Where'd you have in mind?"

"Do you know the big tree on National?"

"The ficus?"

"Yes. Can you meet me there in, say, half an hour?"

"Okay."

For fifteen minutes I thrashed around all the possibilities of the impending conversation. None were good. Finally I got up, washed my face, brushed my teeth. I made it to the tree on schedule.

It's a landmark. Literally. It's got the plaque and everything. It's also the biggest tree I've ever seen, a Moreton Bay fig with branches spreading a hundred feet or more over the grounds of St. John's Presbyterian Church. Its trunk is probably thirty feet around, but it would be hard to measure because the huge buttress roots reach so high up. The ground underneath, if you come at the right season, is littered with thousands of inedible little figs, pretty until they get crushed beneath your feet into a mess of seeds and pulp.

I try to visit the tree once or twice a year. It's a life-affirming experience, sitting under this plant that's been there, according to the plaque, since 1875, and knowing it's lived through earthquakes, smog, and the mayoralty of Sam Yorty.

I found a place on the brick coping atop the foot-high wall surrounding the trunk. Across National Boulevard was a special bonus tree, a eucalyptus with layer upon layer of peeling bark, with an otherworldly shape that made it resemble a cast member from *Fantasia*. A couple of pigeons were in the gutter, playing chicken with the cars as they investigated the dribs and drabs deposited there by the so-called dominant species. Pigeons don't care about romance, I thought. They don't care about murder.

"Hi," said a voice off to my right.

She had on yet another of those sleeveless tops, this one light blue. Her naked arms were captivating. Her shorts, soft navy cotton, had a Big Dog emblem down by the hem. Her legs were as engaging as her arms. She had black sandals on. I could see her toes. These I did not find particularly appealing. I have my limits.

"Hi," I said, patting the brick next to me. "Have a seat."

She crossed in front of me and sat. The sight of the backs of her legs sent an inexplicably strong wave of desire through me. Then she sat a prim foot away, and the wave washed over, and I was back to my normal level of unbuffered testosterone. "What did you want to talk about?" I said.

She gave me a slightly displeased look. "Fine, thank you, and you?"

"Sorry. I guess I got a little shaken. 'We need to talk' is the four worst—"

"Words known to modern man. I read the column too."

"There was a column?"

"Yes. In the *Times*. About a month ago. Some 'My Turn' kind of thing. It was very pathetic."

"I'm sorry I'm pathetic."

"He was pathetic. You're not pathetic." She held out a hand, took one of mine in it, said nothing more. It seemed like a deliberate dramatic pause. Then: "I was going to tell you eventually."

"About what?"

A couple of unidentifiable syllables made it out of her mouth. A tear ran down her right cheek. Just as it arrived at her jawline, another flowed down her left. As it reached her chin, a third escaped, back on the right.

She opened her purse and pulled out a tissue, seemed to

be gaining control, when suddenly she looked at me and burst out in big sobs.

I slid over and took her in my arms and let her outburst wear itself out against my chest. Her tears fell on my shirt. A teenage boy walking by took in our behavior and stepped up his pace, as if afraid of being infected by whatever had come over us.

Eventually the crying stopped. I was aware of Sharon dabbing at the wet spots on my shirt with the tissue. "Don't worry about that," I said.

"I'm sorry," she said.

"For what?"

"For losing it."

"Stop. Just tell me why you lost it."

"Two reasons. One, just thinking about what happened sometimes makes me cry."

"You going to tell me what it was?"

"In a little. I have to tell you the other reason first."

"Which is?"

"I've just been so tentative, so afraid of getting hurt. I really think we might have something together, but I've got all these protective mechanisms in place, and I've been keeping you at arm's length, and I lied to you about some things, and now you probably think I'm a big liar and—"

The crying was about to resume. In my best Archie Bunker voice I said, "Aw, little girl, not the waterworks again."

She laughed, and the new tears dried up almost instantly.

"I don't think you're a big liar," I said. "Just tell me what happened."

She pulled away, opened her purse, took out a mirror. "I'm a mess."

"You look wonderful."

"You really think that, don't you." She ditched the mirror, sat up straighter, and took one of my hands in both of hers. "I always knew I wanted to be an actress."

This had not been included among all the horrible things I was expecting. "An actress?"

She nodded. "Even when I was a little girl watching TV with my parents, I knew. In elementary school and junior high I was in all the plays. And I was the best actress in high school. And I went to Yale Drama School and was the best actress there too."

"I had no idea you were into acting."

A wry smile. "Of course not. I was hiding it."

She looked out toward the street. A young woman was going by, pushing a stroller, with an infant on her chest in one of those backward papoose things.

Sharon shook her head. "I wanted kids someday. I was going to go to New York and be a big star and when I'd established myself be one of those women who has it all." She shrugged. "Now I don't have theater and I don't have children."

"You could still have both."

"No." She turned to face me again. "When I graduated, I worked awhile to save up some money, and then I did go to New York. I gave myself five years to make it. I supported myself waitressing and temping and doing all those other things struggling young actresses do, and I waited for the theater world to discover me."

When she said "temping," I thought of Laura. Sometimes older struggling actresses had to do those things too.

Sharon sighed. "After five years I'd had a number of parts Off-Off-Broadway, and one Off-Broadway. Character roles. And I worked with a group that went around town doing free theater in neighborhoods that usually didn't see any."

"But you didn't get your break."

"I didn't get my break."

"So at the end of five years you gave it all up."

"No. At the end of five years I gave myself another five years."

"What you must have gone through."

She reached up and touched my cheek. "Sweet man."

"That seems to be the conventional wisdom."

She put her hand in her lap, leaving the other still clutching mine. "I started getting better parts. I did a lot of Off-Broadway, *a lot* being a relative term, of course. One or two plays a year. Certainly not enough to live on, but enough to be encouraging. But I had that ticking clock."

"Although no one said if you weren't a star you couldn't just keep working at it. Some people keep working at it."

She nodded. "Like Laura."

"And my friend Diane." Who had, I recalled, recognized Sharon's name. It must have been from when Diane worked in New York.

"And I might have done that. But somehow I was developing a cosmic sense that everything was leading to that ten-year mark. Something wonderful was going to happen to my career just then."

"And what? It didn't happen, so you chucked the whole thing and came to L.A.?"

She shook her head. "Three months before my deadline I auditioned for a new Broadway show. A new drama by a new playwright with a lot of advance word. I talked my way into the audition and, like they say in *Variety,* I wowed 'em." She looked out at the street again. "It was almost too perfect. The part was perfect, the timing was perfect. Well, almost. We were to open four days after my ten-year anniversary in New York." A smile. "I allowed myself a four-day extension."

Now she was looking right at me. The way she kept changing her focus reminded me of someone delivering a monologue. "You would think the play was about the beautiful leading lady until, halfway through the first act, you realized it wasn't. It was about the best friend, the plain one. I was the plain one."

"Not typecasting."

"Thanks, but I know I'm not a leading lady. There's more."

"What more?"

"My social life was kind of slapdash during those years, but shortly after we started auditions I got involved with the director. It was the kind of relationship I'd never had before. Intellectual. Emotional. Intensely physical."

"Spare me the details."

"Of course. In any event, we were cruising along smoothly to opening night. The only fly in the ointment was, I was having a little trouble with the character. Most unlike me. The director thought everything was going too smoothly for me, keeping me from getting in touch with the turmoil the character was going through. I was ninety percent there, just not quite plumbing the emotional depths I needed to. But I thought I'd have it by opening night."

"And did you?"

She looked away again. "The day of the opening, he broke up with me."

"What?"

"He said it was time to move on. It seemed very strange, the timing and all. And I hadn't had a clue it was coming. Everything had been lovely."

"I think I see what's coming here."

"Do you?"

"I've worked with asshole directors before. Guys—women

too—who'll put the cast through anything to get the effect they want onstage. He thought if you were distraught by his breaking up with you, you would, what did you call it, 'plumb the emotional depths' more thoroughly. By being hurt in real life you'd find the character."

"Right on the money."

"And did it work?"

Another one of those wry smiles. "Not exactly. I left his apartment a total wreck. I was crushed by his dumping me, yet I knew I had to get myself together for that evening. And I suspected what he was doing, and even that he'd planned it all along, that he'd taken up with me just to hurt me and make me a better actress, which sounds Machiavellian when you actually put it into words."

"Did it work?"

"We never got the chance to find out. I was so upset I wasn't paying attention to traffic and walked right in front of a taxi. I broke my leg in three places. They took me to the hospital. I tried my best to get out, but they wouldn't let me. At one point I made it as far as the elevator. I was delirious—they'd given me drugs for the pain—and I thought that if I got in the elevator, when the doors opened again I'd be at the theater. And when they didn't, when I found myself in the hospital's basement, surrounded by carts full of towels and refuse, I totally broke down. They found me lying on the floor there."

"And the play went on without you."

"The understudy went on, and she was great. Not as good as I would have been, friends told me, but she did a wonderful job and her career took off. Then the director took up with her."

"Adding insult to injury. How long were you in the hospital?"

"A week. I'd done something horrible to my leg during my elevator jaunt, and it took them a while to get that straightened out. Then I went home and was a vegetable."

What could I say? Gee Sharon, tough break, but you could have picked yourself up and tried again. Would I have done that? "And?"

"I stayed a vegetable for two months. My leg healed, but my psyche didn't. To have everything I was working for this close . . ." She held out two fingers a half-inch apart. "Once I could function again, I packed up and moved to a small town in upstate New York. I went there to sort things out. And to be away from the theater."

"But eventually you came here."

"Yes."

"If you wanted to be away from show biz, Los Angeles was a strange place to pick."

"I wanted to be away from the theater. Not necessarily from show business. L.A.'s not exactly the world's greatest theater town. And, after all those years up north, I wanted to live someplace warm. As I told you before, I was sick of cold weather."

It didn't exactly ring true. I let it slide.

"I was trying to forget New York. I didn't want anyone asking about it, so I made up a background about being in finance. That usually glazed people's eyes enough that they never asked again, and if they did I made something up on the spot. I'm very good at that."

She looked me in the eye. "I haven't let a man get close since. For five years I didn't go out on a date. Eventually I began trying, but I never let anyone in. And I never, never became physical."

"You haven't been with a man—"

"In almost ten years. No matter how nice they seemed on

the surface, I didn't trust them. I thought I could be hurt again, and I'm afraid that my fear of that happening led me to hurt a few very nice men." She looked into my eyes, touched a finger to my cheek again. "You're a very nice man too."

"Nice. Sweet. Those are my most popular qualities."

"Now do you see why I've been so jealous of Gina? Why it was such a horrible thing for me to see her at your house, looking like she'd just spent the night with you? Here I was close to trusting you, and there was this other woman who seemed to have a part of you."

"Uh-huh. But I told you—"

"Nothing's going on." Almost nothing. Just a little coed sleeping. And condom procurement.

"It's time to move on," Sharon said. "And I think you're the man to do it with."

"I think I'm the man to do it with too."

"I'll cook dinner and—why the look?"

"Just, I have tickets to the theater. Remember? My friend's play just opened."

"I totally forgot."

"I promised to go. But if it would be too painful for you to see a play, maybe we can just have an early dinner. I can go to the play alone." I grinned. "Or I can take Gina."

Sharon shook her head. "I'll go. As I said, it's time to move on." She stood. "I'd love to spend the day with you, but I promised to visit a friend in Agoura Hills. Her daughter's having a birthday party. She's one."

"Like a one-year-old knows from birthdays."

"I know, it's so silly. But I promised."

"About tonight. Why don't I come pick you up?"

I waited for her to say no. That her house was a mess, or something.

She surprised me. "That would be good."

She told me the address. We arranged that I would come by at six-thirty, exchanged a kiss, went off to our vehicles. I sat in mine for a minute or two, wondering how I was going to screw things up with Sharon. I knew I would somehow.

27

When your day starts with "We need to talk," you sometimes forget about the little things in life. Little things like people getting killed and you trying to figure out who did it.

So it wasn't until I got home from my big tree rendezvous that I began thinking about murder again. I made myself a fried egg sandwich and took it out to the Jungle and watched the drivers on Madison Avenue negotiate the speed bumps.

I was thinking that Laura might actually have been Albert's killer. They had a lovers' quarrel. She got hold of a gun somewhere and plugged him, then ran home to feed the cat to establish an alibi for the part of the evening not occupied by her imaginary dinner with Helen.

Then who killed her?

If I had half a brain, I would let the police deal with that question, stop sticking my nose where it didn't belong, and get on with my life and especially with romancing Sharon. It would end my dealings with plant smugglers and crazy old ladies. And it would eliminate the torque wrench–wielding maniacs chasing me around piles of tires.

I pictured myself lying dead, out of sight of the traffic on Reseda Boulevard, buried under a dozen or two radials, to be reported on someday on the local news. *Mysterious skeleton found in Reseda. Film at eleven.*

Hold on.

Piles of tires?

Why were there piles of tires? Tire people used to take the old ones and put retreads on them. Did they still do that? And even if they didn't, wouldn't the tires have some salvage value? Why would the Gartners keep them around?

Then I remembered something I'd seen at Albert's. And the piles of tires began to make sense.

I phoned the tire store. The machine said they were closed on Sunday. I remembered Laura telling me the Gartners lived in Tarzana. I called directory assistance and sweet-talked the operator into giving me the address as well as the number. When I dialed and Helen answered, I nearly did the Otto thing, but just hung up instead. Once more I drove up to the Valley. Once again the heat far exceeded that on the Westside.

The house was a white ranch, indistinguishable from thousands of others out that way. The smell of cut grass filled the air out front, where David was pushing a mower that seemed way too loud. He was shirtless, covered with sweat. He had no hair on his chest. No wrench, either, and the mower seemed a mite too cumbersome for him to attack me with.

"Where's my socket?" he said the moment I got out of the truck.

I had to raise my voice to make myself heard over the racket. "Sitting on my nightstand."

"You intending to keep it?"

"No."

"Then bring it back sometime, okay? Those things are expensive."

"Fine. I will. Look, I want to talk to both of you. Where's Helen?"

"Why?"

"Is she here?"

He must have known he wasn't going to get rid of me. "She's in the back."

He turned off the mower. My ears continued to throb. We went down the driveway and through a gate, into a backyard loaded with orchids. Racks, tables, hanging pots, bark plaques. A greenhouse about the size of mine occupied a corner. Next to it was a pepper tree whose trunk was virtually covered with blooming specimens.

Helen had on a tank top and shorts and sandals. Her hair was pulled back into a ponytail. Typical suburban mom, minus the kids. Somehow I knew there weren't any kids.

She saw me and shook her head. "I had a feeling we'd be seeing you again."

"And I didn't want to disappoint you. Tell me something. Whose idea was it?"

"Was what?"

I picked up a five-inch pot housing a bloomless dendrobium. The particles filling the pot were black, not the usual red-brown. There were quite a few plants around in a similar medium. "The plan to turn your old tires into orchid mix."

They traded surprised looks, returned to me. "How did you figure it out?" David said.

"Actually, it was a guess. But, judging from your expressions—and the number of plants I see around here growing in the stuff—it was a good one." I put down the pot. "Once I got to thinking about why you kept all those old tires around, it kind of made sense. I mean, if people are going to use an orchid mix made out of old tires, what better source than a tire store?"

David decided bravado was called for. "Yeah. So you figured it out. So what of it?"

He really didn't seem like that bad a guy, once you got past the bluster and the racism and the penchant for threatening people with hand tools. "So this," I said. "People overheard you talking to Albert, and what they overheard pointed to you guys being in business with him. So I figure it's this tires-to-mix thing. You grind up your tires, throw them in bags, sell the stuff to all the orchid people. Make a million dollars. Albert told me the tire mix had promise."

"Albert had nothing to do with it," David said. "Where'd you get that idea?"

I ignored his question. I was on a roll. "Here's what I don't understand. You look like you're doing well at the store. This is a nice place. Nicely kept up. No kids, I'm guessing, to suck up your income."

Something on Helen's face told me I was on the money about the kids. And that she wasn't entirely happy about it.

"You two aren't lacking," I said. "How come you had to go to Albert for money?"

"We didn't go to Albert for money," David said.

The next piece of the puzzle slid into place. "Of course. It wasn't money. It was expertise. Albert was such a big orchid maven, he would help you figure stuff out. Like how big to make the pieces, maybe. That's it, isn't it?"

Helen smiled. "It's nice to know you have everything

worked out. It's almost a shame that you're so wrong. Please believe me when I say Albert had nothing to do with our plans."

"You're telling me you didn't need his expertise?"

"Or his money."

"I know as much about orchids as Albert did," David said. "Jeez, Hel, we don't need to listen to this."

"Jeez, Dave," I said, "I think you do. So tell me. If you didn't need Albert's help, if you had everything you needed, money, expertise, how come you haven't gone ahead with this grand scheme of yours?"

"There's no market," Helen said. She picked up a pink-flowered phalaenopsis, potted in the rubber fragments. "We made up a batch of the mix and grew some of our plants in it until we were sure it was worthwhile. And it is. It doesn't compact, and we have to repot less often. But when we researched the market we decided that until the medium becomes more accepted, the numbers just aren't there. The start-up costs would be too great."

"So why don't you just sell off your old tires? Get some money out of them."

"We do sell them off. If we didn't, we'd all be buried fifty feet deep in them. We just keep enough around so we can move on a moment's notice. Orchid people move slowly, but when they do, we'll be ready."

"And why didn't you just tell me about this before?"

"You were asking about being in business with Albert. This had nothing to do with Albert. So there was no reason to mention it, was there?"

"I guess not."

I examined both their faces. I was virtually certain they were telling the truth.

So. I'd discovered the Gartner's big secret. And it had nothing to do with Albert. Once again I'd been on a wild-goose chase.

But there was another secret. I caught Helen's eye. "I guess I'll get going, then."

"Good idea," said David. "And don't forget my socket."

I walked back through the gate. I waited at the truck. I wasn't surprised when Helen came out to the curb. "You know, don't you?" she said.

"Yes."

"I suppose you want to ask me all about it."

"Not really. All I want to know is this. Yoichi says he was with you the night Albert was killed. Is he telling the truth?"

"He is."

"You and he didn't have anything to do with Albert's death, did you?"

"No. What reason would we have?"

At the moment I could think of only one. Albert's opposition to illegal activities like Yoichi's. But Yoichi had said Helen didn't know about that.

I could tell her. Measure her reaction. But I'd promised not to. "What would happen if David found out?"

"He'd probably go down to Yoichi's place and try to beat him up."

"And you? What would he do to you? Would he beat you up too?"

"Of course not. There's not any domestic abuse going on here. David's actually a fine husband."

"Then why'd you take up with Yoichi?"

"I don't know. For the thrill of it, I guess."

"Oh. Yes. It seems very thrilling, sneaking around like that."

"Don't make me feel any guiltier than I already do. I dread the day he finds out. I dread hurting him. He's very good to me. His hatred of the Japanese is his only real fault."

"That's like saying Hitler's hatred of the Jews was his only real fault."

"Consider what you just said. It's very stupid."

"Sorry. Bad analogy." I groped for something more intelligent to say. "I won't tell anyone."

"I know." She looked at me for a few seconds more, before turning and walking into the house.

28

I DROVE HOME, CALLED GINA, LEFT HER A MESSAGE ABOUT what I'd found out in Tarzana, threw in a little about the Sharon situation. Then I got in the shower. I washed every part of my body I could reach and let the water beat down on that part of my back I couldn't. I used the nail brush until the last bit of dirt had disappeared from my fingertips, along with a portion of my fingertips themselves.

I took my time shaving, then picked out a nice pair of Dockers from my audition stash, topping it with a colorful, as yet unworn shirt Gina talked me into buying several months before. I stopped at a Conroy's and put together a bunch of flowers, then drove to Sharon's house in Westchester. It was on a quiet side street, not far from Loyola Marymount University, in that area between Lincoln and Sepulveda that Gina calls Whitechester. A magnolia sat out front, with a sprinkling of dead leaves and flower corpses littering the sidewalk and street below. Impatiens and begonias were planted in the thin strip of earth along the front of the house. Several pots full of epidendrums sat by the front door.

My flowers and I went up to the entrance and rang the bell. Half a minute later Sharon showed up at the door. She was wearing a cranberry-colored linen blouse and a long skirt in a muted print.

She spied the flowers. "For me?"

"No, they're for me. I came over to borrow a vase."

"They're beautiful."

"I picked them out myself."

"You did a fine job." She kissed me on the cheek. "I'll just put them in some water and be right back out."

I stood out there awkwardly, then wandered down the driveway and looked over the gate. The grass was patchy. Then again, so was mine. The trees were trimmed, the bushes pruned. Colorful annuals poked out of the ground.

She had a lath house, about ten by fifteen feet, with redwood lattice on top and on three sides, open to the north. A couple of hundred orchids grew inside. Some kinds I recognized and some I didn't. Something in there was broadcasting a fruity scent I could detect halfway across the yard.

I turned at the sound of footsteps. Sharon had added a thin sweater to her outfit. "Maybe you can see the lath house . . . later," she said.

"Sounds good." I checked my watch. "We should get going."

We made it to the play with fifteen minutes to spare. We parked half a block away on Santa Monica Boulevard, and walked over to the theater.

Some things had changed—the marquee was new, and even from outside I could see they'd redone the lobby—but some remained the same. The brickwork above the marquee, punctuated by windows sporting ancient venetian blinds. The industrial-looking pipe heads jutting out of the sidewalk to the left, a perfect place to lean against and stare at traffic when you've had a big argument with one of your artistic co-conspirators.

I stood there motionless as images of the Altair of yesteryear merged with what was there now like some cheesy sci-fi effect. Eventually, the old ones faded. I wasn't looking at the Altair Theater. I was staring at the John Diamante Theatre. Spelled with an *re.* Pretentious.

I picked up our comps at the box office. The young woman guarding the door tore them in half. She looked exactly like the young women who took tickets when I was running the place. Smiling, but with an edge of desperation, of deep disappointment that someone else had gotten the ingenue part. Next time she'd show them. She was only paying her dues, right?

We passed through the lobby and into the theater itself. The seats were new. The walls were a different shade of black. The tech booth still overlooked the last row. I watched a techie climb the three steps and go in. She had dark frizzy hair and her overalls were frayed. Techies never changed.

The set was essentially a couple of easy chairs and a bed in someone's yard, with a porch behind. I guessed having the furniture outdoors was the "experimental" part of "experimental yet commercial."

We spotted some seats in the center, about halfway back. To get to them we had to squeeze by a couple of couples. They had the look of people from Beverly Hills or Bel Air who came to small theaters because they thought it legitimized them as supporters of the arts. You'd hear them in the lobby at intermission, complaining that they didn't understand the play.

We took our seats. "I've been thinking," Sharon said. "And actually being here, in a theater, settles it. I'd like to get back to the stage."

I turned to look at her. I wondered if she was fooling herself. She'd get cast in some play, and opening night would approach, and she'd suddenly be overcome by bad memories and go screaming out into the street. "Just like that?"

She shrugged. "When I really faced what I was avoiding, when I told you about it, it didn't seem so horrible anymore. Sometimes when bad things happen you think you'll never get over them, but when you look at them later, they're nothing. Like relationships that fail. Six months later you run into the person and wonder what you ever saw in them." It was a funny thing for someone who hadn't had a lover in ten years to think of.

She took my hand. "Anyway, I was thinking . . . you were considering getting back to the theater as well. What with your going to Laura's scene study and all. I thought maybe we could sort of lean on each other as we dived back in."

"That implies we're going to be together a while."

"I don't have any problem with that. Do you?"

I shook my head. The house lights went down and the stage lights came up.

The play was much better than I'd anticipated. Both leads were very good, though the woman cast as Grandma Moses occasionally lapsed into Granny from *The Beverly Hillbillies*. The story was set in 1961, right before Grandma died. The Moseses were scheming to embezzle three million dollars from the City of New York. Robert Moses was in on it because he was pissed off over them not naming Shea Stadium after him. Grandma just wanted to do something dishonest before she kicked off. During the first act they assembled their criminal crew, including Diane as the Transit Authority accountant who was going to cook the books.

I sat comfortably beside Sharon, sometimes holding her hand, sometimes not, and not endlessly calculating in my head what that meant. Albert Oberg never entered my thoughts, and Laura only once, when Diane first entered and I thought, this would have been a good part for Laura too.

Intermission came. Sharon stayed in her seat while I went to the rest room. The years stripped away. There was new paint and a new low-volume toilet, but the bare porcelain sink was the same one that had been there since the Cubs won the pennant. I recognized a ding where I'd dropped a pipe wrench on it, way back when.

I hung around the lobby for a while, sucking in the theater atmosphere. Just as they blinked the lights the first time, I ran into Joe Parlakian.

He'd been our token Armenian at the Altair, and never let us forget it. Everyone knew the dates of the Armenian Genocide and what an awful country Turkey was. Our names had been the subject of endless lame confusion. "Hey, Joe." "Which one?" "Joe P." "Which one?" Theater humor.

He came up and wrapped his big arms around me and pounded my back. Then he held me at arm's length and told me I looked good.

"You look good too, Joe."

"What have you been doing? Besides the commercials. 'It takes a bug,' right?"

"Right. That's pretty much it. How about you?"

"Some voice-over, a little movie work. I have a recurring part on a soap, too, can you believe that, me in a soap?" He frowned. "I was up for *Nine Armenians* at the Taper, but the director . . ." Big, exaggerated shrug. "What an *aboush*."

"Sounds great. Not the thing at the Taper, but the rest."

"I got married too. Three little ones. Life is good."

"Sounds like it."

"What about you, any kids?"

"No kids. No wife."

"You should try it. You'd like it." The lights blinked again. "Better find my seat. Good to see you." He started walking away, stopped, turned. "Some friends and I are starting a theater company. Equity-Waiver, or whatever they're calling it these days. You'd fit right in."

"I'll think about it."

"Call me. I'm in the book."

During the second act I thought a lot about Joe Parlakian's invitation. It would be good to be in a theater company again. And Sharon could join too. We could merge our artistic and personal lives into one fabulous synergistic whole. Jumping the gun? Maybe. But it seemed right.

When the last curtain call was over, we made our way to the thronging lobby. We waited until Diane came out and stood in a little semicircle with three or four other friends while she held court. I got to meet Tom, her real husband. He was short, fat, and jovial. Visually, she and I went together better than they did.

A couple of the others were going out with them afterward. I wanted to go. But I wanted to be alone with Sharon more.

We got to her house. We exited the truck. I hesitated on the sidewalk.

"Are you coming in or not?" she said. She unlocked the door and led me in.

The living room was nice. Nothing spectacular. The furniture, tasteful but not memorable, stood on hardwood that could have used a polishing. The right pictures were on the walls and the right knickknacks in the right places. My flowers sat on the coffee table in a cheap vase, the kind that comes with a flower shop arrangement. The place smelled slightly musty, like a long-unused room that's been opened up for company. "This is the living room," she said.

"Is there more?"

"Not much."

"Oh, come on, give me the tour. You've seen enough of my place."

She smiled. "Sure." She stepped over to the kitchen. "This is the kitchen."

"Nice microwave."

"I like popcorn." She led me down a short hallway. One door on the left, one on the right, one at the end. "Guest room on the left. Then the bathroom. This . . ." She took a couple of steps into the room on the right. "This is my bedroom." Like the living room; nice, practical, nothing to write home about. More hardwood flooring. The bed was a queen. It had a blue comforter on it. "Why are you staring at my bed?" Sharon asked.

"I was trying to figure out if that was a down comforter."

"I see." She gave me a Mona Lisa smile, retreated from the bedroom, led me back into the kitchen. She poured us a couple of glasses of Amaretto, handed me one, directed me to the sofa. I sipped my drink, slipped my arm around her. She smiled, put her glass down, turned her face up to mine. I put my glass down too.

It was the first really serious kiss we'd had, with all the

attendant slipping and sliding and hands wandering who knew where. It lasted a minute or two. When it was over, she gave me a big solemn look. Then she stood and took my hand and pulled me off the sofa. Still holding my hand, she headed down the hallway and into the bedroom.

She pointed me toward the bed and said, "Sit." She began to unbutton her blouse. She'd gotten just far enough for me to know she had nothing on underneath when the doorbell rang.

"Ignore it," she said, undoing another button. "They'll go away."

They didn't. They knocked on the door. Then again, louder. "I don't think they're going anywhere," I said.

Then I heard yelling. "Joe! Joe, are you in there? I've got to talk to you."

"That's Gina," I said.

"I know who it is. What's she doing here?"

"I don't know." I also didn't know how the hell she'd found us, but my contemplation of that question was interrupted by more yelling from the front door.

Sharon uttered a disgusted sound. "She'd better have a damned good reason for being here."

She stomped out, fastening buttons as she went, and headed toward the door. I followed. She opened the door. Gina stood there, hand poised to bang again.

"Hi," she said. "Sorry to interrupt." She spied me across the room and pushed in. Sharon made a move to stop her, but wasn't quick enough. "We need to talk," Gina said.

"Not that again," I said. I turned so I was addressing both of them. "You girls know each other, right?"

"Come on," Gina said. "This is important."

"I'll just bet it is," Sharon said. "Look, no one invited you up here. What are you, a stalker? You getting uptight because somebody's about to grab the guy you've been taking for granted all these years?"

"Lady, if I'd have wanted Joe I could have had him any time I wanted him." She turned to me. "Sorry. I know how you hate being talked about in the third person."

"This is really awkward," I said. "Can't it wait until morning?"

"No. It's about Albert."

"Gi. Go away. I'll call you in the morning."

Sharon stormed over. "Get out. Now."

"No."

They glared at each other. Sharon said to me, "Get her out of here or the evening is over."

What to do, what to do. I looked at Sharon. Then at Gina. Back to Sharon. "I have to follow up on this. I'm sorry. I'll be back in a minute."

She went to the door, opened it wider. "Fine. Be with your little friend. Go. Now."

I went out. Gina followed. When we reached the sidewalk, I said, "This had better be good."

"Not yet. In the car."

We got in the Volvo. "Okay. What is it?"

She pulled a big coffee table book from the backseat, dumped it in my lap, turned on the interior light. "Where the dust jacket's stuck in."

I looked at the book. *New York Theater Scene 1986.* I opened it to where Gina indicated. Each page had photos from some play or other, with a paragraph or two about the production and the personnel. On the right-hand page, bottom left, a scene from something called *Pablo and Veronica.* Two actors, one actress. The hair was shorter and black, she was much younger, but the actress was definitely Sharon.

"She wasn't in high finance before she came back here," Gina said. "She was an actress. She's lying to you, Joe."

"Where'd you get this?"

"Larry Edmunds." A big theater bookstore, new and used, on Hollywood Boulevard.

"Why'd you go there?"

"For proof. I mean, I thought I had proof, but sometimes you don't believe stuff I find on the Internet and—"

"You looked up Sharon on the Internet?"

"Yeah, I did a search on her name. Eventually I came to a site where some theater fanatic has records on every show that's run in New York for the last twenty years."

"You went searching the Internet to dig up dirt on the woman I'm going out with?"

"I don't trust her, Joe. I haven't from the beginning. And I don't like what she's doing to you."

"What the hell's that supposed to mean?"

"How can I put this? She's leading you around by your penis."

"What penis? We haven't even done anything yet, although if you hadn't shown up . . . anyway, there's more to this than just my penis."

"Fine. You have a deep emotional attachment."

We were getting nowhere. "You said this had something to do with Albert."

"I think your new friend is mixed up with his death. And Laura's."

"And what's the basis for this amazing intuitive leap?"

"I just thought, she's so full of shit, there has to be a reason. And the reason could be that she's involved in the killings, and, if so, I didn't want you to be alone with her. So I went to your place, but you weren't there, and that left her place, so I called Sam, and he called one of the orchid people who had a membership list, and I got the address and came to save you."

"Save me?"

"She may be planning on doing you in next."

"This is *so* stupid, Gi."

"It's *not* stupid."

I sighed, shook my head. "She already told me about her past. This afternoon."

"She what?"

"She's been covering it up because something crappy happened to end her career and she didn't want to think about those days. She told me about it because she trusts me."

"You've known her for a week and she trusts you enough to expose her big secret life. Do you really believe that?"

"Sure."

An important moment, this. Because, even as I said "Sure" a tiny seed of doubt, smaller than the microscopic seed of an orchid, took root. It sounded all right for me to say, Gee, Sharon trusts me enough after a week to lay her life bare, but when someone else said it . . .

Defense mechanisms sprang into position. "I think you're jealous. You just want to drive Sharon and me apart."

"Jealous? Me? Jealous of an orchid woman?"

"Stop calling her that."

"Your love life is your own, Joe. I'm not interested in it."

"Then why'd you buy those Trojans?"

"I'm telling you, there's something not quite right with that woman."

"There's something not quite right with you, right now."

"Will you listen to me? Wasn't I right last time I got a hunch about someone not being who they said they were?" Something that happened during the Brenda business.

"So lightning's going to strike twice."

She kind of curled into herself. "You're not going to listen to me, are you?"

"No. Goddamn it, Gi, I've got a chance for a normal relationship here. I don't want to blow it." I looked at Sharon's house. Only one light was on. "If you haven't already blown it."

I grabbed the handle and swung the door out. Gina put a hand on my arm. "Where are you going?"

"Back in there. To try to salvage an evening you've probably ruined."

"Don't."

I shook off her hand. "Leave me alone."

I got out of the car and went to the front door. I reached for the doorbell, looked back, saw Gina still sitting in her car at the curb. I made a little motion with my hand, like go away, making it as dismissive as I could. A couple of seconds later I heard her engine start up. Then she left.

I rang the bell. Eventually the door opened. "Well?" Sharon said.

"I told her it could wait. Can I come back in?"

"I'm not sure I should let you."

"Look, I'm sorry I ran out. But what could I do?"

"You could have sent her away."

"I couldn't. She's my best friend."

"Too good a friend, I think."

"I thought you were over that."

"Maybe I'm not." She shook her head. "I don't want you to come back in. I need to think about things."

"What kind of things?"

"Things. I'll talk to you."

"When?"

"Don't try to pin me down." She swung the door closed.

I stood on the front step for a couple of minutes, waiting

for her to have a change of heart, like the star-crossed lover in the movies always does. When she didn't, I went out to the truck. I sat watching the house until that one light went out. Then I went home and straight to bed. I thought I would lie awake, agonizing over the two women in my life and how upset they both were with me. But my body took mercy on me, and dragged me quickly down into restless sleep.

29

WHEN I WOKE UP MONDAY MORNING, I DECIDED I WAS worthless. Not only couldn't I carry on a decent relationship, but I'd reached an impasse in the only other worthwhile element in my life, the search for Albert and Laura's killer or killers.

It took what seemed like hours to gather the wherewithal to crawl out of bed. I seemed to have no particular reason to do so. Finally my eyes focused on the socket I'd spirited away from Gartner's. It had fallen on its side and rolled to within an inch of the nightstand's edge.

I decided to take it back. Getting rid of it would make me feel a little more honest, a little less worthless. It would also give me an excuse to get in the car and go somewhere. It was a bad excuse but, hey, it was all I had.

The sky was clear, the temperature in the sixties. A cool, crisp, perfect Los Angeles spring morning. On another day I would have loved it, thought a morning like that was the most wonderful thing in the world.

The direct route to the Valley and Gartner's would have been up the San Diego Freeway. But there really wasn't any hurry. So I made my way to Pacific Coast Highway, planning to turn up Topanga Canyon Boulevard and take the long way into the Valley, then double back to Reseda. That would eat up more of the day.

I passed Santa Monica and Pacific Palisades. By the time I got to Topanga Canyon, I'd thought of another reason to take it. Austin and Vicki lived up there. Austin would probably be home. He'd have marijuana. I could get high and try to forget that I was worthless.

But once I came down from the temporary euphoria that smoking dope would bring, the miserable state of mind would return. In spades. I needed to think things out, figure out what I had to do to become a useful member of society again. Reverting to my days as a pothead wasn't going to help that effort. I was afraid if I headed up Topanga, even if intending to go to Gartner's, I'd end up at Austin's and descend into reefer madness.

So I kept going on P.C.H., followed it as it turned inland, and drove all the way up to Santa Barbara. I spent hours wandering up and down State Street, first in the truck, then on foot, trying to shake the feelings I was experiencing, being wondrously unsuccessful at doing so.

Eventually I got hungry. I found a mini-mart, came out with some bananas and a bag of pretzel nuggets and a bottle of water. I ate a banana and some pretzels.

Sometime after two I got in the truck and headed back south. I was going to take the freeway all the way home, realized the only advantage to this would be getting there more quickly, and what advantage was that? So I turned off in Oxnard and drove back toward P.C.H. Around Port Hueneme I remembered the socket in my pocket. Too bad. But there was always another day for that. There was always another day when you worked only six days a year.

As I approached Malibu I remembered a rocky little cove full of rounded stones and driftwood, where sandpipers piped and pelicans flaunted their crops. A surfer girl I'd dated in my theater days had shown me the spot. It was a good place to think. I'd spent several fun-filled hours there after she dumped me.

I found it a mile farther on. I parked on the side of the road, grabbed my pretzels, picked my way down the rock-strewn slope. There was a tiny beach, a little oasis of sand among the stones. I found a place just beyond where the sand was wet, kicked away a chunk of Styrofoam cooler, sat down on a round gray rock. I could smell the salt of the ocean, marred by a subtle undertone of rotting vegetation.

Above me, gulls did their thing, swooping and calling. Down by the water, a couple of pelicans squatted on the beach. Just beyond the waterline, a sandpiper—or one of those birds I've always thought of as sandpipers—waded, constantly eyeing the surface and repeatedly plunging its beak in. It didn't seem to be coming up with much.

To my right a taller bird, with a crest on its head, a crane or an egret or a heron, stood on one leg. It looked at me and it looked away. I couldn't figure out what it was doing there. There weren't any fish up on the beach. Maybe it was checking out what *I* was doing there.

I pulled a pretzel from the bag, scraped the salt off with a fingernail, threw a piece in the air. A gull caught it, dropped it, went after it on the ground. Another wheeled in for a landing. I threw it some too. More gulls clustered around, some gray with mottled feathers, others white with gray wings and an orange spot on their lower beaks. A couple of short-necked black ducks too. Or maybe they were loons.

I crunched another pretzel and threw the fragments on the sand. A whirlpool of gulls erupted. One of the white ones opened its mouth and cried at the others, *weep-weep-weep-weep-weep*. Another picked up the call. Then a couple more.

I tried thinking about Sharon. She'd said she'd talk to me. What was she going to say? I spent an hour formulating conversations in my head. They all ended badly.

"Enough," I said aloud, and forced myself to move on to killers and victims and suspects. I thought about Helen Gartner. About her husband, David.

I thought about Yoichi Nakatani. I knew I ought to turn him in. I knew I wouldn't.

I'd gotten the feeling he was glad someone had found him out. But he probably could have gone on a long time without that happening. Why would anyone suspect him of being involved in plant smuggling?

Then I remembered that someone had.

Dottie Lennox had told me Yoichi was a smuggler. She'd actually said it was "a Japanese fellow," but even with all the Japanese-Americans in the orchid club, what were the chances more than one was a smuggler?

Where would she have come up with that nugget? Could it be that she wasn't as crazy as I thought? Why had I been so quick to throw away everything she had to say, simply because she saw the Red Menace where no one else did?

I went back over my conversation with her and realized something else. She'd known about, or at least suspected, the Gartner's plan to turn tires into a growing medium. When I asked her about them, she told me, "Some people have funny ideas about orchid mix." I'd dismissed it as pre-Alzheimerian free association.

Maybe I'd been too quick to discount what she said. She'd been in the orchid group longer than anyone. If only I could ask the right questions, and not be so linear in interpreting the answers, maybe I could find out something about who killed Albert and Laura.

I got up to go. Only one bird remained nearby. A different kind of gull, smaller than the others, with brownish-gray wings and gray spots on its chest. It waited shyly, hoping for a crumb.

There was one pretzel left. I scraped off the salt, broke it in half, tossed the pieces at the bird. It gobbled one on the spot and flew off with the other. I climbed up the slope to the truck.

I felt a little better, but not much. Maybe I had a plan in mind regarding the killings, but my love life was still a shambles.

I stopped in Santa Monica to call my machine. Much as the idea of doing any more commercials pained me, I felt a responsibility to see if Elaine had come up with anything. She hadn't. Nor had I gotten another miracle pardon from Sharon.

But there *was* the next best thing. Gina had left a message. "Guess what? Your girlfriend called. You're forgiven. And she wants me to come over for coffee so she can get to know me better. She says she has some issues to work through. Everyone has issues these days, when they used to have problems." There was a pause. Any longer and the voice activation feature would have cut her off. "I don't know what I was talking about last night. Maybe I *am* jealous. Anyway, I'm going over at four. I'll let you know what happens."

Sometimes I suffer from bipolar disorder. What they used to call manic-depression before everything became so politically correct. It shows up only under certain circumstances.

Like the epileptic who's touched off by a flashing light, I needed a romance to set off my condition.

At the words *you're forgiven,* the gloom that had permeated my being evaporated. I went from woe to ecstasy in three seconds.

A little voice in the back of my head said, Gee, Joe, if she was going to forgive you, wouldn't she have called you first? Rather than let you hear it secondhand through Gina? I chose not to listen to it.

I hit rush-hour traffic, and it was nearly six when I pulled up to the house on Grevillea Avenue. Dottie's daughter, Maureen, was out front, wearing another Jane Austen dress. We got the hellos out of the way. "She's not as crazy as she seems," I said. "Is she?"

"No. But I thought it best that you find out for yourself."

"Is she here?"

"Where else?"

"Can I see her?"

"Of course."

I went through the house again, past the Hummels and the Wedgwood and the Oriental porcelain, all lovingly arranged in their cabinets. The door to the conservatory stood open, as if Dottie had known I was coming.

I entered and stood just inside the door. She was raptly watching the Casio again. I cleared my throat.

She looked up, waggled one frail hand in the air, waved me over. "Oh, goodie. Well, don't just stand there. Come in." Exactly how she'd greeted me the last time. She poked a button and cut off the TV. "Bring a chair," she said.

"That's okay."

"Suit yourself. I'd like my catasetum."

She pointed at a bench off to her left, where a small plant with a yellowish-green flower awaited. I brought it over and handed it to her. "They spit their pollen, you know. They have a little hair on the flower, and when you touch it they spit. Because they think you're an insect." She peered up at me. "I remembered why I was telling you about the bees and wasps."

It took a second to recall the surreal conversation we'd had days earlier. "Why?"

"Because I was talking about those ancient Greeks. And what I wanted to tell you about was the bull semen and the horse semen."

What had I been thinking? Her pegging Yoichi as a smuggler must have been a lucky guess. I was wasting my time.

"They thought bees came from dead bulls, and wasps from dead horses. And so they put that together with the orchid roots looking like testicles and they decided the ones whose flowers looked like bees came from where bull semen fell to the ground, and the ones whose flowers looked like wasps came from where horse semen fell."

"Oh, those Greeks," I said.

I tried to figure out how to leave gracefully. But before I could, she looked directly into my eyes. Her own were perfectly rational as she said, "You found out about the Japanese fellow."

Hmm, I thought. Let's not be hasty. "Yes."

"You didn't believe me when I told you." She anticipated my apology, held up a hand to cut it off. "It's all right. Sometimes I sound like I don't know what I'm talking about."

"How did you know about him?"

"I know everything that goes on in the orchid world.

Always have, always will." She shook her head slowly. "There aren't many of us left now. From when the club began." She smiled, closing her eyes, as if picturing those days. "There was a lot less paperwork then. We had the plants and we showed them off."

"You knew about him and Helen too?"

Her eyes opened. "Then it's true?"

"If by 'it' you mean that they were seeing each other, yes."

"I suspected as much. Now I know, thanks to you."

"You can't tell anyone."

"Of course not. Do you see how it works? My grapevine?"

"Are there other things I ought to know?"

"About what?"

"About who killed Albert. And Laura too."

"Why would I know about that?"

"You said you knew everything that goes on in the orchid world."

"I did, did I?" She held out the catasetum. I took it and put it back in its place. When I returned, she said, "Well, then. Who do you think did it?"

"I'm running out of new ideas."

"Tell me your old ones."

"I thought it might be David and Helen Gartner. Or one of them. Because I was told they'd had business dealings with Albert. But that turned out not to be true."

"Go on. Anyone else?"

"Yoichi, but he was with Helen when Albert was shot. And for a while I thought Laura might have killed Albert, then someone else killed her."

"But you don't think that anymore."

"No."

"Nor do I, young man. All right, then, put these bad

things aside for the moment. I suppose you'll be wanting to know about Sharon Turner."

"I will?"

"You want to be her boyfriend."

"How did you know—"

"The grapevine, young man. I hear things. What do you want to know?"

"What do I need to know?" Why had I phrased it like that? Like there was something specific I'd missed.

"She's a touch fragile, don't you think?" A vague gesture toward the house. "Like one of the figurines. You don't really care for them, do you?"

I smiled. "No. Not to my taste."

"Nor mine. But Mo likes them. So I endure them. The things parents do for their children." She leaned forward. "Why do you want to be with her?"

"She's smart. That's the main thing. I don't have to dumb down my conversation for her."

"It's odd, what you've found out and what you haven't."

"What haven't I found out?"

"Are you sure you want to know?"

"I'm sure."

"All right then. Go inside and ask Mo to give you volume six of the orchid society's history."

Dottie found the place in the scrapbook full of photos and pasted-in sheets of lined composition paper. " 'Monday, March nineteenth, 1990. Monthly meeting.' " Darkness was descending quickly, but she seemed to have no trouble seeing the page. " 'Our speaker was Dr. Ghazarian, who gave a delightful talk on the orchids of Bolivia. His slides were, as always, fascinating. There were many lovely plants on the display table. As usual, several of the members whose turn it was to bring refreshments neglected to do so, but our historian provided several dozen shortbread cookies that took up the slack.' "

She raised her head and smiled. "Before my hips went out on me, I was quite the baker."

"I'm sure you were."

"I'll skip the treasury report and the part about the annual show. Let's see. Ah, yes, here it is. 'Three new members tonight. Tony Kleha's wife Lorraine was one. Also a young woman who just moved here, by the name of Sharon Turner. The poor soul didn't know anyone, so our historian took her in hand and showed her around.' "

"She told me a friend brought her to her first meeting."

"As I said when I saw the two of you at the orchid society meeting, she was wrong about that. She didn't know anybody."

Someone cracked a spigot in my gut. The first drop of acid fell onto my delicate stomach lining.

Dottie closed her eyes and smiled. "The poor thing was living in a motel, so I introduced her to Mel Aspin."

"Who's that?"

"One of the old-time members. He died two years ago, some sort of brain thing. It was very sad, but the club auctioned off his collection, so some good came of it. He had a room to rent. Sharon rented it. At least for a while."

"Then what happened?"

She leaned over, whispered, "She had men over."

The spigot in my abdomen opened a bit wider. "She told me—"

"When Mel discovered a naked Negro in the kitchen, well, that clinched things. He told her to move out. It wasn't the Negro part, of course. Mel liked people of all races. It was the naked part."

"But Sharon told me she didn't see anybody after she moved here."

"Why wouldn't she? She was a normal healthy girl. She had needs, you know." She leaned back. "A girl doesn't take care of her needs, she gets odd. Just look at Mo."

I didn't want to look at Mo. I wanted to look at Sharon some more. "She dated, then?"

"You're being quite dense this afternoon, young man. Yes, she dated. And more."

Whoever was controlling the faucet in my stomach twisted it all the way. I felt like a ferret was gnawing on my innards, like I did back when I was twenty, the day I found my tripping girlfriend in my best friend's water bed.

Or like when I found out about the Samoan.

I knew I'd reached the end of the road with Sharon. I could never trust a woman who had already lied as much as she had.

And I was sure she had lied. Because that voice in the back of my head, the one that had asked earlier why Sharon would tell Gina, not me, that she forgave me, was back, and now I was listening. It was wondering why I was believing what this strange old woman was saying, rather than what Sharon had told me.

And I said to it, it doesn't matter why. It just matters that I do.

Dottie cleared her throat. "You should probably hear the rest of what's here in the archives."

"No, I think I've heard—"

"You need to listen to this too."

There was something about her tone. "Go ahead," I said.

"That's better. Now where was I?" She zigzagged a finger

across the page, found her place. "Yes, here it is. 'Our third new addition this evening also just moved here from New York. He is rather an expert, and will make a fine addition to the society. His name is Doctor Albert Oberg.' "

What a coincidence, was my first reaction. Sharon and Albert joined on the same night.

But a second or two later the rest of my brain kicked in, and I realized she'd said "Doctor," and before that "New York," and I knew it wasn't a coincidence at all.

30

MAUREEN WAS IN THE KITCHEN. SHE SMILED, WIPING HER hands on a towel. "Did you find out what you needed?"

"The phone. Where is it?"

"Right there. On the wall."

I grabbed it, dialed Gina's cell number. It rang once, twice, before it was picked up. "Hello?" Not Gina's voice. Sharon's.

"It's Joe."

"Hi, Joe."

"Let me speak to Gina."

"I'm afraid she can't come to the phone now."

"Is she all right?"

"Of course. Why wouldn't she be? She's just in the bathroom, and asked me to get her phone."

"What have you done to her?"

Silence on the other end. Then, "Well. It sounds like you've figured it out. This puts a bit of a crimp in things."

"Let me talk to Gina."

"She's a bit indisposed. We had a lovely kaffeeklatsch, but

it ended badly. Gina thought it was time for her to go. I thought it wasn't."

"What do you mean, 'indisposed'?"

"I'm sure a little TLC will make everything fine. I'm sure you'll be able to take care of it when you get over here. You *are* coming over here, aren't you?"

"I'll be right there. Please don't do anything else to Gina."

"There's a bit of a whine in your voice, Joe. I don't think I like that. See if you can take control of it before you get here. It's probably improper breathing. You learned how to breathe properly when you were an actor, didn't you? Oh, and Joe? Make sure you're alone. Make sure you don't call the police." *Click.*

I was an idiot. Worse, I was an idiot on two levels.

My grand idiocy was that I'd been led down the widest of garden paths by a lying, scheming murderer. If I got through all this, I'd look back and shake my head at how magnificently stupid I was.

But there was a more immediate problem to deal with, related to my second level of folly: I'd let on to Sharon that I knew what she'd done. If I'd just kept my cool, acted as if everything were okay, I could have called the cops and gotten them over to Sharon's and rescued Gina.

But I'd blown that possibility nicely, thus giving up any advantage I may have had. And thus generating a specific warning not to bring the cops in.

"Something wrong?" Maureen said.

"No." I ran out the door. Halfway down the ramp, I stopped.

If I went over to Sharon's alone, chances were very good that she was going to kill both Gina and me.

Like she killed Albert. I knew why she'd done that.

Like she killed Laura. I wasn't sure about why she'd done that.

I almost ran back in and called the cops. Burns, to be specific, because I didn't trust anyone else not to bring in a thousand SWAT team members with assault rifles and battering rams, thus prompting Sharon to blow Gina's brains out.

But I couldn't really be sure that if I called Burns, she could guarantee what would happen. She might agree to go along with me, but she was a good cop, and she would do things right, and there would be backup. And I didn't know who that backup might be, and I just couldn't take the chance that they might induce Sharon to start shooting.

Maybe I should have called anyway. But I wasn't thinking straight. All I could think of was Gina.

Sharon was wearing a red blouse open at the neck to show the barest hint of cleavage. Farther down was a black skirt that revealed several inches of thigh. Her earrings resembled little African sculptures. Her hair seemed to have a bit of extra body. Its gray color wasn't intriguing anymore. It was just . . . gray.

She looked out at me, made sure I was alone, opened the door wide. That's when I saw the gun. I thought it was Gina's. I wasn't sure. I hadn't actually seen it in a while, just had my hand on it a couple of nights before.

Sharon took a step back, waved me in with the gun, looked out into the darkness, closed and locked the door.

"Where's Gina?"

"It was that Dottie Lennox, wasn't it? That's how you found out."

"Yes. Where's Gina?"

"I *knew* I should have been more careful when I first got to L.A. Done a little more research beforehand. But I didn't really have a plan then. Only an intention."

"Where's Gina?"

"Please, Joe, don't make any more loud noise. We don't want to attract attention. Gina's in my bedroom."

I ran down the hall. The light in the bedroom was off, the curtains drawn. I groped on the wall for the light switch, cursing when I couldn't find it. At last I did.

Gina was on the bed. Her eyes were closed and she wasn't moving. She had duct tape across her mouth, and her wrists were tied to the headboard with rope. Some more looped around her ankles and stretched down somewhere under the bed.

And there was blood on the side of her head, and blood on the pillow, and some on the blue comforter.

31

I RAN TO GINA, FELL DOWN ON MY KNEES, TOOK HER FACE IN my hands. She was pale, but she wasn't cold, and even as I touched her I saw her chest rise. I looked more closely at the side of her head, grabbed a corner of the comforter, ineffectually swabbed the area. There wasn't that much blood after all. It had just been smeared around.

"It's ruined, I suppose," Sharon said. "The comforter, that is. Oh, well. Couldn't be helped. It *is* down, by the way. Not that you really care. That's not why you were staring at the bed last night." She laughed a nasty little laugh, moved to her nightstand, switched on a nondescript earthenware lamp, turned off the overhead. "Much better." She pointed to Gina with her free hand. "Your little friend there's really as gullible as you are."

I looked at her over my shoulder. The lamp painted her face in harsh shadows. "I've got to get her to a doctor."

"Don't be ridiculous. It's just a little bump."

"I've got to—"

"No." She gestured with the gun. "We had a nice cup of coffee before I hit her," she said. "I told her how very sorry I was for my behavior, and that I thought you were someone special and that I hoped she and I would be good friends. At first she was suspicious, but I'm such a good actress that I got her to fall for the whole thing."

I turned back to Gina. Her eyes fluttered open.

"You see," Sharon said. "Nothing to worry about. I really didn't hit her that hard. Just enough to make it easy to drag her in here and tie her up."

Gina's eyes were fully open now, wide, fearful. A corner of the duct tape was loose. I slowly peeled it away. "Careful," Sharon said. "Don't want to cause her any pain."

The tape came free. A tiny spot of sticky residue remained along Gina's jawline. She licked her lips, uttered a couple of nonsense syllables. "I'm sorry, baby," she said at last. "I should have figured her out."

"There was no way you could," Sharon said. "I'm simply too good an actress."

I began picking at the ropes binding Gina's wrists. Sharon watched me closely, but didn't move to stop me. I got the first one off, reached over to work on the other.

"You know," Sharon said, "it was so much fun leading you around by your penis that I would have done it even if I wasn't trying to distract you." Good to know that they agreed on what I was being led around by.

I worried the knot on the second piece of rope until it came undone. Gina struggled to sit up. I pushed her back. "Stay. Rest."

I had to stall until I could come up with something. I looked back at Sharon. "I know the part about the hospital was true. Why don't you tell me what else was?"

She shrugged. "I don't see why not." She made herself comfortable in a soft chair across the room from us, crossed her legs at the ankle. "I like embellishment much more than total fabrication, don't you? I suppose I could have made it *all* up, but I like a mixture of truth and lies. Gives the whole performance more texture."

"How much was the truth?"

"My years in New York. The play. Getting hit by the cab. All of that, sad but true."

"Made you a little crazy, did it?"

"Crazy? I don't think I'm crazy. Getting revenge on someone who ruined your life, that's not crazy." She smiled. "Albert had to pay eventually for not letting me get to the theater. I really wasn't hurt badly. It was only a little fracture."

"What are you talking about?" Gina said.

I threw Sharon a look, turned back to Gina. "Sharon was about to get her big break and got hit by a cab. Albert was the doctor who kept her in the hospital—for her own good, I might add—and prevented her from playing her opening night."

"I tried very hard to get out," Sharon said. "But he gave me a shot. For the pain, he said, and so I wouldn't hurt myself worse. It knocked me out. I couldn't escape. Do you feel it yet? The helplessness of not being able to escape?"

I thought back to the day the whole thing started. Albert's den full of medical diplomas. Why hadn't I realized he'd been a doctor before he retired and moved to L.A.? Why hadn't I found that out before? If I'd just dug a little deeper, I might have—

Might have what? Remembered Albert was a doctor when there was a hospital in Sharon's story, and magically made the connection? No. Not a good thing to beat myself up about. And this was no time to be beating myself up about anything, not when I could better spend my energy trying to get us out of the mess we were in.

Gina was sitting on the bed, working the leg bindings loose. I knew if one of us came up with something, the other would follow their lead. "How come it took you so long to—to do something?"

"You know what they say, whoever *they* are. 'Revenge is a dish best served cold.' I kept track of Albert, and when he retired and moved to Los Angeles, I did too. I was following him one night, just a few weeks after we both got here. He came to an orchid society meeting. So I developed a sudden interest in orchids. It seemed a good way to keep close to him." She gave me another of those wry smiles she was so good at. "And it was kind of serendipitous, because I found out that I really did like the plants. I'd never had a hobby before, and now I had one, and as an extra added bonus it was the perfect way to keep tabs on Albert. Although I have to admit, I'm not really that fond of a lot of the people in the orchid society. Like that old bitch Dottie. I suppose I'll have to deal with her too."

Gina swung her legs over the side of the bed, sat beside me. "Didn't Albert recognize you?"

"I didn't look the same. I wore glasses when he saw me, but I got contacts before I moved here. I changed my hairstyle and let the gray come out. You like the gray, don't you, Joe? You think it's sexy, don't you?"

I didn't answer.

"Besides, it had been two years. I'd been just one of thousands of patients, and he saw me for only a few minutes. Just enough to ruin my life."

"Oh, please," Gina said.

"Don't mock me, dear."

"Okay," I said. "I get the part about serving revenge cold. But, what, eight years? That's a long time to hang around waiting to kill somebody."

"Ten years actually, counting the time before we both moved here." She smiled triumphantly. "The day I killed him was ten years—and four days, that part was the truth—from the day my play was to open. Just as much as the time I spent in New York trying to make it as an actress. A nice bookending effect, don't you think?"

"Very clever," I said.

"And I have to say, I couldn't have picked a more difficult day. I couldn't get him alone. That stupid party early on, and in the evening he was with Laura."

So. When she was supposedly with Helen, before she went home to feed Monty the cat, Laura was with her boyfriend, Albert. Sometimes the simplest explanation is the best one.

"I waited outside for hours," Sharon said. "Finally, Laura came out. She told him she'd be back within forty-five minutes. That's when I realized what was going on between the two of them, and what a lovely suspect she would be. After she drove away, I knocked on the door and told Albert I had an orchid question. He let me right in. I announced that I was going to shoot him, and why. It was pathetic, the way he put his hands up in the air, like I was a Wild West stagecoach robber." A short, harsh laugh. "I knew Laura would come back and find him and the police would think she did it."

"But your frame didn't work out," I said.

"No. Our dear Laura had a story all made up about where she was all evening. And she had Helen to back her up."

"And," Gina said, "you couldn't tell anyone it was a story because that would show you'd been there that night."

"Very good, dear. See, Joe? I didn't scramble her brains at all." She stood and began pacing the room, never letting the gun leave us. "I expected after a day or two Laura would blurt out that she hadn't really been with Helen. But she kept to her story, right to the end."

A residual effect of Laura's est days, I suspected. The keeping-your-word thing. If she told Helen she'd cover for her, she would cover for her.

"Then you showed up," she said. "And Laura had asked you to look into Albert's death. I suppose she thought her alibi was going to fall apart at some point, so the more people she had looking for the real killer, the better. At the very first, I thought your appearance on the scene was a nice piece of luck. Maybe you'd find out Laura wasn't with Helen that night. But that didn't seem to be happening, and I got a bit concerned you might stumble on the truth. So I redirected your efforts. It was rather easy."

"Was it?"

"Setting you to work on Helen and David. David has such a temper, and of course there's that thing about the Japanese. I thought he'd make a fine suspect for you. And if you spent your energy on the two of them, you might unearth the fact that Laura and Helen weren't together that night. Have you found out where Helen really was, by the way?"

"No."

"Well, it doesn't matter, does it?"

"The story about Yoichi and the judging. You made that up too."

"Out of whole cloth."

"But why'd you shoot Laura?" Gina said.

Sharon made a face like, isn't it obvious? "Eventually I realized Laura wasn't going to tell the truth about that night anytime soon. So I had to make it seem as if she really did kill Albert. So I shot her too."

"And tried to make it look like suicide," I said.

"I knew the police would find out it wasn't, but it was a

simple enough thing to do, and it gave them something else to think about."

I looked at her, waiting for more. There wasn't any. I said, "Why did you act like you were interested in me?"

Sharon smiled. "You were obviously going to be a thorn in my side. The only way to keep track of you was to play on your obvious need for a little romance."

"Was it that obvious?"

"From the moment I met you. The way you looked at me. It didn't matter then, but when you wouldn't go away, it was time to become your perfect woman."

"It was all an act."

"That's what we actors do, isn't it? Yes. I decided what I would need to do to control you, and I did it. It was partly planned—I even made notes—and partly improvisation. It was marvelous. After all those years away from the stage, it was wonderful to be able to spend hours with you playing a woman who didn't exist."

She absently brushed her hair back. "The improvisation was my favorite part. Remember, I told you I was good at making things up on the spot. Like that story about being involved with my director, and how it had ruined me romantically. It made me seem terribly vulnerable, didn't it?"

I didn't give her the satisfaction of an answer.

"But my favorite fabrication was not being available Saturday night. I knew you would get crazy when I told you that. Your kind always does."

My kind? What kind was I? "But if you were trying to be my ideal woman, why the twists in the road? Why let me wonder if you'd go out with me? Why the big show when you found Gina at my place?"

"Because your perfect woman is one who gives you grief. You wouldn't know what to do with a relationship that went smoothly. Things have to be twisted for you to be interested. You should have seen your face the other morning. I almost felt bad about making you think you'd queered things by having Gina stay over." She shook her head. "To think I would care whether the two of you are fucking. Are you, by the way?"

"No," I said.

"Yes," Gina said.

Sharon chuckled. "One of you is lying, and do you know what? I don't care which."

Again she pushed back her hair. "Much as I was enjoying things, you were becoming a bit of a nuisance. I thought with your fumbling around you might discover something significant. Then, when you told me yesterday morning you'd resurrected Laura's alibi, I knew what I had to do." She shook her head. " 'We need to talk.' I knew saying that would make you crazy again."

I looked for something to say. Nothing came to mind.

"Then, my show at the big tree. Part improvisation. Part truth. It would make things more of an acting challenge if you knew some of the truth. And it was a little bit of living dangerously, letting you know something significant, setting you up for last night."

"For what last night?"

She looked at me with something resembling pity. "The script was that you came over, had your way with me, then confessed that you'd killed Albert and Laura, and told me you had to deal with me because I was getting too close to finding out. But I would have somehow managed to get the gun away, and to shoot you in self-defense."

"But why would I have done it? I'd never met him, hadn't seen her in fifteen years."

"Because when you met Laura again after all those years,

you became infatuated with her. And you went up to Albert's that night and killed him to clear the field for yourself. And when Laura wouldn't have you, you shot her too."

"That's preposterous. Besides, I was with Gina that evening."

"Ah, yes, Gina." Sharon shifted her eyes to her. "I have to admit, she was very clever, finding me on the Internet."

Gina looked sheepish. "One of the things we talked about before she slugged me."

"I suppose I should have changed my name when I came to L.A.," Sharon said. "But, as I said, I really had no plan at that point. You know, I'm actually glad you burst in last night, because it made me realize you were just as much of a problem as Joe. So I decided to postpone things a day, and deal with you both at once. And, as an extra bonus, I wipe out Joe's alibi for when Albert was killed."

She smiled. She was very impressed with herself. "So I invited you over, Gina. And you came, like a good little girl. And then, Joe, I was going to call and tell you, yet again, that I forgave you. And you would come over expecting to finally get some, and then I could deal with you both at once. But you ruined that by finding out I'd shot Albert."

"And the police know too. I told them. They're on their way."

She whipped her head toward me. "I told you, no—oh. You're lying. I can tell just by looking at you." She shook her head. "But it doesn't matter that you found out. The end result is the same. You and I will be on the verge of consummating our relationship when your jealous little friend will burst in and shoot you. And then I'll get the gun away from her, and that will be that." She waggled the weapon. "It was so considerate of you, Gina dear, to bring this with you."

My eyes went to the gun. Sharon noticed. "I had one

ready, of course. Just like the one I used on Albert and Laura. That's the one I would have used last night. But, with this scenario, Gina's will be so much better."

She smiled at me. "Now it's time to set up the denouement of our little drama. Would you please take off your clothes?"

32

EVEN WITH ALL THE WEIRDNESS, HER REQUEST DUMfounded me. "What for?"

"It will make it much more realistic if Gina bursts in on us when we're already in the throes of passion."

"I'd rather not."

A tiny movement of the gun. "Just do it."

I slowly unbuttoned my shirt and dropped it on the bed.

"The shorts too," Sharon said. "And the shoes."

I took off my Reeboks and stood up. I undid my shorts and let them drop. When they hit the hardwood floor I heard a tiny *clunk,* muffled by the fabric.

I reached down, picked up the shorts. Sharon looked me up and down. "Not bad," she said. "A bit out of shape, but certainly not a 'stack of flab,' as you so cleverly put it the other night."

"I'm glad you approve."

"Now your underwear."

"Come on, Sharon, this has gone—"

"Do it."

I turned away to drop my shorts on the bed. Not that I

particularly cared about being neat, or about being modest, but I had the germ of an idea.

I caught Gina's eye. She knew I was up to something. And, somehow, that I needed a diversion. She got up and headed for the door.

"Stop right there," Sharon said.

"What if I don't?"

Sharon gestured with the gun. "I'll use it."

Her attention was all on Gina. I slipped my hand into my shorts pocket, found what I wanted, palmed it.

Gina looked my way, then back at Sharon. "You're really brave," she said, "with that cannon in your hand."

"Please. Leave the dramatics to me. Now step back toward the bed."

Gina glanced at me again. I reached my right hand up to my ear, as if to scratch it. I thought she knew what I was up to. Or maybe she just trusted that I knew what I was doing.

Sharon turned back toward me. "Well? What are you waiting for?"

"Bitch," Gina said.

The gun went toward her again. "That's the last crack you're ever going to—"

I didn't have time to pull my arm back. The throw was all wrist. I flashed on my fracas with David Gartner, and how I hadn't trusted my aim.

The gun snapped toward me. But before Sharon could squeeze off a shot, the steel socket I'd spirited away from Gartner's Tires hit her directly above the left eye.

She screamed in pain. The gun went off.

Gina sprang toward Sharon.

Another shot. Breaking glass. Another scream.

In the space of a second I contemplated life without Gina. If the shot had hit her, if the second scream were hers, if the worst happened, I would spend the rest of my life wondering why I didn't save the person I cared about the most.

Unless I ended up dead too.

Time resumed its normal pace. Gina smashed into Sharon. Her momentum carried them into the wall. Gina had her hand on Sharon's, trying to wrest the gun from her. A third shot filled the room with clamor.

I cast my eyes around, grabbed the lamp off the night-stand. I'd gone about two feet with it when the plug ripped from the wall and the room was plunged into darkness. A small detail I hadn't anticipated when I was searching for something to belt Sharon with.

I stumbled over to the struggling shadows, raised the lamp over my head with both hands, brought it down on the taller of the two. The lamp shattered. I heard the gun thump onto the hardwood.

I dropped the rest of the lamp, stepped to where I guessed the light switch to be, pawed the wall. The overhead fixture flooded the room in time for me to view the last of Sharon's unconscious slide to the floor.

Gina looked down at her, then at the ruins of the table lamp, then at me. "Isn't it the *girl* who's supposed to hit the villain over the head with a lamp?" she said.

I couldn't think of a clever reply. Or any, for that matter. I stumbled over to Gina, my brave Gina, and enfolded her in my arms.

When things had quieted down—after I'd put my clothes on and we'd called Burns and she'd called Casillas, after they'd both shown up and he'd made a big stink about people messing around in his case, after the paramedics had examined and bandaged both Gina's head and Sharon's—I got a chance to talk to Sharon one more time. I had this scene from a movie in my head. It's the one where the bad person acts like they're attracted to the hero or heroine for some nefarious reason or other, and at the end the bad person's caught, and it's sad because we realize the bad person has, despite themselves, actually fallen for the good person. And, of course, it's too late, and the weepy music comes up as they're carted away, calling to the good person, "I really did love you."

We were outside, after they'd bandaged Sharon's head and handcuffed her and put her in a cop car, pushing her head down like you see on TV. I bent and looked into the car. I caught her eye and said . . . nothing. There was nothing to say.

She looked up at me, seeming to take a second to realize who I was. She blinked several times, but didn't say anything either. A couple of cops got in and slammed the doors and carried her off.

I plunged my hands in my pockets, trying to draw myself into a tight little ball. I needed to walk away, but it was too much effort. Gina came and took my arm and led me to her car.

We were on my couch, each leaning up against one end, with our feet jumbled in the middle, much as we had the night a week earlier when Gina had been dumped and we shared a bed. Gina had listened for an hour as I bemoaned my love-starved idiothood, and my failure to see through Sharon's choreographed attraction to me. At least six times I'd said,

"How am I ever going to trust a woman again?" At least six times Gina had generated an appropriate response.

Finally I sensed I'd beaten the subject to death, at least for that evening. "I've been thinking of getting out of commercials," I said.

She gave me a what-now look. "Why?"

"It's just too ridiculous. I mean, there I am acting like a boob to sell stuff I don't really believe in, taking jobs away from people who really care about doing it. I'd be better off putting my energy into getting back into the theater."

"You want to get back into the theater, is that it?"

"Yeah. It would be much more rewarding. You meet a better class of people."

"Like Sharon."

"Well, she was an okay person, except for the fact that she was a lying, conniving murderer."

"I see. And this isn't just some sort of transference, you thinking that because you've had this incredibly horrible thing happen to you, you need to make a significant change, whether it's related to the bad thing or not."

"No, Gi, I really would like to do some theater again."

"So do it. Get off your ass and do it. And it'd be stupid to give up commercials. You have an easy income source that hardly takes any of your time. Not that you have to worry about time. Your dance card of life isn't exactly full."

" 'Dance card of life'?"

"All I'm saying is, don't make everything harder because of some artistic sensibility you've suddenly developed in your mid-forties."

"I think I'm having a midlife crisis."

"Probably." She untangled her legs from mine, slid over, put her arm around me. "Just let all this stuff soak in, baby.

Just get yourself through it, and don't make any earth-shattering decisions until your head is back to normal."

I nodded, reached out, barely touched the bandage on her temple. "Tell me something."

"What?"

"How come, when Sharon asked if we were lovers, you said we were?"

She grinned. "I thought it might get her pissed off, so she would do something dumb." A small pause, and the smile was gone. "And, maybe, it was a bit of wishful thinking."

I considered what she'd told me. Then I said, "It's time for bed."

She looked at me, nodded, popped up off the couch. "I'll meet you there."

"Remember whose place we're at. Don't get in on my side."

She went off to the bathroom. After a bit I got up, turned off the lights, stood in the dark until I heard her in the bedroom. I went in the bathroom, washed, brushed, got undressed. When I came out, Gina was in the bed, on the proper side, beautiful by the light of the gardening-Asian-lady lamp. Her bare arms and shoulders were outside the bedclothes. She looked me over in a way she hadn't in seventeen years, then patted my side of the bed. I got under the covers and slid over to her. I looked in her eyes.

I said, "Remember what you told me about not making any earth-shattering decisions?"

"Yes."

"I'm about to make one."

"I was hoping you would."

She turned toward me. I took her in my arms and found her lips with mine.

The Joe Portugal Guide to Orchids

WHAT'S AN ORCHID? TO MOST PEOPLE, IT'S A PRETTY CUT flower decorating their teenage daughter's wrist on prom night, or a nifty blooming plant for sale at the local flower shop, Home Depot, or upscale supermarket. To a botanist, it's a member of the Orchidaceae, the largest family of flowering plants. All orchid flowers include three sepals and three petals, with one of the latter modified into a structure known as the lip, whose shape and color are often the key to figuring out just which orchid species or hybrid you have. The male and female reproductive parts are united into a structure called a column, and the flowers are zygomorphic, meaning if you want to cut them into two equal, mirror-image parts, there's only one way to do it. Compare this to a rose. If you intend to whack a rose in half, you can start your cut anywhere along the edge. I don't know why you'd want to cut a flower in half, but if you're so inclined it's good to know the ground rules.

Another common orchid feature is the pseudobulb, a thickened section at the bottom of the stem, which stores water and food as a hedge against drought. Some are so thick and weird that they're attractive to succulent plant collectors like me. Sympodial orchids, or ones whose stems have just a couple of leaves each and in which new growth pops out of the base of the old, often have pseudobulbs. Monopodial plants, which grow a succession of leaves on each stem, don't.

In nature, some orchids are terrestrials, growing at ground level like most plants. Others, usually the more tropical species, are epiphytes, which means they live on trees, wrapping their thick roots around them to stay in place. They're not parasites, though, as they take nothing from the tree they're attached to, picking up nutrients from tiny patches of decaying plant matter.

Orchids grow all over the world. There are hundreds of genera, which is the plural of genus, which is a group of plants in a family with more in common with each other than with other members of the family. (If families and genera seem like Greek, I suggest a session with "The Joe Portugal Guide to Botanical Nomenclature" included in *The Cactus Club Killings,* the story of my first brush with homicide. If you haven't read it, you should. If you have, buy it for all your friends.)

Not content with the tens of thousands of species nature has provided, orchid fanciers have produced over 100,000 hybrids, trying to combine the best characteristics of two parents into that one fabulous plant that will bring them fame and fortune. A look through any issue of *Orchids,* the American Orchid Society's monthly magazine, will show an amazing range of plants painstakingly bred for specific colors, shapes, and textures. The prices are pretty amazing too. Orchid collecting is not a poor person's hobby.

Orchids have a reputation for being tough to grow, supposedly requiring conditions far beyond what a typical person can provide in order to thrive and bloom. They conjure up pictures of stuffy hothouses with foglike humidity and drop-dead temperatures. These perceptions are false. Though some orchids require specialized care, many don't, and can be grown by anyone, inside or out, if just a few basics are kept in mind. Growing them, as with most other plants, is primarily a matter of watching them, seeing what they're up to, and applying a little common sense.

In general, orchids like the kinds of temperatures typically found in our homes. If you get into them, you'll discover that they're classified as warm-growing, intermediate, and cool-growing. The differences aren't huge, but accomplished growers with greenhouses and the like can make them grow and flower better by strict temperature control. Humidity is also an important factor; orchids generally like a lot of it. You can keep a spray bottle handy, or increase the moisture level around your plants by growing them on a tray filled with water and gravel. But make sure the water doesn't rise above the bottom of the pot. This encourages root rot.

Most of the orchids you buy will be potted in a fine bark mix, and the size of the particles makes water run off relatively quickly, but it's still fairly easy to water them too often. This is another fine way to induce root rot. When in doubt about watering, don't. Orchids are tougher than they look. Pseudobulbs and thick leaves help them retain moisture even if the mix dries out.

Orchids like a lot of light and will bloom better if they get it. But a lot of light doesn't mean a bunch of direct sunlight, which will burn many of the plants. You can grow them in filtered natural light, and many people suffering from orchid fever grow them under artificial lighting as well. Ventilation is important too. If your orchids end up somewhere where the air doesn't move at all, it might be worthwhile to keep a fan in the room. Your orchids will thank you. Okay, they won't, but you can hang around and enjoy the flowers while you wait for them to say something.

Fertilizer is another cultural consideration. Many orchidists use one type during blooming season and another when vegetative growth is the goal. The subject of orchid fertilization could probably fill a book by itself.

Like most other plants, orchids suffer from pests. Mealybugs, scale, and aphids all like to suck on them; slugs and snails love chewing on them. Plant viruses are another difficulty. To avoid their spread, experienced orchidists never use the same tool on two plants without disinfecting it in between.

The important thing to remember with all these cultural factors is that dealing with them for orchids is little different from dealing with them for any other house or garden plant. Again, common sense is the key. If you want more details, check out the gardening section of your local bookstore. There are a lot of good orchid books out there.

And now, on to the orchids mentioned in this book. First, the more widely grown genera:

Cattleya species and hybrids are the big frilly orchids popular in corsages. Some have one leaf per stem, some have two or three. They like lots of light. Related genera include *Brassavola* and *Laelia.*

Cymbidium is a genus of terrestrial orchids. They tend to flower early—sometimes in the middle of winter—and the blooms can last for months. Their long leaves give them higher space requirements than most other orchids.

Dendrobium generally has conelike stems, though some form clusters of small pseudobulbs that hug the ground. They like small pots and good air circulation. They're fairly common at nonspecialist nurseries and other places orchids are sold.

Epidendrum is a genus of easy-to-grow plants with reedlike stems and leathery leaves. They often flower year-round.

Oncidium generally has tall flowering spikes with many small blooms. They last well both on the plant and cut, and are often used by florists in arrangements.

Paphiopedilum and *Phragmipedium* are known as slipper or lady's-slipper orchids because of the semienclosed form the lip takes. They often have leathery petals, odd colors, and mottled leaves, making them the weirdest-looking of the popular groups.

Phalaenopsis is a genus characterized by straplike leaves that hug the surface of the potting medium. They're known as moth orchids, a reference to the shape of the flowers, and are the members of the family most likely to be found in places like food markets and hardware superstores. They thrive at typical indoor light and temperature levels.

Vanda is related to *Phalaenopsis,* but forms long stems full of leaves rather than clutching the surface of the medium. They like more light and heat than most orchids mentioned here, and are often grown in slatted baskets with their roots dangling free.

Now, some less commonly seen orchids:

Angraecum and the smaller, related *Aerangis* are from Africa, Madagascar, and the islands of the Indian Ocean. Their flowers tend to be star-shaped and to have long nectar spurs.

Catasetum has a couple of unique characteristics. First, they are among the only orchids that produce male and female flowers rather than ones with both sets of gear. Second, the male flowers have a trigger mechanism that causes them to "spit" their pollen at visiting insects.

Eulophia is a terrestrial orchid genus often characterized by fat, chunky pseudobulbs. Because of this, and because their cultural requirements are similar to those of the South African succulents they often grow with, they're starting to become popular with the cactus crowd.

Ophrys forms flowers that mimic the bees and wasps that pollinate them.

Schomburgkia has columnar pseudobulbs which, in some species, are hollow and house ant colonies.

Stanhopea produces fragrant, fleshy, bizarre flowers. The inflorescence grows downward, into the medium, so they're grown in baskets that allow it to burrow through and escape back into the air.

The following are miniatures, characterized by diminutive individual heads, though an entire plant can sometimes reach a decent size:

Isabelia virginalis comes from Brazil. Its tiny pseudobulbs are covered by something resembling a fishnet.

Maxillaria tenuifolia is best known for its coconut-like fragrance.

Nanodes discolor forms midget clumps of semisucculent leaves. It grows from Mexico all the way to Peru.

Pleurothallis, with over a thousand species, is the centerpiece of an alliance—or group of related species—known as pleurothallids. Their flowers show an amazing range of colors, along with appendages, hairs, and other weirdness.

Obviously, this is only the most basic of introductions to a fascinating group of plants. Invest in an orchid book if you'd like to learn more. But if you just want to see some pictures of the plants mentioned in this book, get on the Internet and surf to http://walpow.com, where one of the members of the Culver City Cactus Club has kindly posted photographs of many of the orchids referred to here. You'll find the plants mentioned in *The Cactus Club Killings* there too.

Nathan Walpow has been collecting cacti and other succulent plants for over twenty years and has over 400 specimens in his collection. He is the president of the Sunset Succulent Society, located in Los Angeles. In 1997 his short story "This Bud's for You" was the first fiction ever to appear in the *Cactus and Succulent Journal,* the publication of the Cactus and Succulent Society of America.

Nathan Walpow has been writing since 1992. Before that he had ten years of experience as an actor, working on the stage and on television shows such as *Moonlighting,* and he is a five-time undefeated *Jeopardy!* champion. He is also the author of *The Cactus Club Killings,* the debut novel in the Joe Portugal mystery series.